PRESUMED SAFE

Hope you like it!!
Love Always,
Kim

Kim MacInnis

outskirtspress
DENVER, COLORADO

This is a work of fiction. The events and characters described herein are imaginary and are not intended to refer to specific places or living persons. The opinions expressed in this manuscript are solely the opinions of the author and do not represent the opinions or thoughts of the publisher. The author has represented and warranted full ownership and/or legal right to publish all the materials in this book.

Presumed Safe
All Rights Reserved.
Copyright © 2016 Kim MacInnis
v3.0

Cover Photo © 2016 thinkstockphotos.com. All rights reserved - used with permission.

This book may not be reproduced, transmitted, or stored in whole or in part by any means, including graphic, electronic, or mechanical without the express written consent of the publisher except in the case of brief quotations embodied in critical articles and reviews.

Outskirts Press, Inc.
http://www.outskirtspress.com

ISBN: 978-1-4787-6950-7

Outskirts Press and the "OP" logo are trademarks belonging to Outskirts Press, Inc.

PRINTED IN THE UNITED STATES OF AMERICA

This book is dedicated to two of the strongest and most amazing women I have had the pleasure to know, my mother Margaret and my friend Rhonda Charest Couto.

May You Both Rest in Perfect Peace

"There can be no keener revelation of a society's soul than the way in which it treats its children."
Nelson Mandela, Former President of South Africa

ACKNOWLEDGMENTS

There are many people to thank and acknowledge. I want to first thank my readers, Tracey Mac Innis, Lorna Mac Donald, Rebecca Chin and Darren O'Neil. Their feedback was invaluable and helped shape the story in a very intriguing way. Many others helped develop the story, particularly the characters. Thank you to my mother, Margie for always inspiring me. Many thanks to my nieces, Reilly Mac Neil, Taylor Mac Innis, Cassie Mac Innis, Bridget Mac Innis, Audrey Austin, and Charlotte Austin for their unique personalities.

I would also like to thank Captain Mike Froio, Kelly Hoye, Nora Lehman, Shantell Cottrell, Kelly Mac Innis, Sarah Simonsen, Janice Wright, Kylie Austin, Keaghan Austin, Henry Chin, Conor Holick, Braden Holick, Tyler Demelo, Eric Couto, Molly Couto, Emma Couto, Marquez Canery, Jeff Kilroy, Eric Chin, Scott Macdonald, Susie Holmes, Jill Holmes, James Kelleher, Christina Mastrangelo, Lorraine Carboni, Baldies, Devan McNeill, Garrett McNeill, Amanda Mac Donald, Stanley Mac Donald, and Jordyn Neves. Finally, I would like to thank my husband, Dave for all of his love and support.

All of the characters in this story are fictional. The only "real" name used is Dana Blades. Dana is not a detective. Dana was a student of mine at Bridgewater State University. He took several of my classes and I would tease him about his name telling him it sounded like a movie star name or a famous athlete's name. I loved having Dana as a student. Dana died on August 4, 2013. He was an amazing person, always smiling and loving life. He was also amazing son, husband, father, and friend. Hopefully Detective Dana Blades will keep his spirit and memory alive.

Doy-en
(noun)
- the most respected or prominent person in a particular field.

PROLOGUE

The Doyen quietly sat drinking a cup of coffee. There were only a few people in the group who had the privilege of a face-to-face with the Doyen. These members of the group explained why they made the decision to take the child without the Doyen's approval. The Doyen listened intently. The members of the group explaining their actions were nervous and didn't want to disappoint the Doyen. After what seemed like several minutes, the Doyen told them they had made the right decision. The Doyen also told them if they came upon such a situation again, they had to make greater efforts to reach the top members of the group.

The group members left the room exhaling pronounced sighs of relief. They wanted to go home knowing their memberships were safe. The Doyen sat for a few more minutes thinking deeply about the group's activities. So many children were missing and so many more would be taken. They were doing good work.

CHAPTER 1

The doctor examined the little boy carefully. She made every effort to be gentle and reassuring. She had seen bruises like this before and it meant only one thing; he was abused and on more than one occasion. There were bruises all over his back. He was so young. His blue eyes were sad and defeated. There was no expression on his face and this broke the doctor's heart. There was a pattern of bruising all over his back. Some looked new and some had yellowed as time passed. These weren't bruises an average, active four year old would sustain through play. His hair was dirty and his clothes were a bit too small. His aunt and uncle had brought him in when they arrived in town to visit. The doctor believed the aunt and uncle when they told her they didn't abuse Sean.

Sean's Aunt Susie explained that they were shocked when they saw Sean. He looked sad and thin. He was very white. She told the doctor about her brief visit with Sean's mother, Elaine, who was Susie's sister. Susie couldn't stop staring at Sean even though Elaine kept talking to her. Elaine was very happy to see them but eager for them to take Sean for the day. Susie wasn't impressed with Elaine's willingness to hand over Sean so quickly. Elaine's apartment was a mess and so was Elaine.

She looked like a crack addict. Her clothes were falling off her. Her eyes were bloodshot and her long hair was a greasy brown and she chain-smoked. Elaine's boyfriend, Colin, was at work when Susie and Reid were at the apartment. Susie hadn't met him but didn't like the sound of him. She spoke with Elaine on the phone several times in the last few months and heard Colin yelling at Elaine in the background. He didn't sound nice. Susie worried about that and worried about little Sean.

Elaine rushed out after talking to Susie for only ten minutes. She told Susie she would be back in an hour and they could catch up. Susie had a feeling Elaine would be gone for more than an hour. When Elaine left, Sean seemed to relax. He half smiled at Susie and Reid. His plaid shirt was dirty and his jeans were too short. He needed a bath. Susie wiped Sean's face gently as he stood very still. Too still. Something was wrong.

Susie and Reid decided to take Sean to the playground just to get him out of the apartment. Susie told the doctor that Sean was very quiet on the way to the park and didn't seem to want to play. Her heart broke as she stared into his empty eyes. She pulled Sean towards her to hug him and he winced. She asked Sean what was wrong and he said his stomach hurt. Susie pulled up his shirt and saw his belly. She tickled him a bit but he didn't laugh. Susie didn't know why but she turned him around. There were bruises all over his back. She turned to Reid and motioned for him to look. Reid was a firefighter/EMT. He took one look at Sean and suggested they take him to a clinic. He didn't believe the bruises were normal bruises for a four year old. Susie asked Sean where the bruises came from. At first Sean just shrugged but Susie assured him that it was okay to tell her. Sean told her Colin hit him a lot. Susie asked him if his mother knew this. Sean told her that she did.

He told her they left him alone a lot and sometimes he was hungry. Susie felt herself fill with rage and pity. She wanted to kill Elaine and Colin. She looked at Reid and motioned for him to get into the car.

Reid asked a passerby where the nearest clinic was and headed in that direction. Susie sat quietly in the passenger's seat. She started to think about how she failed Sean. She had deluded herself in thinking that Elaine was a good mother. She convinced herself that she shouldn't interfere with Elaine. She was now so angry with herself. She hated that she had turned into one of those people who thought a family should stay together no matter what.

When Susie and Reid arrived at the clinic, the doctor reassured Susie that Sean's bruises weren't her fault. She then told Susie and Reid they would have to file a child abuse report. The doctor said she would also file a report. She left the room to make a call. A few minutes later the police arrived at the clinic. This surprised the doctor because she had called the social worker involved with Sean. Instead of coming to the clinic as suggested, the social worker had called the police. The doctor was puzzled because she was sure she reached the right social worker. Elaine and her boyfriend were supposed to be following a plan to get sober and attend parenting classes. They had done neither according to the social worker. The doctor made another call while the police talked to Susie and Reid. She found out that the social worker hadn't checked on Sean for a month and that was the reason she avoided the clinic. The doctor was furious.

The police agreed to leave Sean with Susie and Reid until Child Services came to get him. When the officers stepped out of the room, the doctor motioned for Susie and Reid to step into her office. She told Susie that Sean would end up in foster care if they waited for a social worker to come to the clinic. Susie and Reid would have to petition the court for custody. It might take up to a week for them to even see a judge. Susie didn't want this to happen. She wanted to protect Sean. The doctor told Susie she had to make another phone call but would be right back.

Susie didn't know there was an open case on Elaine with the Department of Children and Families (DCF). Sean's father left a long time ago and no one knew where he was. Susie suddenly felt nauseous. She chastised herself for not seeing Sean sooner than this. Sean looked like a broken little boy. Susie wouldn't let them take him from her for a night let alone a week.

The doctor returned to the room. Surprisingly, the doctor told them she could help them avoid DCF. She told Susie and Reid to take Sean, go out the back door and get into their car. She gave them a phone number. She told them to call the number and the person who answered would give them instructions. She told them to hurry.

Susie was confused. The doctor said to trust her. No one would ever hurt Sean again. Reid looked at Susie and told her they needed to go. He heard about too many kids getting hurt and even dying in foster care. Boston was bombarded with child abuse cases lately, some ending in the deaths of several children. Reid wanted Sean to be safe. They left through the back door of the clinic not knowing that their lives would forever change and Elaine would never see her son again.

CHAPTER 2

Detective Dana Blades was nervous but happy. He was getting married. He and Clare had been seeing each other for over a year now. He proposed to her a few months back and she accepted. He asked her sons, Eric and Tyler, for their permission before he asked Clare to marry him and they thought that was so cool. Blades loved those boys as if they were his own. In fact, he intended to adopt them after the wedding. He wasn't prepared for their reactions when Clare asked them if they wanted to change their names. The boys flung themselves at Blades and told him they would love to be his sons. Clare started crying and Blades took a few minutes to compose himself. His heart was bursting with love for those boys. Clare would have to deal with her ex-husband but he would sign off on any paperwork as long as it didn't cost him money.

Blades looked at himself in the mirror. He never imagined he would get married again. He was still friends with his ex-wife but never wanted to go through another divorce. When he met Clare, he knew he would get married again, if she said yes. He smiled at himself as he adjusted his bowtie. He was very tall at six foot, three and weighed about two hundred pounds. His skin was mocha brown. His goatee was perfectly shaped around his mouth and went well with his shaven head. Blades stayed in shape and ate as healthy as possible unless he was with Clare's family. They loved food.

Blades thought about Clare and smiled even more. She was something else. He had never met another woman like her. She was smart and beautiful. She was about five foot, eight inches and had a lean body probably because she was an avid runner. Plus she was a nurse so was committed to staying healthy. She had long, dirty blonde hair that had a natural wave to it and beautiful hazel eyes. She was a pretty upbeat, happy woman who was crazy about her boys. Blades was amazed at her positive attitude considering what she went through with her first husband, the boys' father. Blades had never met him but hated him anyway. He did a job on Clare's self-esteem despite her positive attitude. Blades wasn't sure Clare told him everything about Dennis and how he treated her. He always felt she was keeping something from him. She claimed she just wanted to forget about that part of her life.

Blade shook off thoughts of Clare's ex and decided to see how the boys were doing. Blades had asked Eric and Tyler to be his best men. They were thrilled beyond belief. Micah and Jake would be groomsmen and Harper and Emily were bridesmaids. Of course Theresa, Jake's wife, was the matron of honor. The grandmothers, Peg and Catherine, were walking Clare down the aisle. They were self-proclaimed feminists and didn't like the idea of a man "giving" Clare away as if she was property. The grandmothers were well liked and everyone loved their new outlook on life.

Blades asked the boys what Jake and Micah were doing,

"Hey guys, have you seen Jake and Micah? Are they getting dressed?"

"They're getting dressed now, Dad," yelled Eric. "I'll tell them to hurry it up."

Blades loved when the boys called him Dad even though the adoption was not official. It seemed that they wanted a father very badly and Blades hoped he could succeed in that role. Clare continually told him the boys were crazy about him. Blades was certainly marrying into an interesting family.

Blades thought about Jake and everything they all had gone through in the last year. Jake had just been released from prison three months ago. He had been convicted of aggravated assault for attacking a local high school swim coach. Blades was actually the one who stopped Jake from killing the coach who was about to be arrested for sexually abusing numerous girls. For some reason, Jake had taken it upon himself to stop the coach from hurting any more kids. The coach eventually went to prison and would never get out.

Jake claimed he just wanted to beat the shit out of the guy, not kill him. Jake served six months because he pled no contest. Most people regarded Jake as a hero but Blades wasn't so sure. Several other accused rapists had been killed before Jake had assaulted the coach. Blades didn't want to think about the possibility that Jake was the killer. Even though he had arrested Jake, he had been taken off the case because of his close relationship with Clare. He and Jake never discussed the case. But Jake knew Blades suspected him. Blades was also curious as to why Jake served any jail time.

Blades did speak to the Chief about it but the Chief basically shrugged him off claiming that they couldn't condone vigilante justice even in assault cases. Jake was made an example in this case. The investigation into the dead alleged rapists continued for a while but reached a dead end. No one seemed to want to resurrect these murder cases. They could find no actual evidence that Jake killed anyone. Blades wanted to believe that Jake had nothing to do with any of it. Whatever the case, he didn't think Jake was dangerous and he also thought he was looking at Jake too much after the assault instead of looking for the real killers. But Blades had no sympathy for the men who were killed because of what they had done to so many girls. It was a complex thought process. Blades always felt there was more to the killings than he understood. Once again, he shook off bad thoughts. This was his wedding day and he didn't want to think about anything else.

"Hey Blades, how are you holding up?" yelled Jake as he ran down the stairs grinning.

"I'm hanging in there," replied Blades. "Don't worry, I won't change my mind! Besides, Theresa would hunt me down and kill me!"

Jake laughed. He seemed happy. Prison didn't seem to have hurt him. He looked great despite his prison time. He was a little under six feet and very fit. He was always smiling and consistently laid back. Blades really liked him. Jake was lucky enough to get a job at a local community college when he was released from prison. The university Jake had worked for before his conviction fired him. Jake understood.

Blades thought about Theresa. She almost had a nervous breakdown when Jake went to prison. Harper and Micah had a hard time, too, but seemed to be bouncing back. Blades wondered if Theresa ever thought about the possibility that Jake was a serial killer. He would never ask her that question. Their marriage had survived the hard times and they seemed closer than ever. Theresa was a spitfire most times and very smart. She was shorter than Clare and more petite. What she lacked in stature, she made up in wit and a sharp tongue. She taught at the local university and was well known as an avid supporter of abused women and children. Blades had met her at a university event over a year ago and she set him up on a date with Clare. Now here he was getting married.

Blades yelled to the boys to hurry up.

"Come on guys, we can't be late!"

"Clare won't be on time," laughed Jake.

"I know but I am anxious to get to the inn," said Blades as he paced nervously.

Clare and Blades were getting married at a beautiful inn and then staying there for a few days for a mini honeymoon. Theresa would take the boys. Thankfully, Eric and Tyler loved staying at Theresa's house.

Blades headed out to the car. It was show time.

CHAPTER 3

Theresa and the girls ran around the house getting ready for the wedding. Harper was so excited to be a bridesmaid and of course so was Emily. They wore cream- colored gowns with lace overlays and spaghetti straps. Theresa wore a coral one. They were all very striking. Theresa was so happy that Clare was marrying Blades. She thought they were perfect for each other and her nephews loved Blades. She watched everyone running around and went to check on Clare.

"How's it going, Clare?" asked Theresa.

"Oh, fine. I'm so nervous," replied Clare with a slight blush.

"You'll be fine. Our mothers are walking you down the aisle, remember?" chided Theresa.

Clare burst out laughing at the thought. Their mothers insisted on accompanying her down the aisle. Peg was Clare and Theresa's mother and Catherine was Jake's mother. They told Blades that they weren't giving her to him but showing their approval. Blades was happy they approved because those were two people even he wouldn't cross.

Clare looked in the mirror. She loved her dress. It was a simple sleeveless cream -colored gown. The entire dress was lace. The halter wrapped beautifully around Clare's neck. Clare was very attractive and even nicer inside. Today her hair was perfectly coiffed. She barely wore make-up and was stunning.

"Speaking of our mothers, where are they?" asked Theresa.

"They're on their way here. God knows what they'll be wearing," said Clare as she shook her head.

The sisters laughed again. Theresa looked at Clare.

"You look so beautiful," she told her.

"Thank you, Theresa. If it wasn't for you, this wouldn't be happening."

"See, it pays to be pushy!" declared Theresa.

"We'll both have great husbands," said Clare with a very serious and sincere look on her face.

Theresa looked at Clare more seriously. She knew Clare meant what she said. She and Clare only discussed Jake's crime and prison time once. Theresa tried to explain to Clare why Jake attacked the coach but Clare told her she didn't need an explanation. She loved Jake and that was that. After all Clare went through with Dennis, that meant a lot to Theresa.

Theresa touched Clare's cheek and thanked her.

"Yes, we will," said Theresa softly.

Just then Grandma Peg and Nana Catherine burst into the room. They looked incredible. Both were dressed in cream colored tailored suits to match Clare's dress. They were in their seventies and both had beautiful white hair and beautiful blue eyes. They were in great health and loved life. Two years ago, they announced their feminist platforms and moved in together.

"You two look great!" exclaimed Clare.

"Thank you," they said in unison.

"We decided against dresses since everyone is wearing them. We thought Blades would take us more seriously if he saw the suits," declared Grandma Peg as she straightened her blazer.

"Oh, mom," said Clare. "He takes you very seriously and loves you both."

"Oh, we know," said Catherine. "We're just making sure. We adore him."

"Okay," said Theresa. "Let's get going. We don't want Blades to think we ran away!"

CHAPTER 4

Reid and Susie drove back to the playground. They wanted Sean to try to relax while they called the number given to them. They had no idea what was happening but given the panicked look on the doctor's face, Susie knew something serious was about to happen. She and Reid decided that they would at least call and if they didn't like what they heard, they would come up with another plan to protect Sean. Reid took Sean to the swings and tried to get him on one. Susie called the number the doctor gave her. A woman answered. Susie told her about the visit to the clinic. She spoke so fast the woman told her to slow down. The woman proceeded to tell her that if she wanted to save Sean she had to go underground.

"What do you mean?" asked Susie incredulously.

"You, your husband, and Sean will have to change your entire identities and move away. I'm not going to sugarcoat anything. You'll not be able to contact your family or friends again. I know this is abrupt but sometimes this is what it takes to protect a child," explained the woman.

"Oh my God," said Susie. "Why can't I just file for custody of Sean?"

"Because even if you get it, your sister will have access to

Sean and so will her boyfriend. Is that what you want for Sean? Are you willing to take that chance?" asked the woman very calmly.

"I don't know what to do. What if Elaine gets help? Wait a minute, how do you know about my sister?" Susie started to panic.

"The doctor called and told me," replied the anonymous woman.

"I'm so confused. What if I can convince Elaine to get help?" Susie asked again.

"How many times has she promised to do that?" asked the woman.

"Sean has no control over his life. He's a little boy trapped in a home with abusive so-called parents. He deserves a chance to have a healthy life and you can give it to him."

"Hold on," said an exasperated Susie, running her fingers through her hair.

Susie got out of the car and rushed over to Reid. She tried to get a hold of herself. Sean was actually playing on the pirate ship. She told Reid what the woman said and Reid took the phone from Susie. He walked away from Susie, talking and listening to the woman on the phone. Susie looked at Sean. He smiled at Susie. Her heart melted.

"Are you having fun, Sean?"

"I love this ship. This is my first time here," commented Sean with a smile.

"I'm so glad you're having fun," replied Susie with a tinge of sadness in her voice.

"Aunt Susie?" asked Sean.

"Yes, Sean."

"I'm hungry." He said hesitantly.

Susie looked at Sean closely. He was thin. She had only

given him snacks before they went to the park, assuming that he ate.

"When did you eat last?" asked Susie.

"Yesterday," said Sean in an all too routine sounding way.

Susie looked at Sean and thought that if a small boy said he was hungry so nonchalantly, what else was he hiding? Susie shook her head out of anger at Elaine and sadness for Sean. She looked for Reid and motioned him to come to her. He came back to where she was standing and Susie moved away from Sean.

"Tell the woman we're coming with Sean. He's never going back to his mother again," hissed Susie with conviction and immutable determination in her eyes. Reid saw that look before and knew she wasn't going to change her mind.

Reid looked at Susie with a serious look on his face.

"We're doing this?"

"Yes," said Susie. "We're doing this."

Susie turned to look at Sean again and then looked back at Reid.

"The last time he ate was yesterday," Susie told him. She tried very hard not to cry. She turned so Sean couldn't see her. Reid hugged Susie and told the woman on the phone to give him the address where they would meet.

CHAPTER 5

Everyone was finally at the inn. There were about fifty people in all. Blades stood with the justice of the peace on a small platform at the end of a slender red carpet. Eric and Tyler stood next to him, to his left, followed by Jake and Micah. Eric stole glances at Blades maybe to be sure he was still standing there. Harper and Emily made their way slowly up the aisle with huge smiles on their faces and looking incredibly beautiful. Theresa came next, also looking gorgeous. They all carried purple hydrangea bouquets. Theresa was smiling and trying not to cry at the same time. Finally, the grandmothers came with Clare. Clare had one on each side of her and held a bouquet of beautiful mixed flowers. As tough as the grandmothers claimed to be, they were trying not to cry, too.

Clare reached the end of the aisle and smiled tentatively at Blades. Blades took her hand and kissed her cheek.

"Hey," said the justice. "That's supposed to come later."

Everyone laughed. The ceremony was short and sweet. Blades and Clare didn't want to write their own vows. They just wanted to be married. Eric and Tyler beamed throughout the ceremony. When the justice told Blades to kiss his bride, everyone clapped. As they finished their embrace, Eric and

Tyler ran to the newlyweds and hugged them. It was an amazing, loving group hug. Now everyone in the place was crying. Clare was trying hard to stop crying.

The justice announced to the guests that there was a cocktail hour followed by a reception. He then introduced the newly titled husband and wife. Everyone clapped. Even Blades' police officer friends were a little teary-eyed. Then Eric asked everyone to wait. Clare looked at him with a surprised expression. Eric told the guests that he and Tyler had an announcement.

Eric and Tyler stood on the platform where the ceremony took place. Eric spoke.

"Blades is our Dad now," said Eric. Tyler nodded in agreement.

"Our names are Eric and Tyler Blades now," declared Tyler proudly.

The room became very quiet as everyone looked at these two proud and happy boys. Everyone started getting weepy again. Blades and Clare walked over to the boys and each took one of their hands. All four left the room as a family and headed to the reception.

"Okay," declared Jake. "Enough with the crying! Let's celebrate!"

They all headed to the reception room.

CHAPTER 6

Susie and Reid arrived at the designated "meet" spot. A man who was probably in his sixties approached them.

"Susie and Reid?" he asked in a serious tone.

"Yes," replied Susie.

Susie was nervous and thought she probably looked like hell. She wore yoga pants and a sweatshirt. She was petite with brown curly hair and green eyes. Reid was well over six feet and perfectly fit since he was a fire fighter. He had blond hair and piercing blue eyes.

"Follow my truck," the man instructed as he walked back to it. He was long and lanky and wore a plaid shirt and blue jeans. He didn't introduce himself.

Reid and Susie found themselves listening silently. They were still in shock about the chain of events. They thought they were visiting Sean today, not kidnapping him. They followed this man and drove for about forty minutes and turned down a dirt road. Reid drove and Susie talked to Sean until he fell asleep. Susie looked at Reid. He was such a good man. He was traditional but in a nice way. He had a happy face, the kind that looked like he was always on the verge of smiling. Reid reached for Susie's hand and squeezed it. He was so matter of fact about this decision. In a way Susie was not surprised because Reid had been abused as a child by his father. He probably wished someone had rescued him. They travelled the dirt road for about twenty minutes and then turned into a driveway. It was a long driveway that led to a farmhouse.

"Are you having second thoughts?" asked Reid.

"Not at all," replied Susie firmly.

Susie turned around and looked at Sean. He was fed and sleeping. She would never leave him. Everything seemed surreal but okay.

"How are we going to do this?" asked Reid.

"We'll know in a few minutes," replied Susie.

Reid parked the car behind the truck. He stepped out and walked toward the man they had followed. Susie stayed in the car with Sean since he was still sleeping. She watched as Reid spoke with the man. The man had long grayish hair pulled into a ponytail and a mustache. He was one of those thin guys who probably ate everything in sight.

"How's this going to work?" asked Reid.

"Well it's complicated but very organized," replied the man.

"What is?" asked Reid.

"Your new life," the man replied.

"Wait a minute. I need to know who you are," said a very serious Reid.

"My name is Sam. Not my real name, of course. You'll stay with me and my wife for a few days until we decide where you should go if you want to go through with this," explained Sam.

"Are you saying we'll be basically kidnapping Sean?" asked Reid.

"You might want to call it that but we call it saving him," responded Sam confidently.

"So, we're going to have to leave everything and everyone behind, aren't we?" asked Reid.

"Yes," replied Sam. "If you really want Sean to have a good life."

"How do you know we're the best option for Sean?" asked Reid.

Sam knew Reid was testing him.

"We don't for sure but you took him to a doctor," said Sam. "You seem genuinely concerned for his safety and he's comfortable with you. Plus we did a background check on both of you after you left the clinic and everything came back clean. We've been watching Elaine for some time now. We were about to make a move but then you and Susie surfaced."

Reid looked at Sam with a shocked expression.

"You've been watching Elaine? Who? How?" asked Reid.

"We have people all over the country helping children live safe lives. As soon as Elaine's case was opened, we started watching her. The social worker assigned to Sean failed to protect him. We're tired of that happening to helpless kids and we're not going to wait until the system gets its shit together," explained Sam.

"How do you really know we're safe? You know as well as I know that a background check doesn't mean much," said Reid.

"I know but it's a start. Besides, we have people checking you out more thoroughly; talking to your friends and whatnot," added Sam.

"What! Don't you think that's a bit suspicious? People might be wondering why you're asking so many questions," said a panicked Reid.

"Not the way we do it," replied Sam calmly.

Reid looked over to where Susie sat in the car. He ran his hands through his hair.

"Who's "we"? asked Reid, sounding very exasperated.

"I'll tell you more about that later. I know we're strangers but you have to try and trust us. We've been watching Sean and his mother. We're especially concerned about the boyfriend," warned Sam.

"Can you give me more details?" asked Reid. "Did Colin hurt Elaine or Sean? I want to be sure about what we're doing."

"Colin has hit both Sean and his mother but not serious enough for some kind of legal intervention. That's what frustrates us. My wife and I belong to a group that gives abused kids a chance at safe lives. It's very complicated but the gist of it is that we save kids' lives and stop bad parents from ever getting their kids back and having any more kids. We also stop some people from ever having kids in the first place," explained Sam.

Reid shook his head in confusion but wanted to hear more.

"Are you saying your "organization" kills people?" asked Reis.

"No," said Sam. "We sterilize bad parents or people the group thinks will be bad parents. They don't know even realize they're sterilized. As far as I know the group has never killed any parents."

"My God, what did we just walk into?" asked Reid.

"Believe me, nothing bad," said Sam. "You won't be associated with the sterilizations and most of our activities. You'll simply be safe so you and Susie can give Sean a good life."

"I think I've heard enough. Okay, what do we do next?" asked Reid.

"Come in the house," beckoned Sam.

Reid walked over to the car and opened the passenger door.

"Susie, let's go in the house. We have a lot to talk about. I'll grab Sean," said Reid.

Reid opened the back door and gently lifted Sean out of the car. He continued to sleep with his arms wrapped around Reid's neck. Susie followed them as they went into the house.

Sam held the side door open as Reid and Susie entered the house. They were greeted by a middle-aged woman named Janice.

"Welcome to our home," said Janice. She motioned for Reid to put Sean on the couch so he could continue sleeping. Reid did just that as Janice placed a blanket over Sean.

"Would you like some tea or coffee?" asked Janice.

"Water would be great," said Susie. Reid requested coffee.

"Okay," said Sam. "I know this is overwhelming but I promise it gets easier."

Susie sat beside Sean on the couch and rested her hand on his back. Sam asked Susie about the doctor's visit and she recounted the day they had with Sean, including what Sean told them.

"Sounds like he was abused on a regular basis," said Janice shaking her head with a look of genuine sadness on her face.

Susie eyes welled up with tears as she processed this. She looked at Sean on the couch. He looked so peaceful.

"Yeah, it seems that way," said Susie. "Why can't we just file for custody of Sean? We can prove he's abused."

"Yes, you could prove he's abused," said Sam. "However, your sister will likely get instructions to clean up her act and keep custody of Sean. She won't give him up because she probably wants the monthly check she gets for drugs. I'm sorry to be so blunt but it's true. Even if you get custody, your sister will probably get to see him on a regular basis. Sean will be bounced around and you can't guarantee that no one will hurt him. Frankly, he is better off being kidnapped by you."

"That's what we're doing," Reid said quietly. "We're kidnapping him."

"We're giving him a safe life, Reid," said Susie as she processed what Sam had just said.

Susie turned to Sam with a determined look.

"What's next?" she asked.

"Well, we have to decide where you're going and buy some time," said Sam.

Susie had a quick suggestion.

"I can call Elaine and ask her if we can take Sean for the week to our house in Connecticut. She won't care because she'll be free of any responsibility. This will give us a week or more to get our things in order."

"Are you sure she'll go for that?" asked Sam.

"Just listen," said Susie.

Susie pulled her phone out of her pocket and called Elaine.

"Hey, Elaine. It's Susie. How are you?"

"Great," slurred Elaine as she giggled.

"Where are you?" asked Susie with an irritated tone.

"I'm at a friend's with Colin."

"Well, Reid and I are wondering if we can take Sean back to Connecticut for the week. We don't get to see him much and you probably need a break," said Susie in a hopeful tone.

"That's a great idea!" exclaimed Elaine. "He loves his Auntie Susie and Uncle Reid. Keep him as long as you want."

Susie's heart sank. Elaine could care less about her son. She didn't even ask about him.

"I'll be in touch," said Susie.

But Elaine had already hung up.

Susie looked at Reid. Suddenly she was filled with rage.

"Elaine will never see him again," she vowed.

"Okay," said Sam. "We have some work to do. Tomorrow

you should go to your house and pack as many things as you can but tell no one what you're doing. If anyone does ask, just say you're going on a trip since it's school vacation. Reid, can you get time off, so to speak?"

"Yeah," said Reid. "I have plenty of vacation days."

"Good, then," said Sam.

Janice was listening carefully the entire time.

"Well, let's eat and get some sleep," she suggested.

Janice showed them their rooms after they woofed down some sandwiches. Susie, Reid, and Sean needed to sleep.

CHAPTER 7

Reilly Simonsen finally graduated with her Masters in journalism. She was an idealist and believed that the media's role in society should be reassessed and redefined. The media's role should be the watchdog of the people according to Reilly. Right now the media continued to be more concerned about profit than truth. In fact, so-called mainstream media was now depending on tabloid programs to provide them with some news. It was disgraceful. Where were the investigative skills? Media personnel printed or broadcasted stuff that garnered the most attention. Who cares if Beyonce decided to try a vegan diet? That was leading news one morning. Jesus, people died all over the world from hunger and Beyonce thinks the answer is a vegan diet? This stuff pissed Reilly off to no end. Reilly wanted freedom of speech to be honored. Everything little thing people said was policed now. Sometimes she was afraid to open her mouth or write down serious thoughts for fear of being accused of some dreaded opinion.

Reilly lived with her great-aunt Loretta. Her mother died of breast cancer when Reilly was six and she didn't know who her father was because her mother had been artificially inseminated. Aunt Loretta had never married and had no kids of her own. Upon Reilly's mother's death, Aunt Loretta was given custody. Reilly's other relatives didn't question this choice because Reilly's mother was very close to her Aunt Loretta and everyone knew she would take care of Reilly. Aunt Loretta had a lot of money. Her father had left her a pile of it when he died and Aunt Loretta had invested it wisely. She put Reilly through private schools and paid for her to go to university.

Reilly adored her eccentric aunt. She was very liberal for her age. She did a lot of volunteering and charity work and she was brilliant. She would put people to shame on Jeopardy given the chance. Reilly begged her to apply to be a contestant but Aunt Loretta would just laugh and say she didn't want to embarrass anyone with her genius. Reilly certainly got a kick out of her aunt. She loved watching her pick out her outfits for the day. Aunt Loretta wore a dress or skirt everyday and she had coats and shoes to match every outfit. Her bluish gray hair was always perfectly coiffed as was her make-up. Reilly wasn't the skirt or dress type. She preferred jeans and a sweatshirt but loved when her aunt displayed her fashion sense.

This particular evening, Reilly was practicing for a job interview with her aunt's help. Most of the time they just ended up laughing because Aunt Loretta would ask outrageous questions that had nothing to do with a job interview. Reilly was nervous but confident about her job prospects. Aunt Loretta had a lot of contacts because of her charity work but Reilly wanted to find a job on her own. She was very interested in working for the Boston Globe but didn't think she had a chance. She wanted to be an investigative reporter and there was a lot going on in Boston all of the time. Reilly was particularly interested in crime stories.

Even though Reilly didn't want her aunt's help, her aunt had already made some calls. Reilly would get the job because she was qualified but Aunt Loretta just wanted to make sure. No one at the Globe would know about Aunt Loretta calling in a favor, as they say, except for the person interviewing Reilly. It wasn't a "pity" hire. Reilly was damn good at what she did, sometimes a bit too passionate, but good.

CHAPTER 8

Dana and Clare settled into their new home with ease. It wasn't new for Blades but was new for Clare and the boys. It was probably new in a special way for Blades because he now had a family living there. The boys were happy; everyone was happy. Clare's ex-husband, Dennis agreed to let the boys change their names to Blades probably so he wouldn't have to pay child support. On one hand, Clare was glad but on the other she was sad that Dennis didn't care about the boys. She knew it was better in the long run because Dennis had been cruel. Clare hadn't shared everything about her marriage to Dennis with Blades because it was too painful.

School break was almost over and everyone was sad it was coming to an end. Clare, Blades, and the boys were having a blast. They spent a lot of time with Theresa and Jake. One day during break, Blades took the boys into work and introduced them to everyone as his sons. The boys beamed with pleasure. They came home on cloud nine. Claire noticed that whenever Dana was home, the boys followed him everywhere. It was endearing. On the last night of break, everyone went over to Theresa's for dinner. This was a common occurrence.

The grandmothers made a big dinner as usual. There was

always way too much food but everyone would get doggie bags. They brought everything over to Theresa's. They cooked an entire turkey dinner with all of the trimmings. They even made pumpkin pie. They announced that people shouldn't have to wait until Thanksgiving for a good turkey dinner. No one complained.

"So Blades, any new and exciting cases?" asked Micah as they ate.

Micah was Theresa and Jake's fifteen-year old son. He was genuinely interested in police work and wanted to be a police officer when he got older.

"Unfortunately, there's always something going on," said Blades.

"Crime never sleeps," said Harper, Micah's sister.

"Let's talk about something more positive," said Theresa. She didn't like talking about crime especially given Jake's experiences.

"Yeah, like when are you and Clare going to have a baby?" asked Jake.

Everyone started hooting and hollering while Clare turned as red as a beet.

Blades laughed so hard he almost choked.

"What's so funny?" asked Grandma Peg.

"We just got married," said Clare. "Stop bugging us!"

"Besides," said Blades. "We already have two kids. We couldn't get a better family if we tried."

Eric and Tyler aimed wide toothed grins at Blades and Clare. Their smiles were certainly contagious as everyone looked at them. They were ten and twelve years old, respectively. They were both still in the lanky stages and loved basketball. Tyler was darker than Eric, who was very fair. They were both very handsome boys and did well in school. Blades thought it was interesting that they never mentioned their father. This nagged at Blades. Something more must have happened to them that Clare didn't share. He didn't want to push the issue. He figured Clare would open up when she was ready.

Nana Catherine broke the brief moment of silence by announcing that everyone needed to bring their plates to the kitchen. Everyone did just that and then was ushered into the living room for coffee.

"Are you looking forward to going back to work?" asked Theresa as she and Clare helped clean up.

"Not really," laughed Clare. "But I'll be fine once I get there."

"Believe it or not, the boys want to go back to school," Blades informed her.

"I'm not really that surprised," said Theresa. "They're at the age where school is one big social event."

"It's getting harder to keep up with them," said Clare.

"They grow up so fast, Clare. You'll miss keeping up with them," said Theresa.

Clare knew that she was thinking about Harper now being in college.

"We'll always have our kids," Clare assured Theresa with a smile.

Blades' phone rang breaking the sullen moment.

"Blades, here," he answered.

Theresa and Clare changed the subject and started planning a shopping day for Harper. Theresa always had to warn Clare not to buy her too much but Clare never listened. She loved buying for Harper because she was like the daughter she didn't have. They decided on a date as Blades walked back into the room.

"Clare, I have to go. There's an Amber Alert in town. A newborn was taken from Children's Hospital."

"Oh my God," declared Theresa. "That's terrible."

"Go ahead Dana. I 'll see you at home," added Clare.

Blades gave Clare a quick kiss on the cheek and headed toward the door. He yelled to the boys that he would see them at home. Eric came running down the stairs.

"Wait!" he yelled.

Blades stopped in his tracks and turned to Eric. Eric ran to him and gave him a big hug.

"Be careful out there, Dad," he said.

Blades kissed the top of Eric's head as his eyes welled up with tears. He was overwhelmed by the affection the boys showed him.

"Thanks, buddy. Give Tyler a hug for me."

"No way," declared Eric. "You can hug him when you get home!"

Blades laughed and went out the front door. Theresa and Clare watched as he left.

"Wow," said Theresa. "Those boys love their Dad."

"So do I," said Clare. "So do I."

CHAPTER 9

Susie woke before Reid and discovered Sean sleeping between them. She kissed the top of his head and quietly slipped out of bed. Sean started out on the cot in the room when he went to bed and obviously changed his mind about his sleeping arrangements. Susie didn't mind one bit. She walked downstairs and immediately smelled coffee.

"Good morning," said Janice with a huge smile on her face.

"Good morning," replied Susie.

"Sit down dear and I'll get your breakfast. The coffee is right on the table," Janet said as she pointed in that direction.

"You don't have to make my breakfast," said Susie.

"It's already done, dear," declared Janice.

Janice took a heaping pile of pancakes out of the oven followed by another heaping pile of bacon. She placed the plates on the table.

"Dig in, Susie," she said.

"If she doesn't, we will."

The two women turned around to see Reid carrying Sean into the kitchen. Sean had a huge smile on his face. Reid put him down and he ran to Susie. He jumped up on her lap. Susie heart melted once again. Sean was so relaxed with them.

"You hungry, Sean?" asked Susie.

"I love pancakes," he said.

Reid made a plate for Sean and himself. They both ate like they hadn't eaten in days.

Janice and Sam joined them at the table. They each poured themselves a second cup of coffee. They watched the new and happy family eating together. They looked like they had always been together.

"What's next?" asked Reid.

"Finish your breakfast," said Sam. "Then we'll talk."

Susie and Sean finished eating. Janice suggested they wash up and come back down when they were finished. Susie understood this as removing Sean from the room. She challenged Sean to a race to get him moving. Of course she let him win.

"So," said Sam. "I believe we came up with a good plan. Tell me what you think. Janice and I spoke with some other members of our group and thought it would be best for you guys to go to your house."

"Really?" replied Reid.

"Yeah. This will give you more time to move. Elaine said to keep Sean as long as you want. Susie is still on vacation so it'll look like she just has her nephew for the week. No one will be suspicious. Gather as many things as you can. Close your bank accounts. Susie mentioned you're renting your house so that's good. You told me earlier that you have a lot of vacation days to use. No one will ask questions at least for a week or two and by then you'll have your new life," explained Sam.

"Okay. I'll have to talk to Susie about this. What do we tell Sean?" asked Reid.

"That's the tough part," said Janice. "You're going to have to tell him the truth. He may only be four but he knows that his home life is not healthy or safe. He'll probably be happy that you're taking him away from that."

"This is so surreal," said Reid.

"I know," said Janice. "You're saving a child's life. A lot of kids don't get these second chances. We know." Her eyes welled up with tears.

"Our granddaughter died when she was two," explained Janice.

"Our daughter was in a terrible realtionship with an evil man. We kept telling her to leave him but she wouldn't mainly because she was afraid of him. We took Anna as much as we could. We went back and forth about getting custody of her. We waited too long because everyone around us convinced us that she belonged with her mother. We fell for the "keep the family together" philosophy. Our daughter's boyfriend got drunk one night and hit little Anna in the head. She never woke up. He's in prison for life. Our daughter committed suicide shortly after Anna died. We lost our family. We should have been more insistent about having Anna live with us. I'll never forgive myself."

"Janice, you have to stop blaming yourself, " said Sam as he touched her hand. "It won't do you any good. We're doing this for Anna. She's our guardian angel now. She's at peace with her mother at last," said Sam.

"I'm so sorry," said Reid.

"Don't make the same mistake we did," said Janice, looking directly at Reid.

"Let me go talk to Susie," said Reid as he headed to the stairs leading up to the bedrooms.

Susie was tickling Sean when Reid walked in the room.

"Hey guys," said Reid.

"What's going on?" asked Susie as she sensed Reid's semi-serious tone.

Reid told Susie what Sam suggested. He left out the part about their granddaughter. Sean listened intently and kept looking at Susie for her reaction. Susie knew what he was doing. He was checking to see if she really wanted to take him with her. Susie turned to Sean and put her hands on his shoulders.

"Sean, do you understand what Uncle Reid is saying? We'll move far away and you'll have to change your name. You'll never see your mother again," explained Susie softly.

Susie tensed and her stomach turned as she waited for Sean's reaction. Telling him he will never see his mother again was tough.

Sean's bottom lip trembled as his eyes filled with tears.

"I don't want to go back there," he whispered as a tear slid down his cheek.

Susie believed Sean knew what they were asking him to do and she was trying very hard not to cry. She wasn't sure if she was sad that Sean didn't want to be with his mother or glad that she and Reid would raise Sean safely. Reid and Susie both knew that Sean didn't fully comprehend the seriousness of the situation but knew in their hearts it was the right thing to do. Susie breathed a long sigh of relief and hugged Sean.

"You don't ever have to go back there," Susie promised as she held Sean's cheeks and looked straight into his eyes.

Sean wrapped his arms around Susie, squeezing tightly. He buried his face in her chest. Without picking his head up, he raised his left arm toward Reid. Reid looked surprised and hesitant but stepped into the hug. All three hugged silently for a long time. Susie had never felt this depth of love before for a child. She now understood that kids always come first.

CHAPTER 10

Blades arrived at the hospital where Clare worked. He headed to the maternity ward. When he reached the main desk, he spotted Dr. Kelly Lehman. He met her before when he was investigating a case involving another doctor from the hospital a few years ago.

"Well hello, Detective Blades," said Dr. Lehman with a smile on her face.

"Hello to you, Dr. Lehman," replied Blades.

"I assume you're here about the missing baby," Dr. Lehman stated.

"Yes, I am. Do you work in this department now?" Blades asked.

"No, I was checking on a baby I performed surgery on. Any leads on the missing child?" she asked.

"Not that I know of," said Blades. "I just arrived."

"Nice to see you again. I hope you find the baby," said Dr. Lehman.

"Thank you, Dr. Lehman. Me, too," said Blades as he watched the doctor walk away.

Blades always had a weird feeling around her like something was off. Dr. Lehman intrigued Blades. She was incredibly smart and confident. She was tall for a woman at five foot, eleven. She probably played basketball in university. Even though Dr. Lehman was friendly, Blades always felt her holding back. He couldn't explain it. There was just something about her that didn't feel right even though he had never heard a bad thing about her.

Blades decided to speak with a group of officers and detectives already at the hospital before he spoke with the baby's parents. He checked in with the group of officers who told him that according to the baby's mother, she fell asleep and when she woke up the baby was gone. The mother assumed the nurse took her to feed her. That was all they knew at this point. Blades decided to talk to the mother first and the father second.

"Hello, Alissa," said Blades as he walked into the mother's room. "I'm Detective Blades. Can I ask you a few questions about your daughter?"

"Of course," Alissa replied. "I can't believe someone took her. I'm going crazy with worry."

Blades noticed Alissa was jittery and glancing around the room frantically. She kept wringing her hands, too.

"What do you remember?" asked Blades.

"I fed Ivy and then put her in her basinet. Then I fell asleep. When I woke up an hour later, she was gone. I thought the nurse had her so I went back to sleep," explained Alissa.

Alissa continued to rub her hands together and glanced about the room. Blades recognized her behavior as that of a drug addict detoxing. He tried not to look disgusted.

"No one came in to visit you?" asked Blades.

"Just Darren, Ivy's father," Alissa replied.

"Would he take her from you?" asked Blades.

"No, never," said Alissa. "We plan to get clean and start fresh. Ivy changed our lives."

"Where's Darren now?" asked Blades, ignoring her sudden devotion to her child. He wondered where her devotion was when she used drugs during her pregnancy.

"He's talking with another officer," explained Alissa.

"Okay, I'll be back. Try to think about who might have taken the baby," Blades suggested.

Blades left the room and headed toward the nurse's desk. He had little patience for drug- addicted parents. Blades asked to speak to the nurse on duty at the time of the alleged kidnapping. Nurse Bridget came forward.

"Hi Detective Blades, I'm Bridget. I was working when Ivy was taken."

"Hi, Bridget, thanks for talking with me," replied Blades. "Tell me what you were doing when the baby was taken."

"I left Alissa's room and went to check on another mother. Ivy was sleeping peacefully," explained Bridget as if she rehearsed her explanation.

The nurse appeared to be very upset.

"Okay, calm down. What's the story on the mother? Is she using?" asked Blades.

"Yes," said Bridget. "She's a crack addict and so is the baby's father. Ivy was born addicted to crack but had finished withdrawing. Alissa has an open case on her with social services. The social worker is trying to get her into a program so she can keep the baby. The father is supposed to go into one, too."

"How old is Ivy?" asked Blades.

"She's a little over a week old now. Under the circumstances she's very healthy," replied Bridget.

"Alissa just told me she has every intention of staying clean and raising Ivy," said Blades.

Nurse Bridget's eyes clouded over.

"This is her third child from a third father, Detective Blades. She lost the other two children because of her addiction. It's beyond my comprehension that a social worker would try to help her keep Ivy but that's the system today. I don't know what to think," said Bridget with obvious disgust.

"I see," said Blades. "You seem to be saying Alissa doesn't deserve to mother Ivy."

"She doesn't," said Bridget. "But that's not up to me. I want the baby to be safe. Just because she's gone doesn't mean she's safe."

"Does the mother have any family interested in the baby?" asked Blades telling himself to calm down.

"There's a grandfather who's involved but not in a custody sense. That's all I know," shared Bridget.

"Would the grandfather take the baby?" asked Blades.

"He wasn't in the hospital today, so no. I only met him one time and he seemed very concerned about the baby but he didn't appear able to care for her," replied Bridget.

"Okay, is the social worker on her way?" Blades inquired.

"As far as I know," said Bridget.

"Okay, I may have to talk to you again," said Blades.

"I'm not going anywhere. I'm under lock and key. I'll be lucky if I keep my job," responded Bridget.

As Blades walked away, he wondered how the baby got through the wired exit. All newborns wore sensory bracelets. If someone tried to leave the ward, the alarm would sound. Clearly someone removed the bracelet. He walked toward the group of officers once again.

"Anything new?" asked Blades.

"No, nothing," replied Officer Kilroy. "The father's on his

way. Turns out he has an alibi. He was busy getting high with his friends when his daughter disappeared."

"So much for cleaning up his act," said Blades. "I'm going to talk to the social worker. If anything new develops, find me."

"Will do," promised Kilroy.

Blades approached the social worker standing at the nurse's desk. She looked shaken up. Blades introduced himself and asked her to sit in a private office provided for the investigation.

"Nice to meet you, Detectives Blades. I'm Charlotte Cole."

Blades got right to the point. He was trying hard not to immediately dislike the social worker who wanted little Ivy to stay with a crack addicted mother and father.

"How long have you known Alissa and Darren?" asked Blades.

"I was just assigned the case a month ago. Alissa lost her two other children to foster care and eventually the department found out she was pregnant again. A doctor reported her for using crack during the pregnancy when she landed in the emergency room one night. Apparently she was bleeding. The doctor believed she was punched in the stomach but couldn't say for sure," explained Charlotte.

"So, I understand you implemented a plan for Alissa and Darren to get clean so they could keep the baby?" asked Blades trying to hide his sarcasm.

"Yes, Ivy was going to be placed in temporary foster care while they went through a program," replied Charlotte rather proudly.

"You realize Darren is using right now?" asked Blades.

"I was just told that but that might be just a little slip up," explained Charlotte.

"Are you serious?" asked Blades raising his voice. "You're still considering letting them raise that baby?" he asked incredulously.

"Well, they didn't harm the baby," replied Charlotte defensively.

"So, if they take the baby home and get high, that's a slip? Maybe when they're high, they'll forget they have a baby! Did you ever think about that?" asked Blades in an agitated voice.

"I think you're overreacting, Detective Blades. I'll be watching them closely," Charlotte assured him.

Blades couldn't believe what he was hearing. He was a big proponent of using the system but this baby had no control over who raised her.

"Do you know of anyone who would want to take the baby?" asked Blades.

"No. No one ever asked and Alissa never mentioned anyone. I believe she's estranged from her family. Darren's father wants to be involved in the baby's life but he is in no position to raise a child," explained Charlotte.

"Would Alissa have given the baby to anyone or God forbid sell her?" asked Blades.

"Absolutely not! She couldn't wait to be a mother to Ivy," exclaimed Charlotte.

Blades looked at the fresh-faced social worker. She couldn't have been more than twenty-three years old. She knew nothing about life and here she was making major decisions about a child. She was so naïve. How could she think for a second that Alissa would be a good mother? He thanked the social worker and told her he would stay in touch.

Blades walked back to the nurse's desk and saw Bridget talking with what he assumed to be her supervisor. They were short staffed when Ivy was taken, according to Bridget. That was a problem in itself. Bridget seemed upset but was trying to keep it together. Blades saw her nod her head and then leave. He walked over to the supervisor.

"Where's Bridget going?" asked Blades.

"I'm sending her home," said the head nurse. "She's going to take some vacation days but isn't leaving the area."

"Okay," said Blades. "I need her number and address in case I need to reach her."

The supervisor walked over to the nurse's desk and gave Blades the requested information. As Blades finished up at the hospital, Bridget headed to the parking lot and got into her car. She immediately made a phone call.

"It's done," she said. "They don't suspect me at all. They think I messed up at work but have no idea I took the baby."

"Where's the baby now?" asked the voice at the other end.

"She's with Cliff who's bringing her to Greg and Nancy. Then Greg and Nancy are bringing her to Ricky and William. I talked to Greg earlier and all of the paperwork is ready," Bridget informed the person known as the Doyen.

"Okay, get rid of the sensor bracelet," ordered the Doyen.

"I will," Bridget promised.

"Did you give the mother an injection?" asked the Doyen.

"Yes, she'll never have another baby," said Bridget proudly.

"It's too bad we couldn't give one to the father," replied the Doyen.

"I know, but at least we got to one of them. If he does decide to get treatment for his drug abuse, we have some connections in a few places. We can also pay him a visit at his home. He'll get the injection," Bridget said with confidence.

Bridget hung up and took the cut sensor bracelet out of her bra. She would get rid of it when she got home. Normally if someone tried to cut a sensor bracelet off, the alarm would sound. Bridget turned off the monitor/alarm system for a few minutes while she cut the bracelet off Ivy. She smiled to herself. She was so happy for Ricky and William. They just got married but had been trying to adopt for years as a couple. Being gay didn't help because of so many discriminating obstacles. They weren't sticking around, though.

Ricky and William would move to Ottawa, Canada where all three would start a new life. Ivy was Lily now. Ricky and William were her parents' new names. All three had passports, birth certificates and adoption papers. Of course Ricky and William could never return to the United States. They would meet another couple in the same situation in Ottawa. Jobs were also arranged for them that would eventually ensure their permanent residency in Canada. Lily would have a great life. If she stayed here, the Department of Children and Families, also known as DCF, would put Lily through hell by giving her parents a chance to raise her.

Bridget thought about the injections the group routinely gave to particular people. The group had been sterilizing people for decades. The leader of the group was known only as the "Doyen". No one suspected anything. If the group had to take a child from abusive and neglectful parents, it made sure the parents were sterilized. A member of the group was a chemist. She concocted a drug to cause infertility. It was actually a combination of drugs. The drug cocktail included various individual antineoplastic agents and combinations of chemotherapeutic drugs. Sometimes people had reactions but most didn't. The group didn't care about the reactions, just the results.

Millions of parents had been sterilized across North America. Group members were unanimous when it came to sterilizing bad parents. Group members weren't so unanimous when it came to sterilizing potential parents. This was definitely a bone of contention within the group but with a minority of people. As long as the majority of the group agreed with requested actions, the actions would be justified. The group could not get to everyone but it tried. It was always very busy in Boston and surrounding areas. Too many children were hurt and too many social workers neglected their cases.

Bridget agreed with most of the decisions the group made concerning who would or wouldn't make great parents or who were already bad parents. The major glitch was adoption. The people who were sterilized could always try to adopt children. The group ran interference there, too. All of the injected were flagged by adoption agencies or the Department of Children and Families. The group had people placed in every occupation particularly any occupation dealing directly with the welfare of children. The group wasn't a perfect establishment but all members believed they were doing great work. Yes, it seemed like the group was playing God but God wasn't an issue. The system failed children, so the group stepped in.

The group didn't just monitor parents or potential parents. The group dealt with pedophiles as well. Not everyone in the group knew this. Pedophiles included parents, grandparents, uncles, cousins, coaches, priests and so on. Known pedophiles whether convicted or not, were simply killed if the group could get to them. Most members involved in relocating children had no idea about these killings.

Pedophiles had no second chances with the group. The group vehemently agreed that since there was no cure for pedophilia, child molesters should die. There was no value in these people. The group had killed thousands of pedophiles in various ways all over North America. Some were simply killed in prison; others killed in their homes, in their cars, at their work, etc. The group didn't discriminate; all pedophiles identified by the group were exterminated.

Priests, especially, infuriated most group members. Priests

were supposed to be doing good work, providing comfort and support to people of all ages. They preached on a regular basis about being kind and spreading God's good work. God's work didn't include molesting children. Priests, like most pedophiles, took advantage of their positions of power. They convinced people to trust them. Parents learned to trust priests by handing over their children to serve churches. Many children ended up serving the priests in the vilest ways possible.

Before pedophiles were actually killed, they were informed that they would die. Members of the group wanted them to know that what they did to children was evil; they wanted them to be terrified before they died. A lot of the deaths were made to look like suicides. Many pedophiles were forced to write suicide notes admitting to their crimes and stating that they wanted to die. Pedophile priests generally agreed to let the group stage a suicide. Some pedophiles just "disappeared" and were considered cold cases by law enforcement agencies. For the most part, law enforcement agents didn't fall all over themselves trying to find people responsible for killing pedophiles.

Bridget thought about the Doyen in her group. She was impressed with the Doyen's dedication to children. Very few knew who the Doyen was even though the Doyen attended every meeting. He or she was never identified. There was a Doyen in every designated area in North America. The Doyen ordered all of the injections, kidnappings and kills after the meetings. Everyone involved with the group would receive instructions via other members. Very few questioned decisions because for the most part, the Doyen approved whatever the majority of the group approved. Doyens remained anonymous in order to maintain as much objectivity as possible. Bridget's group had a very strong Doyen.

CHAPTER 11

Reid and Susie left Sam and Janice's home and headed back to Connecticut. Their plan was to stay in Connecticut for a few days and then drive to the next location. They were nervous about going home but were committed to the plan. Susie tried calling Elaine several times but she kept getting Elaine's voicemail. Susie couldn't believe Elaine had not even checked on Sean. She really shouldn't be that surprised. They drove for over four hours and reached their home. It was late afternoon and they were all tired.

All three went into the house. Sean was thirsty so Susie got him some juice.

"This is a nice house," said Sean. "It's clean."

Susie looked around at their little home knowing she would never see it again in a few days. They were renters but had been interested in buying the house. It was a simple raised ranch with a great back yard. It would be perfect for Sean if they could have him legally.

Reid was on the phone making arrangements for his so-called vacation. He would miss his co-workers who were also his friends. He hung up and looked at Susie.

"All set," he said.

Susie felt bad for Reid but the alternative would destroy Sean.

"Sean and I are going to Target to get some clothes and a few toys," announced Susie.

"Yay!" yelled Sean. "I get to have some toys!"

Susie smiled and walked out to the car with Sean, holding his hand.

Reid looked around the house and decided to start packing. He still couldn't believe what they were about to do. They were actually kidnapping a kid. He second- guessed himself almost all the way home in the car. But every time he looked at Sean he knew they were doing the right thing. He saw a lot as a firefighter and EMT. He saw endless families who were clearly dysfunctional and children who were victims and collateral damage of the dysfunction. He was tired of waiting for the system to protect children. On one level he was angry that the system let so many kids fall through the cracks. He was angry that so many parents were given too many chances to keep their kids. There was nothing proactive about the system; it was reactive. The most common response was to wait until something happened to kids before the system kicked in appropriately and even then it failed miserably for far too many children. Abusing children was routine in the U.S.

Reid was determined to give Sean a healthy life, a second chance to be a child. He would miss his friends terribly but he would make new ones. He wished someone had helped him as a boy. Reid hoped they wouldn't get caught. He thought about Susie and how devoted she was to Sean already. They would be okay. One thing he kept thinking about was the idea that Sam's group was actually sterilizing people. This should really spook Reid and Susie but for some odd reason, it didn't. The sterilizing didn't bother Reid. The fact that Reid wasn't bothered by it bothered him.

CHAPTER 12

Reilly aced the job interview. Devan Ferguson was the senior editor and seemed like a great person. She was very encouraging when they talked about Reilly's ambitions. Reilly's references were impeccable. She was a well-respected grad student. Before Reilly left the office, Devan Ferguson offered her the job.

"Well Reilly, you are most impressive and there's no need for me to drag this on. I would like to offer you the job," Devan informed her.

"Wow, are you serious? Oh my God, I can't thank you enough. I'm so excited. When do I start?" asked Reilly.

"Would you like to know your salary first?" laughed Devan.

"Oh yeah, sure," said Reilly as she caught her breath.

Devan offered Reilly quite a package for a first time job. It was a more than respectable salary and benefit package.

"I'll take the job," said Reilly with a huge smile on her face. Wait until Aunt Loretta hears this, she thought.

"Can you start tomorrow?" asked Devan.

"Absolutely!" said Reilly. "I have a great idea for my first story."

"Tell me about it, tomorrow. Go celebrate!" ordered Devan.

"Thank you," said Reilly for the hundredth time.

Reilly left the building and skipped all of the way to her car. She pulled out her cell phone and shared the great news with Aunt Loretta. They would definitely be celebrating. Aunt Loretta hung up the phone with a smile. She would do anything for Reilly.

CHAPTER 13

Blades headed home. His first day back to work was hectic but he looked forward to going home to his family. He couldn't believe how his life had changed. All of a sudden he had a wife and kids. He was so happy. He was crazy about Clare and the boys. He thought about the baby who was missing and wondered how her mother really felt. Clare would be an absolute mess if anything ever happened to the boys.

Blades thought about Alissa. She was not overly distraught about her missing baby but people react in different ways. The nurse was more interesting to Blades right now. She was very matter of fact with her answers. He expected her to be a bit more concerned about the baby since she disappeared on her shift. She seemed to be more concerned about her job and not a big fan of Alissa's. He would have to question her some more.

Blades pulled into his garage. He could hear Clare laughing. The boys must be up to something. Blades went in through the garage door and was greeted by two excited boys.

"Hey, Dad!" they both yelled.

"Hey, guys. How was your first day back?" asked Blades.

"It was good. Just a bunch of school work," said Tyler.

"We have basketball practice tonight. Can you take us?" asked Eric excitedly.

"Let him get in the door, boys!" laughed Clare.

"It's okay. I like when people are happy to see me. Most aren't, you know!" declared Blades.

"That's true," said Clare laughing.

"Of course I'll take you to practice," said Blades with a smile. "Mom must need a break from you two crazies."

"Finish your homework boys," instructed Clare. "Supper will be ready in twenty minutes."

"I can get used to this," said Blades. "I get supper and happy people?"

"Today, anyway," joked Clare. "How was your day? I heard more about the missing baby on the news."

"She's still missing and we really have nothing to go on right now," shared Blades.

"The mother must be devastated," said Clare.

"That's hard to tell," said Blades. "She's a drug addict and already had two kids taken from her."

"Oh boy," said Clare. "Not good."

"We'll have people on the case 24 hours a day," said Blades.

"I find it really interesting how fast and furious the police respond to missing children. I know it's to find the child and keep her safe but DCF should rethink their so-called philosophy on keeping families together. If you ask me, it's more concerned about protecting parental rights than children's rights," declared Clare.

"I think you're right, Clare. The social worker on the case didn't seem concerned that the mother was an addict and the father was actually using at the time of the abduction. She was so focused on reuniting the family. That's not always a good idea," agreed Blades.

"I wish there was some way to stop some people from having babies in these situations. You wouldn't believe what I see at work," shared Clare.

"There's nothing we can do about that," said Blades. "Anyone can be a parent."

"Well, let's eat. We're having lasagna and salad," Clare informed Blades.

"Supper is ready boys," yelled Blades.

CHAPTER 14

Dr. Lehman received confirmation that Lily, the former Ivy, was safely on her way to Ottawa. She was relieved. There had been some close calls with this one. The police responded faster than she thought. Bridget did manage to get the baby out with no fuss but Dr. Lehman imagined the police would focus on Bridget for a while since she was the last one to see the baby.

Dr. Kelly Lehman had been involved in the group for five years now. Everyone just referred to the organization as "the group". Dr. Lehman was propositioned to join the group when one of her patients lost custody of her son. She was a battered woman that Dr. Lehman had treated in the hospital. Her husband had broken her jaw and Dr. Lehman repaired it. The woman eventually told her that her husband was given temporary custody of their son because she was in the hospital. This was the guy who broke her jaw. He was out on bail and a judge actually believed that the boy would be better off with his father because she didn't want the family disrupted too much. So, here was another case where the traditional family unit was more important than the safety of a child and his mother.

Dr. Lehman thought about that woman again. She was

living in Pennsylvania as far as she knew. Dr. Lehman helped re-locate her on one of her son's visitation days. The boy's father dropped him off with the mom and never saw him again. The group had arranged everything. When the mother and son headed to the park, they were picked up by a van and whisked away. Dr. Lehman didn't even know their new names or where exactly they were in Pennsylvania. All she did know was how sick and tired she was of children being victims of a system committed to keeping dysfunctional families together or ignoring them.

Why people believed that if they were in a family, they would be safe was beyond Lehman's comprehension. That was the problem with this society. The family was always touted as the foundation of society: the safe haven. There were millions of broken families. Some of these families needed to stay "broken". In other words, if a child was taken from a parent for good reason, leave it be. What the system often perceives of as broken is really fixed. It's fixed because the bad parent is removed from the equation. She worried about Boston and its increasing rate of abused children and children who died at the hands of their caretakers. Dr. Lehman knew Boston wasn't the only city in the country to have these problems but she was in the midst of it so made it more real for her.

The millions of social workers trying to fix the family needed to be re-trained to focus on the children, not the family. It wasn't just the social workers Dr. Lehman had beef with. It was the mothers who stayed with abusive husbands and boyfriends when children were involved. Lehman knew that it wasn't easy to leave abusive men and she knew she wasn't being fair when she was frustrated with battered women. Sometimes she was just too black and white probably because she focused more on the children. Unfortunately there were battered women who chose their boyfriends and husbands over their children. Dr. Lehman of course blamed the batterers, too. They were the true abusers. But there was too much emphasis on women believing they had to be in a relationship to be whole. This type of thinking had to stop for the sake of women and children finding themselves in violent homes.

Throughout all of this, children were just told which direction they should go. They were bounced all over the place. They went through family members and foster homes and throughout it all had no say in where they were placed. Some people just shouldn't have children but society impresses upon everyone that they really would never be complete unless they were married with children. People just follow a social script that doesn't give power to any kids. Kids are just thrown into the socially constructed play that is directed by adults who are given too many re-takes, so to speak.

Dr. Lehman eventually became an elder in the group. This meant that she had a lot of say in decisions regarding children, parents, and pedophiles. She believed that the group gave children some power. Dr. Lehman really believed the group rescued children and gave them second chances. Their parents, at least one of them, deserved to lose their rights to parent. Procreation might come naturally but parenting didn't. Kids are gambled on. Some couples even think having a child will save a marriage. People delude themselves.

Dr. Lehman was one of the elders who helped capture and kill pedophiles. It didn't bother her in the least. Before Dr. Lehman killed pedophiles, she gave them two options. They could write a suicide note detailing their crimes and be put to sleep peacefully or if they didn't want to write a suicide note, they would be put to sleep not so peacefully. The second option involved Dr. Lehman using a drug called Tetrodotoxin.

This was a potent neurotoxin that caused paralysis and eventual death. The drug could easily be extracted from puffer fish. The group referred to the drug as PFV, puffer fish venom. Those injected would experience paralysis including the inability to breath. They were immobilized but clearly knew what was happening.

During the period of paralysis, Dr. Lehman looked into the pedophile's terrified eyes. She calmly asked them how they felt. Of course, they couldn't answer. She then told them she knew they were terrified. She wanted them to know what it felt like to be terrified. She told them this was how innocent children felt as they were molested and sometimes killed. Pedophiles choosing this route died painfully. Sometimes the bodies would be dumped deep into the ocean but most of the time the bodies were incinerated by members of the group who specialized in cremation.

Dr. Lehman was very devoted to the group and its mission. She grew up in foster care and was bounced all over the place. She knew what it was like to have no power. She knew what it was like to be sexually abused and ignored.

Dr. Lehman spent most of her time caring for people or saving children. She didn't have much of a social life but there was one guy in the group who intrigued her. Jay Hastings was his name. He was a physical therapist who joined the group a year ago. Unfortunately he dealt with a lot of injured kids, too. They went out to dinner once and had a great time. Dr. Lehman thought about Jay a lot and hoped she would see him more often.

CHAPTER 15

Susie and Sean had a blast at Target. Sean was overwhelmed by the fact that he could pick out a ton of clothes and a fair amount of toys. Susie was laughing a lot but still preoccupied. She would have to call in to work in a few days and claim to have the flu or something. She couldn't just disappear from work. She had to think about what to do after that. Susie's phone rang. She didn't recognize the number.

"Hello," said Susie.

"Hi Susie, it's Elaine."

Susie's heart skipped a beat.

"Hey, Elaine. How are you?" asked Susie.

"I'm fine but you have to bring Sean back," insisted Elaine.

Susie started to panic. She motioned for Sean to be quiet.

"Why? We just got him. I want him to spend the week," responded Susie.

"Well, his social worker called and she's coming by tomorrow. I was supposed to tell her that Sean was with you and I didn't. If he's not here when she comes I might lose my apartment and welfare check," explained Elaine.

"What did you say?" asked Susie incredulously.

Susie was astounded that Elaine was more concerned about

her check than having Sean. Elaine didn't care that she might lose Sean. She was more concerned about losing her check and her apartment.

"I said I won't get any money if he's not here. They'll take him," replied Elaine impatiently.

"You're more concerned about the check than Sean?" asked Susie.

"Whoa, that's not what I said," yelled Elaine.

Susie noticed that Sean was staring at her with a confused look. She calmed down.

"Oh, okay. Sorry Elaine. I'm at Target and can't hear well," said Susie.

"Can you bring him home tomorrow?" asked Elaine.

"What time is the social worker coming?" asked Susie.

"Late afternoon. She didn't exactly say. They like to surprise us," explained Elaine sounding panicked.

"Okay, I'll have him back by 1pm. Is that okay?" asked Susie.

"That sounds good. Oh, Susie, you can have him back when the social worker leaves," added Elaine in an almost cheery voice.

Susie said nothing for a minute because she thought she would explode.

"Susie, are you there?" asked Elaine.

"Yeah, I'm here. I heard you. See you tomorrow," said Susie coldly.

Susie hung up and looked at Sean. His face was blank again.

"You said I didn't have to go back, Susie," whispered Sean as he wrung his hands together.

"You don't, Sean. I just told your mother that so we would have more time to move to our new place. I know I lied but it's safer for you. Do you understand?" asked Susie.

Sean nodded. Susie knew he didn't understand the entire situation but she knew she had to keep him away from Elaine.

"Okay, let's get out of here and pick up Uncle Reid. We're going on an adventure," announced Susie.

"Yay!" said Sean. His happy face came back.

As soon as Susie got home she told Reid about the phone call.

"We need to leave now," he said. "Gather your stuff. I'll call Sam."

Reid immediately got in touch with Sam who told him to drive to New Hampshire. Sam gave him an address and told him another couple would be expecting them. Sam also told them to get rid of their phones and buy disposable ones. An hour later, all three were on the road again. They took what they could from the house and emptied their bank accounts. There was no turning back. Elaine would have to live without her check.

CHAPTER 16

Blades took the boys to basketball practice. He loved watching them play. They constantly looked to see if he was watching which he found endearing. They practiced for about an hour and then they grabbed frozen yogurt on the way home. When Blades walked in the house he immediately knew something was wrong. Clare had a panicked look on her face.

"What's up, Clare?" he asked.

"Nothing, nothing," she said. "Boys, go shower and get ready for bed."

"Are you okay, Mom?" asked Eric in a worried voice.

"Yes, I'm fine. I was just watching the news and there was an upsetting story," she replied.

Blades knew she was lying so she wouldn't worry the boys. He motioned for them to go upstairs.

"What's going on?" asked Blades.

"Dennis called. He won't sign off on the adoption papers. He said that the boys should know their real father," said an anguished Clare.

"Why all of a sudden is he interested in the boys?" asked Blades angrily.

"He probably wants money. He's an asshole," declared Clare.

Eric and Tyler were already using Blades as their last names. That wouldn't change if Blades had anything to do with it.

"I'll talk to him," said Blades. "It'll be fine."

"He's very difficult, Dana," warned Clare.

"So am I when it comes to my family," said Blades with obvious determination.

Clare looked at him with loving eyes and calmed down.

"I knew you would make me feel better, Dana. But he's hard to deal with and he's a lawyer. There is nothing more I can do so I guess you could call him. Do you want his phone number?" she asked.

"No, I'm going to pay him an unannounced visit," decided Blades.

"I don't know if that's a good idea," warned Clare.

"Well I'll find out, won't I?" asked Blades rhetorically.

Clare and Blades sat down and finished their yogurt. They were both quietly thinking about her ex-husband. Here was a guy who hadn't seen his sons in seven years and hadn't paid one ounce of child support. All of a sudden he has the urge to see his kids. Something was up.

Blades and Clare said good night to the boys and settled in the living room to watch "The Voice." This was the only show Clare recorded. The boys watched it sometimes but Blades and Clare really enjoyed it. It was like a huge variety show. It was very entertaining. The coaches were also hilarious, especially Blake Shelton. Clare was rooting for Jordan.

Clare snuggled close to Blades and he loved it. How could someone treat Clare so badly? Blades wasn't really a traditional guy but it pissed him off that Dennis, Clare's ex-husband was trying to worm his way back into her life. He would go see him after he checked him out a bit.

Blades got up from the couch and asked Clare if she wanted anything to drink. He told her he had to make a quick phone call. He headed to the kitchen and took out his cell phone.

"Hey Grant, it's Blades."

"Hey Blades, how's it going?" asked Grant.

"Everything is pretty great. I assume you know I got married," Blades informed him.

"I heard that. Congratulations, man. What can I do for you?" asked Grant.

"I need you to check on someone for me. His name is Dennis Clark. He's a lawyer in Whitman. He's actually Clare's ex-husband. He's up to something and it involves money," explained Blades.

"Say no more. I will check him out and get back to you," promised Grant.

"Okay, great. Keep track of your hours so I can pay you properly," replied Blades.

"Oh no, this one's on the house, Blades. You helped my sister with my nephew and I'll never forget it," said Grant leaving no room for argument.

"You don't owe me anything, Grant," replied Blades.

"It's on the house Blades, whether you like it or not," quipped Grant.

"Well at least let me take you out for a beer when you're finished with Dennis," Blades relented.

"I never turn down a beer. Talk to you soon," said Grant as he ended the conversation.

Blades had known Grant for a long time. He was one of the best private investigators around. Blades helped his sister when her husband beat the shit out of her and took off with their son. When the police tracked down Grant's brother-in-law, Blades convinced him to let his son go home. It took a while but the boy was released unharmed. Grant's brother-in-law was arrested for domestic violence, aggravated assault and non-custodial kidnapping. He was eventually tried and found guilty. He got twenty years from a judge who had no sympathy for batterers.

Grant would find out what Dennis was up to. Blades felt good about calling Grant. Blades walked back to the living room in time to see Adam Levine steal a singer from Blake Shelton.

CHAPTER 17

Reid and Susie arrived in Manchester, New Hampshire and followed the directions to another big house. They pulled into the driveway and a woman immediately came out.

"Hi, I'm Emma. Come inside," she ordered with no room for argument.

"I'm Susie and this is…"

"I know who you are," finished Emma.

Susie, Reid and Sean entered the house and were ushered into the living room. They were tired and hungry. Emma left the living room for a minute and returned with sandwiches, coffee, and juice. She was accompanied by her husband, John.

"Eat up," said John. "We don't have a lot of time. Sam says we need to get you guys on the road."

Reid nodded in agreement and wolfed down a sandwich. He was starving. Sean happily opened a juice box and slowly ate a sandwich. Susie held a cup of coffee and stared at John.

"You need to eat," said John.

Susie reached for a sandwich.

"What now?" she asked.

"After you eat we'll go to the basement and I'll take photos for new passports and licenses. Emma will do the birth certificates. You have to pick new names," John told them.

Susie looked at Reid. She couldn't believe all of this was happening. Four days ago she was on school vacation and now her school vacation had turned into a kidnapping. She had to change her name. Susie and Reid couldn't use their middle names or their parents' names because that would be too easy for someone to figure out once it was discovered Sean was missing.

"Sean, what name would you like to use? It'll be your new name and you can never use the name Sean again. We will have new secret identities, like we're spies," explained Susie, trying to sound playful.

Sean looked at Susie with a half-smile.

"Is this part of the adventure?" he asked.

"Yes," replied Susie with a smile.

"I like the name Isaac. There's a show on TV that I like with an Isaac," declared Sean.

"Isaac it is," said John enthusiastically. "That's a very cool name!"

"Reid and I could be Sawyer and Paige," said Susie as she looked at Reid.

"That's fine with me," said Reid. "Are those names from a soap opera?" asked Reid, laughing.

"No," laughed Susie. "I always liked those names."

"Okay," said John. "Now we need a last name. It has to be simple so Isaac will remember it," said John.

"What about Fox?" asked Reid. "It's simple."

"Great," said John. He turned to Emma and told her to get the paperwork started.

"You guys will leave first thing in the morning. Your new home will be in Wahoo City, Nebraska."

"I've never heard of it," said Reid.

"That's why you're going there. The population is just over 4500 people. It's nice and rural and far away from Dorchester. There's a couple there in similar circumstances as you. They've been there for three years so at least you know you have one set of friends. They have a little girl Sean's age. She was taken from her father who was extremely abusive. The father is related to the man you'll meet. That's all I can tell you. Now, let's go downstairs and get those photos done," ordered John.

"Wait a minute," said Emma. "Susie and Reid have to change their hairstyles before we take the pictures."

"You're right," said John. "Let me call Christina."

"Who's Christina?" asked Susie.

"She's our niece," said Emma. "She has a hair salon in town called Dolce. She always helps out if we need to change someone's looks."

"Does she know what's going on?" asked Susie.

"Yes," said Emma. "She can be trusted."

John returned to the kitchen and told them Christina would be there in thirty minutes. They decided to have dessert while they waited. They all sat in surreal silence, at least Reid and Susie did.

Christina arrived right on time. She was a very happy, beautiful young woman. Sean took to her right away. She asked him how he wanted her to cut his hair.

"I'll have a buzz-cut," said Sean.

"Cool," said Christina.

Susie and Reid were surprised that Sean even knew what a buzz-cut was.

"Do you know what a buzz-cut is, Sean?" asked Susie.

"Yeah, Isaac has one on the show. You're supposed to call me Isaac," he said with a grin.

Reid threw his head back and laughed.

"He got you there, Paige," said Reid using her new name.

"Yes, he did, Sawyer," said Susie with a grin.

They both turned to a smiling Sean who was getting a buzz-cut.

"What do I call you and Uncle Reid?" asked Sean.

Susie only hesitated for a second.

"Mom and Dad," said Susie very softly. "Call us Mom and Dad."

"I like that," said Sean.

CHAPTER 18

Blades was still busy trying to find Ivy. He would head back up to the hospital and speak to the parents again and the medical staff. First he had to call Grant back. He had left a message for Blades.

"Hey Grant. Tell me you have some good news," implored Blades.

"I do and I don't. Dennis has a bad gambling problem and owes some pretty heavy people a lot of money," Grant informed Blades.

"I knew it," said Blades. "I knew that prick needed money."

Grant shared more information on Dennis. He was definitely not interested in gaining custody of his boys. He was hoping for a pay-off. Blades thanked Grant and hung up. He was seething with anger. He would deal with Dennis later.

Blades headed back to the hospital and looked for Alissa. Blades walked to where he thought her room was but couldn't find Alissa. He went to the nurse's desk and asked where she was. Nurse Gloria told him she signed herself out.

"What?" exclaimed Blades. "Where did she go?"

"She went home with her boyfriend," Gloria told him, shaking her head.

"I thought she was being placed in a drug program," said Blades clearly exasperated.

"We can't force her to go and her social worker isn't helping in that area. Alissa has convinced her that she and Darren want to be home so they can help find Ivy. The social worker agreed," explained the nurse.

"What the hell," said Blades. "Do you have Alissa's address? I need to ask her more questions."

Gloria handed Blades a piece of paper with Alissa's address.

"Do you want her phone number, too?" asked Gloria.

"No, I'm going there unannounced. I like to surprise people. She's number two on the surprise list today," said a visibly angry Blades.

Blades left the hospital and drove to Dennis Clark's law office. He was partnered with some pretty big names. He walked into the firm and asked the clerk if he could see Dennis. She told him Dennis didn't want to be disturbed and he should make an appointment.

"Oh, really," said Blades as he let himself into Dennis' office.

"Stop," yelled the clerk. "You can't do that."

"I just did," said Blades as he glared at Dennis.

"I'm Dana Blades, Dennis and you're a prick."

"It's okay Sandy," Dennis said to the clerk.

"What can I do for you, Detective Blades? Did you come here to scare me with your gun?" taunted Dennis.

"What exactly do you think you're doing?" asked Blades.

"I want to see my sons," sneered Dennis.

"So all of a sudden you want to see your sons who you haven't seen in seven years?" asked Blades.

"That's right," said Dennis determinedly with an obvious sneer.

"Well guess what, asshole. They don't want to see you," declared Blades confidently.

"You can't stop me from seeing them. I didn't sign off on the adoption papers," countered Dennis.

"Not yet, but you will in two minutes," warned Blades.

Dennis chuckled and loosened his tie.

"You might think you're this big tough detective but you can't force me to sign anything. I'll take you all to court unless of course we can come to some agreement," replied Dennis.

"What kind of agreement?" asked Blades.

"Well, I would be more than happy to sign the papers for a small price," Dennis suggested.

"What price?" asked Blades through clenched teeth.

"Forty thousand dollars," answered Dennis.

"What makes you think we have forty thousand dollars?" asked Blades.

"Oh, I'm sure you and Clare will come up with something if you want to keep your happy little family together," said Dennis with sarcasm.

"So, you're willing to sell your own kids to me?" asked Blades.

"Well, sell is kind of a harsh term to use," Dennis retorted.

"Is blackmail a better term?" asked Blades.

"Come on Blades. If you want them that much you'll pay," replied Dennis.

Blades grabbed Dennis by the shirt collar and dragged him across the top of his desk. Everything on his desk went flying on the floor.

"Listen to me, you piece of shit. You're not getting a dime from us, ever. I know all about your gambling problem. That's your problem. You're going to sign those forms while I'm here or I'm going to play this recording for your big time partners and then I am going to mail copies to every major paper so they can print a nice story about your firm blackmailing families. I 'll also let your partners know that you have never paid a dime in child support," Blades promised with venom in his eyes.

Blades shoved Dennis back into his chair. Dennis looked shaken. Blades held up the recorder and handed Dennis the papers. He watched as Dennis signed off his rights to the boys. Blades took the paperwork and turned to leave.

"What are you going to do with that recording, Blades?" asked Dennis.

"I'll keep it in a safe place for leverage. Stay away from my family. Is that clear?" warned Blades without turning around.

"Yes," whispered Dennis.

"What about my gambling debt? They're going to kill me," declared a newly timid Dennis.

Blades turned and looked at Dennis. The prick actually had the balls to ask him for help.

"Who do you owe the money to?" asked Blades.

Dennis straightened up and looked hopeful.

"Sheldon Hawkes," he replied.

"Oh, that's a doozy," said Blades. "Good luck with that."

"You're not going to help?" asked a desperate Dennis.

"Sure I am. I'll let Sheldon know your calendar just got cleared for the day," declared Blades as he left the office and headed to his car. Dennis was still yelling that he was a dead man. Blades looked at the paperwork and smiled.

CHAPTER 19

Nurse Bridget sat in her living room sipping red wine. She was enjoying her so-called vacation days and looking forward to giving her notice at the hospital. She'd have to stay a few more months but that was okay with her. She would move to another state and get a new identity. She pledged her allegiance to the group a long time ago. She grew up in the system. She was removed from her alcoholic parents' home when she was just four years old. A neighbor found her wandering in the snow at eleven o'clock at night in the bitter cold.

Bridget was never given back to her parents even though they tried to get her back. They promised to sober up all of the time but never did. Even when they had supervised visitation, they were drunk. The visit would start out all nice and sweet and then her mother would tell her how ungrateful she was and blame her for breaking up the family. Bridget would sit there and take the abuse until the social worker stepped in and ended the visit.

In the system, Bridget was shuffled from one foster home to the next until she aged out at eighteen. While in foster care, she was mentally abused, physically abused, and sexually abused on numerous occasions. Eventually Bridget became "too old" to be adopted. This meant that she wasn't a newborn or a toddler. No one in her mother or father's family came forward for her during her years in the system. She was numb throughout her entire teenage years.

As Bridget was deep in thought her cell phone rang. It was Charlotte. Bridget remembered the day she met her best friend. She was in nursing school and nineteen years old. She mainly kept to herself. One day her research methods professor broke the class up into groups. Charlotte was in her group and she struggled with the subject. Bridget immediately helped her and they became instant friends. She later learned that Charlotte also went through foster care but an aunt eventually adopted her.

Bridget and Charlotte told each other everything. Charlotte had also been abused in every way. Finally, Bridget met someone who understood her. They talked about the abuse every now and then. Nothing shocked Bridget. She remained calm in every circumstance and this made for a great nurse. Charlotte went on to become a lawyer but they remained in touch. Charlotte knew what Bridget was involved in and she knew she changed her identity frequently but she kept quiet about it. She wouldn't become involved but she would never reveal the group's work. She understood what they were doing.

There are over 400,000 children in foster care in the United States waiting to be adopted. This didn't include the number of children placed in foster care waiting to be reunited with their families. Over 1500 children die of child abuse and neglect every year in the United States. Children under three are the most common victims. The number of children sexually abused is underreported but the annual average number of substantiated cases each year is over 60,000. Charlotte knew these statistics by heart and she saw a lot of kids who were abused. Because of this she turned a blind eye to Bridget's work but did let Bridget know about cases Bridget could help with. Children can't protect themselves against abuse. Charlotte knew this firsthand.

Bridget missed Charlotte and promised herself she would call her soon. She wanted to wait until Lily was safe. She smiled as she remembered handing Lily to Robert who brought her to Ricky and William. Lily was sleeping peacefully at the time. There was a warm bottle of formula waiting for her in the car and two gushing parents ready to protect her for life. She would have a good life in Ottawa. No one would question a gay, white couple with a black baby. People would assume she was adopted and that was that.

Bridget did come up with an ingenious plan to get Lily to Canada. Ricky and William would be crossing the border with "Luke", a boy baby. Two birth certificates and two passports were created. One set identified the baby as Luke, the other as Lily. The authorities were looking for a little girl. Ricky and William had a little boy with them as far as customs was concerned. Newborns were gender neutral looking. That's exactly why they were dressed in pink or blue so everyone would know how to respond to them. Lily was dressed in blue.

Bridget's thoughts were again interrupted but this time by the doorbell. She wondered who would be at her door. She looked through her peephole and recognized Detective Blades. She opened the door.

"Well hello, Detective Blades. I didn't expect you," stated Bridget.

"I like to surprise people. Do you have a few minutes to talk?" asked Blades.

"Did you find Ivy?" asked Bridget.

"No, we didn't. That's why I'm here. I have a few more questions," he explained.

"Come in," beckoned Bridget.

"Thank you," replied Blades as he entered the home.

"I would offer you a glass of wine but I am assuming you'll decline," commented Bridget.

"Thanks, anyway. I just want to go over one more time when you last saw Ivy," replied Blades.

"Okay. Like I told you, I saw her in her mother's room. That was about eight o'clock. Another mother buzzed me so I went to her room. It turned out she hit her button by accident so I immediately returned to the desk. I looked at the monitor and noticed that Ivy wasn't in her basinet so thought maybe her Mom picked her up. I waited a few minutes and then went to check on the baby. When I went into Alissa's room, she was sound asleep and the baby was gone. It couldn't have been more than five minutes," relayed Bridget.

"Did you notice anyone around the floor that you didn't recognize?" asked Blades.

"No, it was pretty quiet," said Bridget shaking her head.

"How long were you in the other mother's room?" asked Blades.

"Maybe two minutes," guessed Bridget.

"Long enough for someone to take Ivy," suggested Blades.

"I guess so. Whoever took her must have gone in the opposite direction I did," declared Bridget.

"So, someone waited for you to leave the desk and then went into the baby's room, cut off the sensory bracelet and left through the back exit," Blades surmised.

"I guess so but you're the detective, not me," answered Bridget as she took a sip of wine.

"You didn't seem too distraught about a baby disappearing on your watch," said Blades.

"I'm not sure how you expected me to react but it was a

serious situation and I was trying to stay calm and focused," Bridget said defensively.

"Of course. I don't mean to imply that you didn't care," replied Blades half-heartedly.

Bridget felt that the detective was testing her but she was fully prepared. She could put a wall up in a mille second. Nothing could frazzle her. She had a history of stoicism. Detective Blades could slap her across the face and she would barely react. He would get nothing from her.

"I know you're just doing your job, Detective. I want to find Ivy as much as you do," proclaimed Bridget.

"Well, thank you for your time and I'll be in touch," said Blades.

"Have a good night, Detective," said Bridget.

"Oh, one more thing," said Blades. "Why didn't an alarm go off when the bracelet was cut off the baby?"

"I don't know," replied Bridget. "That's a good question."

"Okay," said Blades. "Good night."

Blades left Bridget's house with mixed feelings. There was something weird about her. She was too calm. He couldn't shake that feeling that she wasn't telling him everything. He headed to Alissa's apartment.

CHAPTER 20

Ricky and William crossed the Maine/New Brunswick border with no problems. In fact, the customs officers were incredibly friendly and welcoming. Ricky told the officers that they would be vacationing in Nova Scotia. One officer checked the car, saw "Luke" and wished them a great vacation. Ricky and William followed directions to the "safe house" in Nova Scotia. They would stay there a night or two and then drive to Ontario. An apartment was waiting for them. The group arranged everything. They even found employment for Ricky, an occupational therapist. William was a photographer and would be the primary caretaker for Lily.

Everything was downhill from here. Lily would have a great life, free of abuse. Ricky and William felt they had the whole world in their hands. They left everything behind without a second thought. Their families didn't approve of their lifestyle, as they called it, so Ricky and William found it easy to leave them behind. They now had their own family and would hopefully expand it. Their families would probably not even look for them. If they did, they would have a hard time finding them because of their new identities.

The group actually found Ricky and William. They were

on a list of potential adoptive parents in the Massachusetts foster care system. A social worker visited their home one evening and interviewed them. She was very thorough and seemed to already know a lot about them. They were eager to be foster parents. The social worker promised to visit them again. She came back several days later and talked to them for several hours about a possible newborn. She had them fill out a thick pile of paperwork.

The next time she came, another woman came with her. She spoke to them for a long time about the problems with the system and how many children got hurt or died while under the so-called watchful eye of the state. She then asked them if they wanted to help save children from abuse. Ricky and William initially thought this was a strange question until she told them about Ivy. They were shocked that Ivy would be returned to her drug-addicted mother. They agreed that this would be disastrous. They agreed to do whatever it took to save Ivy.

The second woman who came to see them explained how things worked. Ricky and William immediately agreed to everything. They had some money but were concerned about having enough until they were settled. The woman assured them that money was not an issue. The group had hundreds of generous benefactors. About two weeks after this, they had Ivy who was now Lily. Ricky and William were on cloud nine.

CHAPTER 21

Sean, now Isaac had his picture taken first. None of this seemed to be bothering him yet. Susie went next and they finished with Reid. Susie told Reid she had to go to the bathroom and went upstairs. Reid stayed with Sean while the paperwork was being compiled.

Susie finished in the bathroom and nearly ran into Emma as she came out to the hallway.

"I'm sorry. I didn't see you. I'm so mixed up right now," said Susie hesitantly.

"Are you having second thoughts?" asked Emma.

"I don't know what I'm having. What if we're making a big mistake? What if it's possible for us to legally gain custody of Sean? What if we get caught and go to jail? Who'll take care of Sean then?" asked Susie, clearly beginning to panic.

"I understand what you're going through. We raised our niece. Unfortunately we chose to go through the system and it took years for us to get her. She went back and forth between us and my brother for five years. It really messed her up. She didn't have a stable environment. When we finally did get custody of her, it took years for her to trust us. She had been abused by her father even while we were fighting for her. Of course, the social worker in charge of the case claimed that we had no evidence of abuse. Carly was too young to explain the mental torture her father put her through. She's fine now but every day I regret not running with that child. She didn't have to experience half of what she went through because a system set up to protect children is more concerned with keeping biological families together. Most judges like to give parents contact with their children. Not everyone deserves a second chance to parent," said a determined Emma.

Susie could feel Emma's anger.

"But you just said she's fine now," said Susie in a hopeful tone.

"She's fine now but it took ten years for her to process everything. She learned to cope. She still goes to therapy and she still remembers her father leaving her alone for hours with no food or drink. She remembers missing school because her father wouldn't get up with her. She's anxious about being on time for everything now. So, she may be fine in terms of coping and living a healthy life but we could have prevented some of what she went through," said Emma.

"Where is she now?" asked Susie.

"She lives in town and teaches at the high school," said Emma proudly.

"I just can't believe we can't fight this legally without Sean being hurt," said an exasperated Susie.

"You can't take that chance. You promised him that he didn't have to go back to his mother. The minute you go back to Dorchester, he'll be given back to his mother until the situation is assessed. Then he'll never trust you or anyone again. You said yourself that his social worker is big on keeping families together. Sean has no choice about what happens to him; he has no power. Your sister's boyfriend will hit him again.

He'll be left alone. Your sister will keep using and only care about that check," declared Emma.

Susie looked surprised at this.

"Yes, Sam told me what she said to you. We're so conditioned to just think the real family is the best place for kids but sometimes it isn't. What you're doing seems drastic because most people don't choose this path. They trust the system either because they think it works or because they don't want to disrupt their lives. Sean's life is disrupted and he has no power over that. You can make a choice for him to be safe. You've lived a good life so far. He needs a chance. He's a little boy who needs to know someone will care for him. You might think you're sacrificing your life but you are really saving his. You have to decide if it's worth it," said Emma with conviction.

Susie listened to every word Emma said and took a deep breath.

"You're right. He needs us and you know what? We need him," claimed Susie.

"Okay, then Susie, let's check on the boys in the basement," directed Emma.

"My name is Paige," said Susie with a determined smile.

Emma smiled and squeezed her hand.

CHAPTER 22

Reilly was on cloud nine about her new job. Aunt Loretta insisted on celebrating. They went out for dinner at the Tavern at Quarry Hills, a beautiful restaurant with amazing food. They watched a movie together when they got home.

As Reilly got ready for bed, she thought about her idea for her first real story.

A couple of years ago, Reilly started following a case involving murdered rapists.

The news covered the story very well. The public didn't have much sorrow for the dead rapists and showed some love for the vigilante. What Reilly didn't understand was that the cases just went cold. The police never caught the killer and gradually just gave up. Reilly assumed they gave up because they didn't care about the rapists. The cases were discussed in many of Reilly's graduate classes and Reilly never forgot it.

Reilly shared the idea with her new boss that the story should have had a better ending. She wanted to interview the police and anyone else involved in the case to try to find out why the cases went cold. Reilly was a firm believer in letting the system work and didn't think the police should have stopped looking for the serial killer. Her supervisor thought it was a great idea and gave Reilly some leeway. Reilly knew she had to check in with her boss routinely. She wanted to start with the police.

One story that was somewhat related to the rapists' deaths involved a swimming coach who was accused of sexual assaulting many girls. A professor from the local university beat the coach up and went to jail for a short time. Reilly always thought there was something strange about that case. This was around the time the police stopped looking for the vigilante serial killer.

Aunt Loretta loved Reilly's spunk but warned her to go slow. She reminded Reilly that a good investigative reporter had to be thorough and not jump to conclusions too fast and without facts. Aunt Loretta wasn't sure about any facts for Reilly to find.

CHAPTER 23

Blades knocked on Alissa's door. There was no answer but he could hear something going on inside the apartment. He knocked again. He then heard someone moaning.

"Alissa, open up. It's Detective Blades," shouted Blades.

All went quiet and then Blades heard another moan. Fearing something was wrong, he tried the doorknob and it turned easily to open the door. He let himself in and identified himself again. The kitchen was a disgusting mess. He stepped over garbage on the floor. He walked into the living room and saw Alissa on the couch. She was stoned or drunk or both. Darren came staggering out of the bedroom.

"Who the fuck are you?" he asked Blades.

"Detective Blades," said Blades as he glared at Darren.

"Oh, sorry Detective, I thought you might be our nosy neighbor," said Darren defensively.

"I'm sure you did. What are you two up to?" asked Blades.

"Just settling in," said Darren with a sideways grin.

"Yes, you look like you're incredibly worried about finding Ivy," Blades said sarcastically.

"We are. We just needed to relax," declared Darren.

Blades saw the meth pipe on the coffee table and empty

beer bottles strewn all over the floor. He took his cell phone out of his pocket and called for back-up and an ambulance just in case Alissa was overdosing.

"Now, wait a minute," said Darren. "Why are you calling this in? We're not hurting anyone."

"Just yourselves, apparently. You're clearly using illegal drugs, dumb ass. I'm going to make sure you never see your daughter again. You don't deserve a child," said Blades with disgust.

"Ivy is our baby and we want her," whined Darren.

"Sure you do," said Blades. "You can't have her if you're in jail and that's where you're both going."

Darren stepped towards Blades. Blades put one hand up and one on his gun.

"It'll be my pleasure to shoot you so step the fuck back," demanded Blades.

Darren saw the look in Blades' eyes and stepped back with his hands up.

"Okay, okay, I'm cool," he claimed.

"Believe me when I say no one will care if I blow your head off, you piece of shit," said Blades.

Alissa moaned again and Darren sat next to her. Darren started to cry or at least attempt to cry.

"We need help," he claimed.

"That's on you now. I'm just going to make sure you never see Ivy again," promised Blades. "God help you if you hurt her or someone else did," added Blades.

Other officers arrived at the apartment in minutes and arrested Darren for drug possession. Alissa was taken by ambulance to the hospital. Blades didn't have a chance to ask her any questions. Ten minutes later she died of an overdose and Darren went to jail.

Blades drove home thinking about that baby. Blades hoped she was safe but he wasn't sure if he would ever know. He was mad at himself for losing his temper with Darren but he knew why he did. He was angry that they couldn't be good parents and he was still pissed at Dennis. Even though Blades forced Dennis to sign the adoption papers, he couldn't shake the thought that Dennis didn't love those boys. How could he just walk away from them? As happy as they seemed to be with Blades, they must think about why their father just disappeared from their lives.

During many conversations with Blades about Dennis, Clare told Blades the boys knew their father chose not to see them but the boys also chose not to see him. He had been abusive and they didn't want anything to do with him. Blades just couldn't believe they didn't think about their father or feel hurt by his neglect. Eric and Tyler were rejected by their father. That had to hurt. Clare did say the boys were in therapy for several years after the divorce and it seemed to be very helpful. She never spoke ill of Dennis and always answered their questions. One day they just stopped asking.

Blades pulled into his driveway and felt a wave of fatigue wash over him. He grabbed the adoption papers and walked into the house. As usual, he received a warm welcome. He caught up with Clare and the boys and then watched the Red Sox with the boys. Clare only watched the game when Big Papi was at bat. Both boys fell asleep on the couch before the game ended. Blades walked both upstairs and tucked them in. When he returned to the living room, Clare was waiting for him.

"Did you see Dennis today?" she asked tentatively.

"Yes, I did. We had a nice chat," replied Blades.

Blades walked into the kitchen and took the adoption papers

out of his briefcase. He handed them to Clare. She screamed in delight.

"Oh my God, he signed them! How did you get him to do that? He wanted money, didn't he?" asked Clare.

"Yes and no," said Blades. "He hinted at needing money but I convinced him that he should just sign the papers."

"Dana, I'm not stupid. Did you threaten him?" asked Clare with concern in her voice.

"I just told him that if he didn't sign the papers, we would go after him for retroactive child support which would add up to be tens of thousands of dollars. He didn't like that. I also told him I would let his partners know that he walked away from his kids. He decided to sign the papers," stated Blades.

"This is wonderful news! Oh, Dana, this is the happiest day of my life. The boys will be thrilled! We can go to court and make this official," exclaimed Clare.

"Yes, we can. I'm glad we don't have to deal with Dennis again," said a relieved Blades.

"You're the best thing that ever happened to us, Dana." Clare started crying.

Blades held her tightly and whispered in her ear that, no, they were the best things that ever happened to him.

CHAPTER 24

Elaine was agitated. She paced back and forth across the kitchen floor. It was three o'clock. Susie was supposed to be at the apartment at one o'clock. The social worker would be arriving at any time. Elaine called Susie's cell several times but kept getting voicemail. She left several messages for Susie to call her. It wasn't like Susie to be late.

"Where the hell is your sister?" asked Colin.

"I don't know. This isn't like her. She's not answering her cell," said Elaine nervously.

"Well if she doesn't get here soon with Sean, you're screwed. You know they'll take him again," warned Colin.

"I know, I know. She'll be here. She knows I need that check," said Elaine.

"You need Sean right now. If he's not here, there'll be no check. If she does get here on time, she can always have him back," claimed Colin.

"I told her that already, Colin," replied an irritated Elaine.

"At least Sean's good for something," Colin sneered.

"He's a good boy!" yelled Elaine.

"He's a pain in the ass," declared Colin. "All kids are."

Before Elaine could respond, there was a knock on the door.

"That must be them," she said excitedly.

Elaine opened the door to see the social worker standing there.

"Hello, Elaine. How are you?" asked Jordan.

"I'm fine." Elaine just stood there.

"May I come in?" asked the social worker.

"Of course," said Elaine. "Come right in."

The social worker entered the apartment and looked around. The place looked clean and orderly. Of course, she assumed that Elaine cleaned because she knew a social worker was coming over.

"The place looks nice, Elaine," said Jordan with a smile.

"Thank you. You remember Colin?" asked Elaine.

"Yes, I do. Where's Sean?" asked Jordan.

"My sister came to visit and took him to the park. They must be running late," explained Elaine.

"Can you call her?" asked Jordan.

"Yes, of course," replied Elaine.

Elaine called Susie's cell again. She didn't answer.

"She's not answering," said Elaine.

"I can wait a while. We can go over your long-term plans," suggested Jordan as she sat at the kitchen table.

"Okay," said Elaine.

An hour went by and then another. Elaine tried Susie's phone several times. The social worker was getting perturbed. Elaine seemed more panicky than expected under the circumstances.

"What's really going on, Elaine?" asked Jordan.

"Nothing is going on," stated Elaine.

"Elaine, start talking," demanded Jordan.

"Okay, okay. I let my sister take Sean for a few days. She was supposed to be back today," explained Elaine.

"Where did she take him?" asked Jordan.

"She took him to Connecticut," said Elaine.

"Elaine, he's not supposed to leave the state without my permission. I don't even know who your sister is. She's not on our approved list of caretakers for Sean," said Jordan reproachfully.

"My sister is great. Sean loves her. She'll be back," promised Elaine.

"If she's not back soon, I'll have to write you up and send out an Amber Alert," declared Jordan.

Elaine started pacing again and tried Susie's phone for the hundredth time.

CHAPTER 25

Susie's hair was now a blonde pixie. Her brown eyes were now blue thanks to new contact lenses. She looked good. Reid got a buzz cut along with Sean. All of the paperwork was in order. They stayed with John and Emma for the night and left for Nebraska in the morning. They drove to Nebraska in a used Honda Accord. It would be their new car. The police would be looking for their Hyundai Elantra. The group provided the Honda for them and Emma explained that the Honda Accord was the most commonly driven car in the country. The car was grey; a color that didn't stand out.

Susie got rid of their phones and bought portable ones. She knew Elaine would be calling her. She kept telling herself that she was only calling to get her check. This thought kept Susie focused. Sean was very happy. Several days later, they arrived safely in Nebraska. It was a beautiful state.

Reid, Susie, and Sean were welcomed by a young man named James in the designated Home Hardware parking lot. They introduced themselves using their new names. They weren't sure what to say to James. Thankfully he did all of the talking.

"We have a nice house for you guys. Isaac can start school

next week. You guys can spend some time getting the house set up. You'll meet my wife, Penny, and we have a daughter the same age as Isaac. Her name is Jill."

"Won't it be weird if all of a sudden you know us?" asked Reid, who was now Sawyer.

"No, because I won't know you until the family dance this Friday. You guys should come and meet people. Penny and I will be there and we'll introduce ourselves again," explained James.

"How long have you been in Wahoo City?" asked Susie.

"Four years now. We were also re-located with new identities. We took Jill from my brother when she was one. Her father broke her arm. A doctor made arrangements for the "steal" after she treated Jill. We had been on a list to adopt a child and along came Jill. Her father would have killed her eventually. I really believe that. Jill doesn't remember her father or the trauma as far as we can tell. She thinks my wife and I are her parents," explained James.

"This is all so crazy," said Susie.

"It does take some getting used to but sooner than you think you'll feel like everything was meant to be," promised James.

Susie and Reid followed James as he drove to their new house. They all got out of their cars.

"This is your house," said James.

"Wow, it's great," said Reid.

The house was a nice bungalow style home with three bedrooms. It was a beautiful shade of blue with white shutters. The yard was huge in the back. It was also fenced in.

"Who do we pay rent to?" asked Susie.

"You don't have to pay anything until you both get work.

Your bills will be taken care of until then," explained James. "The house is a gift."

"Where does the money come from?" asked a surprised Susie.

"The group pays for everything," replied James.

Susie and Reid became more and more intrigued with this group. They all walked into the house. It was beautifully decorated. The cupboards were filled with food as was the fridge. There was even cold beer.

"Where's my room?" yelled Sean.

"Come on, I'll show you," said James.

James and Sean walked down the hall and into a bedroom. Sean squealed in delight when he saw his Lightning McQueen bedspread. There were also toys in the room.

"Mom, come and see!" yelled Sean.

Susie hesitated since she wasn't used to that name. In this new world he was her son. Susie felt proud. She joined Sean in his new room and yelled to Reid to come. Reid made a big fuss over the room. Sean jumped up and down on his bed, clapping his hands. Reid opened his arms for Sean to jump into and they all laughed.

James watched the new happy family with a lump in his throat. The group had made the right decision.

"I'll let you guys get settled," said James. "I'll check on you tomorrow."

"Thanks for everything, James," said Susie.

"Any time," said James. "We're here for you."

CHAPTER 26

Dr. Lehman was getting ready for the reception at the governor's mansion. She was excited because Jay Hastings would be there. The governor was going to say a few words about revamping DCF. A boy went missing from Waltham and his mother and boyfriend were suspected of hurting him. He was actually missing for a month before anyone even noticed. A social worker had failed to visit the home where he lived but filed papers as if he did check on the boy. Even the boy's teachers didn't report his absence. It was despicable all around. Heads would roll. Unfortunately, he wasn't the first boy to fall through the cracks and wouldn't be the last. Dr. Lehman was sure the Commissioner of DCF would be at the event tonight but she would avoid him. He needed to be replaced. She had already spoken to the Governor about him.

Dr. Lehman knew the missing boy would never be found. His mother and her boyfriend were sitting in jail and not talking. This was not an isolated event. It was a systemic problem. Two social workers were fired. That didn't mean everything was fixed. Social workers were overworked and underpaid but these two deserved to be fired. Dr. Lehman believed they should be criminally charged. Even though their caseloads were supposedly unreasonable, they should have asked for help. When a social worker fails to check on a child and knows she's failed to do so, that's on her and her supervisor. She should have asked for help. On top of this, the Commissioner should know how the entire Department was running. He should be checking on the supervisors and managers and making sure they were doing their jobs. Lehman knew it wasn't as simple as this but clearly the system was failing.

Jacob, the boy who was missing, was feared dead. It still blew Lehman's mind that mothers would side with their boyfriends and allow them to hurt their children. She had no sympathy for this mother. Maybe she was battered; maybe she wasn't. Lehman didn't care. She failed to protect her child. If she wanted to stay with an asshole that was her decision but that little boy had no choice. The social worker should have had the boyfriend removed from the home. But again, she probably thought it was best to keep the so-called family together. Now, look at it. Dr. Lehman was sure many other people knew there were problems but turned a blind eye. Family matters were still considered private. Privacy is the essence of any abuser's power.

Dr. Lehman thought about how people stand by and watch parents and caretakers slap their kids in public. They say nothing because they have been socialized to believe that it is private. But if we saw a random stranger walk up to a child and hit him, he would be arrested immediately. Someone would intervene. The child would be defended and protected. The same act with different reactions. It made no sense.

Dr. Lehman was ready to leave for the big event. She checked herself in the mirror one more time. She looked forward to the evening. She was happy to be going out socially and she was happy the group saved yet another child today. A little girl had been found wandering around a neighborhood. She was only eighteen months old. The social worker who was in charge of the open case was a member of the group. She visited the apartment on a regular basis and the little girl loved when she came to the house.

Amanda, the social worker, noticed that the little girl was a bit thin and unkempt. She talked to the parents several times a week about caring for Deidre. Part of their plan was to go to AA meetings and parenting classes. They did for the first two weeks and then made excuses for not going the third week. It was now the fourth week and Deidre's parents started drinking again. A group member had been watching the house and happened to see Deidre outside. He called Amanda right away. Amanda told him to keep watching the child and she would be there in five minutes. Her mother and father were both passed out from drinking too much the night before. Amanda came and scooped up Deidre. Deidre was not at all startled because she knew Amanda, so she went willingly.

Deidre's parents kept on sleeping. They had no idea they would never see their daughter again. Dr. Lehman knew the Doyen would be supportive of the move even though Amanda had made no contact to get permission for this "scoop". The Doyen trusted group members to make decisions in emergency cases like this.

A few days went by and finally Deidre's parents called the police. They were genuinely frantic but only for themselves. The parents were arrested and charged with child abuse and neglect. The police suspected they hurt the child but the parents proclaimed their innocence. They didn't know where their daughter was. Lehman knew. She knew she was safe and actually happy. She wasn't even asking for her parents. Her grandmother was distraught but Dr. Lehman felt nothing for her. She should have stepped up long ago but didn't want to butt in. Can you imagine? She wanted to mind her business while her granddaughter was being abused and neglected. No one was protecting that little girl. She would have a great life wherever they placed her. There was now an Amber Alert for a little girl named Deidre who was now Molly. As far as Dr. Lehman was concerned, her parents would remain suspects for a long time. Molly was now safe.

CHAPTER 27

Everyone gathered in the courtroom. Jake, Theresa, the grandmothers and cousins were all there. Emily even came to witness the official adoption of Eric and Tyler by Blades. Emily was one of Theresa's students who eventually became part of their family. Clare and Blades signed all of the forms in front of the judge. The judge asked them to step forward.

"Dennis Clark has signed away all rights to the boys as far as I can see. He isn't responsible for child support and cannot see the boys under any circumstances. Is this correct?" asked the judge.

"Yes," said Clare. "He has no interest in them."

Eric and Tyler sat back far enough so they couldn't hear the conversation. They were busy smiling and chatting with everyone.

"That's pretty sad," said the judge. "He's going to regret this."

"I doubt that very much," said Clare. "He walked away a long time ago. He hasn't seen the boys or tried to contact them in seven years."

"Well then, he doesn't deserve them, does he?" stated the judge.

"No he does not," said Clare with determination.

"I'm happy to see that you're eager to adopt them, Mr. Blades."

"So am I, your honor," agreed Blades.

"Then it's official. May I have a few words with the boys?" asked the judge.

"Certainly," said Clare. "Eric and Tyler, come here, please."

Eric and Tyler ran up to the judge.

"Hello Eric and Tyler. It's nice to meet you. Do you understand the proceedings today?" asked the judge.

"Yes, Blades will become our real Dad," said Tyler with a huge grin.

"You're both okay with that?" asked the judge.

"Yes," they said in unison.

"Your other father agreed to this. Are you okay with that?" asked the judge more pointedly.

"Our other father wasn't very nice to us," said Eric. "So, yes, we're okay with everything. Blades is the best father ever!"

Clare's eyes welled up with tears. She looked at Blades who was smiling ear to ear.

"Okay," said the judge. "Blades, as you call him, is now your father." The judge signed the paperwork and handed it to the clerk to file it.

"Detective Blades, I've heard about you. You have an impeccable reputation as a detective and a person. I'm more than happy to sign these forms," the judge claimed.

"Thank you, your honor," said Blades.

"Yes, thank you," said Clare.

The boys also thanked the judge and everyone left the courtroom to celebrate at Theresa's house. The grandmothers had prepared a feast in advance. Eric and Tyler invited some friends from school. Harper and Micah had friends come over as well. It was a joyous time. Theresa was so happy for Clare. Dennis was an asshole. She looked at Blades with Clare and was so glad she set them up, so to speak.

In the meantime, the judge hung up his robe and sat at his desk. He pulled out his second cell phone and made a call.

"Hi, I just wanted you to know that Blades is officially the father of his wife's boys. There were no problems. They'll be fine. They'll never have to see their biological father again," the judge informed the person at the other end.

"That's great news! Will I see you tonight?"

"Yes, Toni and I will be there," said the judge.

"I'm looking forward to it."

Dr. Lehman ended the phone call and headed to the governor's gala.

CHAPTER 28

Blades was having the time of his life at Theresa's. The boys hugged him every fifteen minutes it seemed. He never imagined loving two kids so much. Clare was happy. Everyone was happy. Jake cracked open a second Sam Adams for Blades when he felt his phone vibrate.

"What's up?" asked Blades. "I'm off duty."

"I know you are," said Captain Froio. "I just thought you should know there are two more kids missing. An Amber Alert was just released for a four year- old boy from Dorchester and an eighteen month old from Brockton. This has never happened before on the same day."

"That's interesting," said Blades. "Do we have extra officers canvassing the neighborhoods? Are there social workers involved?"

"In both cases," said Froio. "We're still gathering information on the eighteen month old. I'm only calling you so you don't hear this somewhere else. I know you're celebrating the adoption of your sons."

"Okay, keep me posted. Unless there is a serious break in the case, I'll see you in the morning," promised Blades

"Will do," promised Froio.

Clare was looking at Blades when he hung up.

"Everything is fine," he told her. "Just work. I don't have to leave."

"Good," said Clare. "The boys need their father here tonight."

Blades kissed the tip of her nose and smiled. Clare left his side to get another glass of wine. Blades thought about the fact that there were three missing kids. What was going on? He'd be questioning a lot of people tomorrow. Right now he would concentrate on his boys and this wonderful family.

CHAPTER 29

Elaine was in full panic mode. Susie had not returned with Sean. She was more concerned about getting in trouble and losing her check than being reunited with Sean. Colin was furious about the whole situation. He depended on Elaine's check for his drugs. Elaine was afraid Colin would leave her because now she might lose her apartment and her monthly check.

The social worker had called the police when Elaine's sister hadn't returned with Sean by the next day. Blades arrived at Elaine's apartment and was greeted by two other officers.

"They're in here," motioned one of the officers.

Blades walked into the living room and saw Elaine and Colin. Colin was sitting far away from Elaine and looked angry. Elaine was wringing her hands continually and couldn't keep still.

"I'm Detective Blades. I take it you're Sean's mother?" asked Blades looking at Elaine.

"Yes, I am," replied Elaine.

"And you're his father?" Blades said as he turned to Colin.

"Ha, no I'm not. That kid is nothing but trouble," declared Colin.

Blades was immediately ticked off by Colin's callous remark but kept his cool. He would get nothing out of them if he got angry.

"How much trouble was he?" asked Blades, looking directly at Colin.

"Wait a minute. I didn't hurt the kid. He really did go with Elaine's sister," explained Colin.

"She said she wanted to take him to her house in Connecticut for the week but then I missed him so much, I asked her to come back with him," Elaine told Blades.

"Is that right?" asked Blades. "As I understand you weren't supposed to let your sister take Sean across state lines. The social worker told you to get Sean back here."

"That's true but I trusted my sister," said Elaine defensively.

"Did you call your sister?" asked Blades.

"Yes, and I told her Sean had to come back. She promised me that she would have him back here yesterday at one o'clock. I waited until this morning to call the police because I couldn't get in touch with her. Our social worker called the police, too," said Elaine as she fought back tears.

"Would she take Sean from you for any reason?" asked Blades.

"No, she would never do that. Sean is my son," said Elaine.

"Is there any reason why she might think Sean was abused or neglected by you or Colin?" asked Blades.

"No!" yelled Elaine.

"Then why is there an open case on you and Colin?" asked Blades.

"We get stressed out sometimes and need a little help but we're trying," explained Elaine.

"So, if I ask the social worker if there might have been a

good reason for taking Sean from you, what will she say?" asked Blades.

"She'll say no!" yelled Elaine.

"So when you last spoke with your sister, she was in Connecticut?" asked Blades.

"That's what she said," confirmed Elaine.

"Okay, we have an Amber Alert out on Sean. If you hear from your sister, let me know," said Blades as he handed her his card.

"I will," agreed Elaine.

Elaine's social worker walked into the room. Elaine jumped up and went straight to her.

"Jordan, tell the detective we would never hurt Sean," Elaine implored.

Jordan looked at Blades and introduced herself.

"Can we speak in the kitchen?" asked Blades.

"Certainly," replied Jordan.

"What do you know about their relationship with Sean?" Blades asked as he motioned to Elaine and Colin.

"It's problematic. A neighbor called the police a few weeks ago claiming she heard fighting. Elaine and Colin were fighting and Sean got hurt in the midst of the fight," Jordan explained.

"How serious was he hurt?" asked Blades.

"Mainly bumps and bruises but enough to re-open a case on Elaine. This isn't her first run-in with DCF. Two years ago we got involved because there was fighting in the apartment. A previous boyfriend was smacking around Elaine. Sean wasn't hurt but he was in the apartment. We kept a case opened for about six months and Elaine seemed to pull herself together. Then she met Colin," explained Jordan.

"Do you think Elaine or Colin hurt Sean?" asked Blades.

"I don't think Elaine would but I wouldn't be surprised if

Colin did. Sean was afraid of him but we couldn't prove that he abused Sean," stated Jordan.

"How do you know Sean was afraid of him?" asked Blades.

"He told me but wouldn't say why. I'm the newest social worker for Sean. The last one he had failed to show up for a family check so was fired," said Jordan.

"Did you know the sister?" asked Blades.

"No, I never met her but Sean talked about her. He loved her. She seemed to be very nice to him. Elaine seemed to like her, too," said Jordan.

"Sean was last seen with Elaine's sister. We're starting to think she took Sean," explained Blades.

"That's possible, I guess. But I still wouldn't rule out Colin," said Jordan.

"Well the sister isn't answering calls or returning them. That's a bit suspicious," said Blades.

"I guess," said Jordan.

"Is it possible that Elaine just let Susie take Sean?" asked Blades.

"No, because she would lose her subsidized apartment and monthly check if she didn't have Sean. Unfortunately that's her first priority," shared Jordan.

"Thank you, Jordan. If anything comes up or if you think of anything that might help find Sean, please call me," asked Blades.

"I will. Detective Blades, I don't trust Colin at all. I'm not a police officer but if I were you, I would watch him," cautioned Jordan.

"Thanks, we'll do that," promised Blades.

Jordan walked back into the living room. Elaine once again rushed over to her.

"Does this mean I'll have to move? Will I still get my check for Sean?" asked Elaine.

Jordan breathed deeply.

"You won't lose anything just yet, Elaine. I think you should be more concerned about Sean than money," suggested Jordan.

"I am, I am," claimed Elaine.

"I'll talk to you tomorrow," said Jordan as she left the apartment.

Jordan said good-bye to Blades and left the apartment. She made a phone call when she got into her car.

"The police will probably head to Connecticut to look for the boy at some point. I did tell the detective that Colin was trouble and emphasized that he might have hurt Sean. I was trying to buy some time for Susie and Reid," explained Jordan.

"We've already moved them. They'll never find them," said the voice at the other end of the phone.

"Did you give Elaine the injection?" asked the voice.

"Yes, I did. I was at her apartment on the weekend. They were both passed out from drinking and God knows what else. I injected both of them," said Jordan with an obvious smile in her tone.

"Well, now," said the Doyen. You did great work."

CHAPTER 30

Susie was adjusting quite nicely to her new life. Reid and Sean seemed to be doing well, too. Sean enrolled in the preschool in town. Reid had an interview with the hospital nearest to the town. He applied for an EMT position. He was also a volunteer firefighter for the town for now. Susie was thinking about substitute teaching but didn't want to jump into everything just yet. Sean made new friends and joined a soccer club.

Susie and Reid missed their friends but actually liked their new lives. They followed the news regarding Sean's disappearance. Susie's sister was interviewed on television and shown pleading for Sean's safe return. She looked like hell. The news showed a picture of Sean as well as pictures of Susie and Reid. They expected this. James told her there would be a lot of intense media coverage at first but it would die down because there were really no leads. Susie knew the police would get involved in Connecticut but she hoped they wouldn't be able to track them.

No one in town talked about the missing kids in Massachusetts. James didn't even talk about it. Susie and Reid didn't bring it up. Occasionally Sean asked if they were going back to where he lived and Susie would simply say no and his face always showed relief. He called them Mom and Dad and so far had not slipped up regarding their old identities. It helped right now that Sean was shy. Reid and Susie were nervous about him slipping up but it was getting easier every day to live their new lives. It actually felt like this was really who they were. They were almost 1500 miles from Boston. There would be no reason for anyone to suspect they moved to Nebraska, although Susie and Reid did believe the police knew they took Sean.

CHAPTER 31

Kelly Lehman spotted Jay Hastings as soon as she was ushered into the Governor's mansion. She waved as he smiled at her. She exchanged pleasantries with many people as she made her way through the crowd to Jay. She finally reached him.

"Hello, Jay," said Kelly with a smile.

"Hello, Kelly. Wow, you look great," said Jay.

"Thank you. So do you," responded Kelly.

"How are things?" asked Jay.

"Pretty busy but in a good way," said Kelly slyly.

"I know what you mean. Would you like a drink?" asked Jay.

"I would love a drink, thank you," replied Kelly.

"The usual?" asked Jay with a devilish grin.

"Sure," replied Kelly.

As Jay looked for a waiter, Kelly looked around the room. She caught the eye of the Governor and walked toward him. He greeted her warmly.

"Hello, Dr. Lehman. I'm glad you could make it," said the Governor.

"I wouldn't miss it," replied Kelly.

"I'd like to talk to you in private for a few minutes. Can you meet me in my office?" asked the Governor.

"Of course," said Kelly noting the serious tone.

Dr. Lehman spotted Jay and gestured that she would be right back. She had a feeling she knew what the Governor was about to say. She knocked on his office door and went in.

"Hi, Kelly. I'm going to get right to the point. We have to slow down with the scoops. Three is too many in one month," said the Governor worriedly.

"I know but one was pretty serious. The baby would have been seriously hurt or worse," explained Kelly.

"Okay, I get that but we don't want a lot of attention in the state. Lay low for a while. I'll do what I can at my end when I meet with the police commissioner. Get the word out to our heads and tell them all to keep tabs on their targets but to lay low. The Doyen is concerned," said the Governor.

"Okay, those targets will never be located, Jake," Kelly assured him.

"I hope not, for everyone's sake," replied the Governor.

The Governor and Kelly headed back to the gala. Kelly found Jay who was waiting patiently for her. He handed her some wine and they found a table. Dinner was about to be served.

"What was that about?" he asked.

"We have to lay low for a while," explained Kelly.

"I figured we would get those orders," said Jay.

"Just make sure our spotters stay in place," warned Kelly.

"Will do," agreed Jay.

They clinked glasses and settled down to eat. Kelly had been attending this gala for many years. The group had a long history with governors. It formed fifteen years ago when Governor Sally Danner came into office. Her sister's daughter was abducted by her father who had a history of abuse against women. The Department of Children and Families, then called the Department of Social Services opened a case on her sister's family. Her sister did get a restraining order against her husband and had him removed from the house. A social worker bent on endorsing a family reunification philosophy recommended that her sister's husband have visitation. It was supposed to be supervised visitation. The Governor's niece was three at the time.

One day during a visitation, the social worker decided it was okay if the father took the little girl to the park alone. She told him she would meet him there in a few minutes. Of course when she arrived, he was gone. He had taken the Governor's niece. The Governor's sister was frantic. An all-points bulletin and Amber Alert were initiated. A few days later, the little girl was found in a dirty hotel in Maine, terrified and hungry. A guest in the adjoining room heard her crying and alerted the manager. When the manager opened the door after no response from the father, he found the little girl alone. The Governor's brother-in-law just left her there all alone.

The Governor's niece was returned to her mother relatively unharmed. Her father was eventually apprehended, pled guilty to non-custodial kidnapping and assault and was sentenced to prison for ten years. Governor Danner was in her second term at the time. She was devastated that her niece went through what she did. She swore to her sister that the father would never see her again. Sure enough, he died a year later at the hands of another inmate who was never identified.

The Governor's reaction to her niece's abduction was so deep she decided to help other children in similar circumstances. This is how the group was formed and the Governor was the first Doyen. It was a very prestigious position. When

Governor Danner's second term came to an end, she surprisingly pardoned a convicted killer. His name was Teddy Alden and he had killed a rival gang member many years earlier. The Governor was very evasive about why she did this, simply stating that he was a model prisoner and many good citizens had petitioned for his release. She didn't mention that he killed her brother-in-law.

Kelly Lehman knew that there was a connection between the former Governor's brother-in-law's death and the release of this prisoner but she didn't care. When the Governor left office she slowly built "the group" that vowed to protect children. There were doctors, lawyers, teachers, police officers, social workers, hairdressers, nurses, politicians, waitresses, plumbers, and many others in the group. Groups emerged in every state and eventually spread to every province and territory in Canada.

Kelly didn't know how many people belonged to the group but knew the numbers kept increasing. The group had saved thousands of children from horrific lives and continued to do so. The group had an ironclad system. There were code words and communication largely took place in meetings, big and small. Phone calls were permitted but only from burn phones since these phones could not be traced with a SIM card.

The group was very organized. People were placed in positions for job purposes but also as spotters or informers. Males and females were directed into police academies for the sole purpose of serving as informants. Of course, they did want to be police officers as well. People were sent to nursing school, medical school, and law school in order to sustain the group's work. Benefactors paid for everything as long as those receiving funding would pledge allegiance to the group. Background checks were conducted on potential group candidates. Students and non-students were observed for years before they were approached about joining the group. If they agreed, their education was paid for and they were strategically placed in positions that would help save children. No paperwork was kept. Every piece of information was saved on flash drives that would later be destroyed when the information was no longer needed. The group was very careful. No one ever quit; they just retired. No one had ever betrayed the group. Many members of the group had families who had no idea about their extracurricular activities.

Governor Danner passed the torch so to speak to another member of the group. The group remained strong and effective. The current Governor was approached before he ran for office and readily agreed to be part of the group. He strategically placed people in positions to support the group's work and kept it confidential. The Commissioner of the Department of Children and Families was a member of the group. Dr. Lehman wasn't a big fan of his because he didn't always share enough information about some cases as far as she was concerned. She tolerated him, though, because he meant well.

Kelly's thoughts returned to the current dinner and Jay. She was glad to be out for a change. Jay offered to get her another glass of wine and she readily accepted. She even felt herself blush.

CHAPTER 32

Susie watched the news to see if Sean's name was mentioned. Her sister gave an interview about how much she missed Sean. Her sister still looked like hell. She couldn't believe she agreed to an interview in that condition. She kept crying and asking for any help she could get. Susie was sick to her stomach. What had she done? Should she have taken Sean? She was having second thoughts again. She called James and asked if she could meet him somewhere. They decided on the park.

Susie spotted James as soon as she arrived at the park.

"My sister was on the news," said Susie nervously.

"I know. I saw her," replied James.

"She wants Sean back and she seems genuine," said Susie.

"She wants her check and her apartment," said James firmly.

"You don't know that," Susie retorted.

"Yes, I do," said James. He pulled a recorder out of his pocket.

"What's that?" asked Susie.

"We bugged her apartment because we knew you would keep second guessing yourself. My wife and I did the same thing, so I understand. It's normal," explained James.

James pressed the play button. Susie listened intently and immediately recognized Elaine and Colin's voices.

"Why the fuck would your bitch sister take Sean?" asked Colin.

"I don't know, Colin. I'm surprised. I don't know," replied Elaine.

"Well you better get him back soon or we'll lose this apartment, not to mention the skimpy check you get each month," warned Colin.

"She'll bring him back and when she does I won't let her near him again. I'll get him into a Head Start program or something so we don't have to deal with him so much," whined Elaine.

"We better not have to deal with him much. He's a pain in the ass," said Colin.

"He's not that bad, Colin. I know I shouldn't have had him but I did so we have to deal with him. I need a fix, Colin," implored Elaine.

There was a brief moment of silence and then Susie heard Elaine giggling.

"Okay, baby. It's coming," said Colin.

Susie looked at James in disbelief. James shut off the recorder.

"I'm sorry you had to hear that. There's more but I think you've heard enough. They don't want Sean and from what I see, Sean doesn't want them," said James.

"Oh, my God. I didn't think Elaine was that evil," exclaimed Susie.

"Colin is worse," said James. "They both got high and he was pretty abusive to Elaine."

"Did she get hurt?" asked Susie.

"Mentally, she did. He didn't touch her but he was pretty mean," replied James.

"As much as I didn't want to hear that I'm glad I did. Sean needs us," said Susie with conviction.

"Yes, he does," agreed James.

"The police are looking for us in Connecticut. Eventually, they'll find our car and know we're gone," said Susie.

"I know," said James. "All three of you look different so you're safe for now."

"The missing kids are all over the news, James. People may start cluing in," said Susie worriedly.

"They won't. I'm going to a meeting tonight and I'll talk to you after, okay?" James promised.

"Okay, thanks James. I don't know what we would do without you," Susie said with relief.

"You're doing the right thing, Paige," said James gently.

"I know. It just hurts to know your sister is a drug addict and doesn't give a shit about her own son," said Susie.

"I'm sure it does but it also feels good to save a child," said James.

CHAPTER 33

Blades was headed to Connecticut to meet with the state police about the missing boy named Sean. His mother claimed that her sister took him so he had to check out every lead. He arrived in Connecticut around noon and drove to the state trooper barracks. He was given a warm welcome and then followed some troopers to Susie's house.

There were really no clues to Sean's whereabouts at the house. There was a car in the driveway and it was registered to Reid Thomas. The house was in a bit of disarray as if they had left in a hurry. There was nothing at the house suggesting Sean had been there but that didn't mean he hadn't. As Blades and the troopers looked through the house, one of the troopers got a call saying Susie's car was found abandoned in New Hampshire.

"Did they find anything in the car?" asked Blades.

"No," answered Trooper Adams. "There was nothing in the car."

"We should check out the toll booths they might have driven through to confirm Sean was in the car," suggested Blades.

"I'll make a call," said Adams.

An hour later Blades received confirmation that Reid's car

did go through a few toll booths and there was a boy in the back seat. The pictures were not perfect but Blades believed it was Sean. This was good news but might also be a dead end. Susie and Reid had obviously switched vehicles along the way. Blades had his hands full. There was nothing new about Alissa's baby and there may be no leads to where Sean was taken. Blades thanked the troopers for their time and headed back to Massachusetts.

Clare and the boys were home when Blades arrived. Clare could tell he was worn out. She heated up his supper and sat down with him.

"Not a good day?" she asked.

"We're not getting too far with the investigations," shared Blades.

"The news showed pictures of that boy Sean in a car going through a toll booth," said Clare.

"Already?" asked Blades. "I just found out about the photos. How does this stuff get to the reporters?"

"Who knows? But isn't that good to know? Maybe people in Connecticut will pay closer attention to people," said Clare.

"Maybe, but if Sean's aunt is watching the news, they'll know what we know and be more cautious," said Blades.

"I saw Sean's mother on the news. She looks pretty rough," said Clare.

"She is rough," said Blades. "She and her boyfriend are drug addicts."

"Then why is everyone trying to give Sean back to them?" asked Clare.

"Her sister broke the law, Clare. She would still have a chance to get custody of Sean if she came back. It's pretty clear his mother can't take care of him," explained Blades.

"Why don't you broadcast that to his aunt?" asked Clare.

"She won't believe us. She'll think we are just trying to get her back here," said Blades.

"Why was Sean in that situation in the first place? Why wasn't he removed from his mother's home and given to the aunt?" asked Clare impatiently.

"I'm not exactly sure but it probably has something to do with helping the mother parent him. Believe me, it's a lot of bullshit," said Blades.

"You know Dana, Sean is probably better off with his aunt," said Clare.

"From everything we gathered, she and her husband are great people. You're probably right but if we let it go, there might be a kidnapping craze," said Blades.

"It does suck," said Clare. "Eat your supper. The boys are about to attack you!"

Clare didn't finish the sentence when Eric and Tyler burst into the room to say hello to their father.

CHAPTER 34

Amanda took Deidre to her own apartment for the time being. The little girl was sleeping peacefully. Amanda's supervisor had called and told her Deidre was missing and she should go talk to the parents. Amanda assured her that she would do so in the morning. She lied and told her supervisor that the police asked her to wait until then. Amanda called one of the elders in the group.

"I have Deidre, Dr. Lehman. I can keep her tonight but we have to move her first thing in the morning," said Amanda.

"I know. I have the perfect family for her. After we move her, you have to go back to work. There won't be any more scoops for a while because there are too many people asking questions about the missing kids. We usually don't take three kids at once but as you know we have had extenuating circumstances," stated Dr. Lehman.

"Yeah, I know. Who am I meeting in the morning and where?" asked Amanda.

"I don't know yet but I will in a couple of hours. Talk to you then," replied Dr. Lehman as she hung up.

Amanda put her phone down and settled in the living room to watch the news. Deidre was all over the news as the latest child to disappear. The mayor of Boston was outraged. The police commissioner had as many officers on the cases as she could. Even the Governor had a few words to say. Most reporters asked him about the Department of Children and Families. They wanted to know why these kids had open cases on them. He wouldn't divulge that information. Amanda smiled. He was smooth. He knew that the kids were in great hands and would play along with the social and legal systems involved. Although he was heavily involved in the group, he never asked the whereabouts of the children. He just wanted to know they were safe. He played his public role well. He appeared angry and disgusted with DCF. He promised to revamp the whole institution. The media loved his response but also believed it was for the cameras.

The phone rang again. It was Dr. Lehman and she instructed Amanda to meet Robert at the Christian Science building on Huntington Avenue at nine in the morning. Amanda didn't ask any questions. After she hung up, she watched a few shows and got ready for bed. She checked on Deidre who was still sleeping. She loved that little girl and wished she could keep her. She knew that was impossible. She also knew Dr. Lehman had found a great home for her. She always did.

CHAPTER 35

Dr. Lehman let herself into the old farmhouse in Rochester. The group owned this hundred-acre farm and used it often for meetings, transferring children and killing pedophiles. Tonight it was pedophile time. Garrett and Liam were playing cards at the kitchen table when the good doctor walked in the house. James was watching a baseball game. Garrett lit up when he saw Dr. Lehman. He had a crush on her but knew he didn't have a chance. Rumor had it she was dating Jay Hastings. Garrett was a computer technician and James and Liam were businessmen. It was their turn to stand guard at the farmhouse for the weekend.

The farmhouse took one pedophile at a time. Tonight it was Trevor Daigle. This particular guy hailed from New York City. He had molested at least eight little boys. He was a Cub Scout leader. Everyone in his community loved him until now. They thought he was so good to the boy scouts. He took them camping and hiking. He spent as much time as he could with the boys. His background check came back unblemished when he applied for the leadership position. Of course this meant nothing. He just hadn't been caught and arrested yet. He liked spending time with the boys because he liked molesting them.

As much as he knew this was wrong, he was too self-centered to stop. He would try and convince himself that what he did to the boys was relatively harmless so he could continue to attract victims.

The group decided to watch Trevor because a young woman made a comment to her teacher that she thought it was weird that Trevor wanted to spend all of his time with young boys. One of the boys was her brother but she wouldn't let her brother spend time alone with Trevor. She said she had "bad vibes" about Trevor. The teacher was a member of the group and passed on the girl's concerns. Sure enough, the group confirmed that Trevor spent far too much time with little boys. He also had quite a collection of child pornography on his laptop and boxes full of pictures displaying naked boys.

The teacher pushed the girl to tell her parents about her concerns. Soon a number of parents started to panic and asked their boys about Trevor. Several boys said Trevor had touched them. Several more said Trevor made them do "sexual things". Before Trevor could be arrested, he fled town but the group caught up with him in a seedy motel in upstate New York and took him back to Rochester, Massachusetts.

Dr. Lehman asked the guys how Trevor was coping at the farmhouse. They said he was frantic for the most part. She opened the bedroom door where Trevor was being detained. He was secured to the double bed with zip ties. The mattress had no sheets and was very uncomfortable. Trevor had a desperate look on his face. He kept pulling at the posts of the bed trying to break the ties. Dr. Lehman noticed that the guys gave Trevor something to eat and drink. Trevor had been detained at the farmhouse for two days. He admitted to everything in the hopes that they would let him go. He offered to turn himself into the police. He was desperate to live. Dr. Lehman felt a sarcastic smirk growing on her face. His pleas didn't move her.

"Hello, Trevor. I hope you're comfortable," said the doctor sarcastically.

"Please, just let me go," he said as he started to sob.

"Now that's an interesting request. Did the little boys you molested request that, too?" asked Dr. Lehman.

"I need help. I'll turn myself in." Trevor looked like hell. There were tear tracks on his face and dried snots.

"You're not going anywhere, Trevor. No one knows you're here and no one can hear your pitiful cries for help. You're a disgusting human being," said Dr. Lehman.

"I'm sick. Please listen to me," implored Trevor.

"Actually, I am quite sick of listening to you," replied Dr. Lehman. "Are you going to write the suicide note or not?"

"No, I'm not. I'm not admitting to anything on paper," declared Trevor.

"I have absolutely no sympathy for you, Trevor. Either way you're going to die. I can give a lethal concoction of drugs that will simply put you to sleep forever or I can give you a painful concoction of drugs," explained the doctor with no expression on her face.

"Fuck you, you bitch. You'll never get away with this!" yelled Trevor.

Without missing a beat, Dr. Lehman opened her black doctor's bag and took out several needles. She proceeded to prepare the needles with her potion that was actually puffer fish venom. She didn't bother to swab Trevor's arm as she drove the needle into a vein. She watched as he slowly became completely immobile. The look of terror slowly made its way across Trevor's face and into his eyes.

"Oh, I'm sorry Trevor, are you afraid?" asked Dr. Lehman.

Trevor couldn't answer since he was completely paralyzed. His brain worked, though. He was in pain and losing his capacity to breathe. He was afraid.

"How are you feeling, Trevor? I hope you're terrified. I hope you're in pain. What you're feeling is exactly what those little boys felt as you molested them. You destroyed a piece of their lives you pig. You knew better Trevor, but you chose to continue molesting them. You're a sick, selfish son of a bitch," sneered Dr. Lehman.

Dr. Lehman watched as a tear rolled down Trevor's cheek.

"Crying will do you no good, Trevor. I bet those boys cried but you still molested them, didn't you?" asked Dr. Lehman.

Dr. Lehman waited a few more minutes and then gave Trevor the antidote. He gasped for air and then started to hyperventilate.

"Save the dramatics, Trevor. You're going to die. I gave you the choices. You can write a note confessing everything you did and I'll give you a nice little cocktail that will put you to sleep. Or if you don't write the note, you will get more venom. What's it going to be?" asked the doctor.

"Please let me live. I'll get help. I can change. I'm sorry," cried Trevor.

"Venom for vermin it is," said Dr. Lehman.

"Wait, wait! I'll write the note," yelled Trevor.

Dr. Lehman yelled to James and Garrett to bring in the notepad and pen. Both men came into the room. They knew the drill. James cut the zip-tie on Trevor's right wrist since he was right-handed. Trevor was able to sit up at an angle and write. Dr. Lehman told him what to write. As soon as he signed his name, a new zip-tide was secured. Trevor was silent. He knew he had been defeated.

Dr. Lehman pulled three more needles out of her bag. One drug relaxed Trevor, one slowly stopped his heart and the last one made sure he was dead. She watched as Trevor's eyes changed from terrified to drowsy to empty. These were the only empty eyes she was happy to see. She hated seeing the empty eyes of abused children. There were too many. At least now there was one less pedophile in the world. When it was done she left the room. James and Garret followed her out.

"Okay, boys, he's gone. Take him to Randolph's. I'll let him know to preheat the oven. It's cremation time," declared Dr. Lehman.

"Will do," said Garrett. "Have a good night, Doc."

"I did," said Dr. Lehman as she let herself out.

CHAPTER 36

Reilly was up at the crack of dawn and in her new office. It was pretty empty given that she just started. She would have to spruce it up some time but she was surfing through some old articles on those mysterious rape cases. She wasn't sure where to start. She really wanted to talk to that swim coach in prison but thought it was too soon. Foundation is everything, she learned from her Aunt Loretta. Begin at the beginning was her favorite saying.

Reilly decided to call the police station handling the cases of the alleged rapists' deaths and asked to talk to the investigating officer. His name was littered throughout the articles online. Dana Blades. Maybe he would have a great explanation for not catching the serial killer yet.

Reilly called the main desk and asked for Detective Blades. He wasn't in. She asked if she could make an appointment and the person who answered the phone laughed.

"We don't take appointments. You can leave a message for Blades if you want."

"Does he check his messages often?" asked Reilly.

"Well, I'm not his keeper but I believe so," said the receptionist.

"Okay, I'll leave a message," said Reilly.

"I'll transfer you," responded the receptionist.

"Wait, do you know who else I could talk to about the serial killer case?" asked Reilly.

"Which one?" asked the receptionist.

"The one the media called the serial vigilante," Reilly informed her.

There seemed to be a long pause before Reilly got an answer.

"I don't know off hand but you may want to speak to the Chief about this," suggested the receptionist.

"Okay, is he in?" asked Reilly.

"Let me check," said the voice at the end of the line.

Reilly was on hold for what she thought was an eternity. Finally the receptionist spoke.

"What's your name and what paper did you say you worked for?" she asked.

"My name is Reilly Simonsen and I'm a reporter for the Boston Globe."

Reilly liked how that sounded.

"Okay, the Chief said he could see you later today, around two o'clock. Does that work?" asked the receptionist.

" Yes, thank you very much," said Reilly.

Reilly hung up and was so excited. She decided to do more research on the story and craft some questions for the Chief. She would have to run this by her new boss.

CHAPTER 37

James knocked on Susie's door. Susie was surprised to see him.

"Hi James. I didn't expect you. I thought you were going to call me," said Susie.

"It's better that I tell you this in person," said James.

"Come in, then," said Susie.

"I have what I hope you'll consider good news," James began.

"Okay, let me get Reid, I mean Sawyer." said Susie.

Susie yelled upstairs for Reid to come down.

"What's up?" he asked.

"James wants to tell us something," replied Susie.

"I'm assuming Paige filled you in on our talk in the park," said James.

"Yes, she did," replied Reid, reminding himself that Susie was Paige.

"I know you guys are still worried about being detected. I may have a great solution," said James.

"What?" asked Susie.

"Well, one of our members had to take an eighteen month old girl off the streets yesterday. She was literally roaming around. One of our social workers had an open case on the family and the parents were not following through with the plan given to them. The group was watching the house when the little girl went outside by herself. That little girl can't be placed back with her parents or she'll get hurt or worse. Now the little girl needs a new home," explained James.

"What are you saying?" asked Reid.

"You want us to take her?" asked Susie with a shocked look on her face.

"Hear me out. You're both worried about being recognized. The police are looking for a couple with a small boy not a couple with a boy and a girl. You just moved here and for all anybody knows, you have two kids," explained James.

"But we've been out in public with just Sean," said Susie.

"Did anyone ask you any personal questions?" asked James.

"No," said Reid.

"You both have been laying low because of the news so no one will be surprised to see you have two kids. In fact, you should be seen more often with two kids so you won't look like the missing family," said James.

"What about Sean? He needs our attention. He may not want a sister all of a sudden," said Reid.

"Feel him out and see how he reacts when he meets Molly," suggested James. "If it doesn't go well, we'll place her with someone else."

"I don't know if we're ready for two kids," said Susie.

"It's really up to you. Molly's parents are both alcoholics. As I said she was found wandering outside by herself. Her parents were passed out. She could have been killed," said James.

"Or kidnapped," said Susie sarcastically.

"Look," said James. "Again, it's up to you but she would

help you avoid suspicion and you would help her live a normal life."

"I don't know what normal is anymore," said Susie.

"My wife and I will help with anything. My wife stays home full-time and loves kids. She would be happy to help you get used to having two kids. It's honestly up to you. Like I said, if you're not ready, we have other options. I was instructed to ask you first," explained James.

"Why not?" asked Reid looking at Susie. "We might as well jump in with two feet. She might be good for Sean. We're already in deep."

Susie looked at Reid and was quiet for a minute.

"Okay," said Susie. "Let me talk to Sean see how he reacts. When will we meet Molly?"

"Tomorrow morning," said James.

James left and Susie went to find Sean.

CHAPTER 38

Six months had passed since Sean had disappeared from Dorchester. Blades was tired and frustrated. He knew that Sean's aunt had taken him, but where? He hit a dead-end in Connecticut and he checked all surrounding airports within a reasonable distance with no luck. Sean and his aunt and uncle didn't fly to wherever they went as far as he knew.

Alissa's baby was probably long gone, too. They had absolutely no clues to her disappearance. Deidre, the little girl from Brockton, was also still on the missing list. Blades found it hard to believe that these kids could just disappear but it did happen all of the time. He had a weird feeling about these cases, though. He didn't think any of the kids he was investigating were in harm's way. All three kids were taken from parents who were abusive in some way to the children. This was conjecture of course, but Blades' gut told him the kids were probably safe.

Blades thought about the parents. The only ones who stayed in some touch with him were Deidre March's parents. They called the station maybe once a week and asked if they were close to finding her. They were usually drunk when they called and Blades had little patience with that but he was professional when he dealt with them. As for the missing newborn, Alissa was dead and her boyfriend stopped calling a long time ago.

Elaine, Sean's mother, called twice since her son disappeared. Blades was in touch with all of their social workers and none of the parents were in any condition to raise a child. This infuriated Blades. Why are so many social workers trying to save the "family" at the expense of the children? Blades sometimes thought it would be best to stop looking but what if the kids were taken by someone who would hurt them? He was very conflicted. He saw so many kids fall through the cracks but maybe these kids were actually wedged out of the cracks. He still had to keep looking. Lately, there was a new case of kids being horribly abused every week in Massachusetts. Something had to be done.

Blades had issues with DCF in Massachusetts. Kids died under its care. Blades also had issues with family members who stood by and ignored abuse. He thought of that little boy from Brockton who was beaten to death by his mother's boyfriend. The boyfriend punched the four year old so hard that an organ actually hit his spine and burst. He eventually died of internal bleeding. The boy had been abused for a long time. Social workers had been involved months before but determined that claims of abuse were "unfounded". They also filed false reports of no-show visitations. Teachers noticed bruises on the boy and did nothing. They chose to believe the boy's mother who attributed the bruises to roughhousing. What the hell was wrong with people? Where was the kid's father? Blades would never get used to this.

Blades thoughts went back to Sean. He would start from scratch again and try to piece the puzzle together. He reluctantly decided to visit Sean's mother again and review the case. He grabbed his coat and started to leave when his phone rang.

It was an officer from Mattapan. He told Blades he recognized Sean from a clinic he had been to about seven months ago.

"You're telling me this now?" Blades said angrily.

"We didn't put it together until lately because the kid was at the clinic a week before he actually disappeared. When we asked the doctor about Sean, she told us she sent him to the hospital with his aunt and uncle and the boy's social worker would meet them there. We filed the report but were told not to follow-up."

"Who told you not to follow up?" asked Blades.

"Our Chief. He said it was taken care of," replied the officer.

"So, what do you think happened? You think something stinks?" asked Blades curious to hear the officer's thoughts.

"Yeah. I thought it was strange for the Chief to tell us to back off and for the doctor to send the kid away while we were at the clinic," replied the officer.

"Jesus, I wish I had known this then. Who was the doctor?" asked Blades.

"Hold on, I have her name written down."

"Alright," said Blades patiently.

"Her name is Dr. Kelly Lehman."

CHAPTER 39

Mary made her way into the doctor's office. Hopefully this would be her last appointment. She was tired of going to the doctor but she did love Dr. Lehman. Mary had her knee operated on about six weeks prior and Dr. Lehman was the surgeon. She had been going to physical therapy and was walking well after several weeks of rehabilitation. Dr. Lehman wanted to see her to check on her progress. Mary walked into the waiting room and waved to the receptionist to let her know she was there. She sat down and grabbed a magazine to leaf through. She had a lot on her mind. She was very worried about her brother. Bobby was her only sibling and younger than Mary. They were very close.

Mary's brother was married and had a beautiful little girl named Chloe. She was about three months old. Mary was her godmother. Mary hated Bobby's wife, Ashley. She was pure evil. Mary thought back to when she first met Ashley and remembered how much she did like Ashley at first. In fact, they had been great friends. Ashley was the only child of a very wealthy family. Her father owned some type of pharmaceutical company. As Mary got to know Ashley, she realized she was a spoiled brat. Mary was now convinced she married Bobby to spite her parents. Bobby was a contractor and not considered good enough for Ashley. Mary did believe that Ashley loved Bobby at some point but she treated him like shit right now. Bobby also loved Ashley at one time but that love was long gone. Despite their lost love, Ashley did get pregnant during what Bobby called "drunk sex." Chloe was now the love of Bobby's life and her grandparents on both sides of the family adored her.

Ashley was a great partner for Bobby for the first two years of their marriage. After that Ashley decided it wasn't fun being married any more. She was bored. She started going out and partying almost every night. She completely ignored Bobby's pleas to work on their marriage. Ashley's parents were disgusted with her but still enabled the crap out of her. When Ashley got pregnant, everyone thought she would ease off on her night-life. She did for a while but during her second trimester she started drinking again. She had at least one glass of red wine every night. When Bobby protested, she would claim that the doctor told her it was just fine. Bobby didn't think it was fine. Fortunately, Chloe was born with no problems that they could see right now.

Ashley barely paid any attention to Chloe and hired a full-time nanny. Bobby worked all week and spent every other moment he had with Chloe. He adored her. Ashley continued to go out every night. One day, Bobby asked Ashley for a divorce. Ashley just looked at him and started laughing. She told him they would never get divorced because she wasn't giving Bobby half of her fortune. Bobby told her he didn't want her money; he just wanted Chloe. Ashley laughed even harder and told him he would never have Chloe. Her parents would hire a team of lawyers who would make sure Bobby paid child support and would only see Chloe every other weekend and one day during the week, if he was lucky.

Mary cringed at the thought of Bobby losing Chloe. Bobby knew Ashley would fight for Chloe not because she loved her but because Bobby wanted to divorce her. Ashley actually wanted to continue being married but do whatever she wanted to do. Bobby tried talking to Ashley's parents but even though they knew Ashley was a problem, they didn't want a divorce in their family. It would look bad. Mary laughed at the thought of that because everyone already knew Ashley screwed around on Bobby and was a raging alcoholic.

Mary stayed awake at night and thought about how she could help her brother and Chloe. Chloe would be so neglected if Ashley got custody of her. Bobby would die inside if he didn't see his little girl every day. Mary actually thought about killing Ashley. She really thought about it. She knew it meant that she would go to prison probably for life but sometimes she didn't care. She wasn't married and had no children. She would do that for her brother so he and Chloe would have a good life.

Mary was called into Dr. Lehman's office.

"Good morning, Mary," said Dr. Lehman in a cheery voice.

"Good morning to you," replied Mary.

Dr. Lehman and Mary had developed somewhat of a friendship over the last year. Sometimes they spent the majority of the appointment talking about their lives or what was going on in the news.

"How's the knee?" asked Dr. Lehman.

"It's actually feeling great," replied Mary.

Mary walked around the room to show the doctor how well she was moving.

"Looks great," said Dr. Lehman.

Dr. Lehman then asked Mary to bend her knee, stand on one leg, and crouch down.

Mary went through the motions quietly. Dr. Lehman knew something was bothering Mary.

"What's going on, Mary? You seem preoccupied," said Dr. Lehman.

"Oh, I'm still worried about my brother. Now the bitch is threatening to hire a team of lawyers to get full custody of Chloe," explained Mary.

Mary and Dr. Lehman referred to Ashley as "the bitch" for quite some time now. Dr. Lehman knew all about Bobby's problems.

"I thought Bobby found a great lawyer," said Dr. Lehman.

"He did but Ashley's parents have a lot of connections," said Mary.

"That's true," agreed Dr. Lehman.

"You're not going to like this doc, but I'm actually thinking about killing the bitch. That way Bobby gets custody of Chloe," said Mary.

"Now, Mary, you know that's not a good idea. You'll end up in prison and Chloe will grow up knowing her aunt killed her mother. That's not good for anyone," said Dr. Lehman.

"I don't know what else to do," said Mary with an exasperated tone. "Bobby can't run with Chloe because he'll get caught and lose Chloe forever. Ashley's parents have a lot of resources."

"Don't give up yet, Mary. I have a few connections myself and will see if I can find a better lawyer for Bobby," said Dr. Lehman.

"Bobby can't afford an expensive lawyer," Mary responded.

"Don't worry. I have a few friends who owe me a favor," said Dr. Lehman.

Mary felt a flicker of hope.

"Thanks, Dr. Lehman. You're too good," said Mary with a look of relief.

"No problem, Mary. You have to finish the next few weeks of physical therapy and come back to see me," said Dr. Lehman.

The appointment ended and Mary left feeling like maybe Bobby had a chance. She opened her cell phone and called Bobby. She left a message about the potential new lawyer.

Dr. Lehman sat at her desk and thought about Mary. The group was meeting tonight and she would bring up Bobby's dilemma. She looked forward to these meetings. The meetings took place every three months all over the country. Every state had a "group". Twenty governors belonged to the group not to mention a lot of other politicians. Everyone felt they were doing good work saving children from horrible lives. Dr. Lehman thought about Mary's brother. She would help him.

CHAPTER 40

Sean was thrilled with his new sister. Molly, in turn, loved Sean. She knew him as Isaac. Susie and Reid explained to Sean that they decided to adopt a little girl so he would have a sister. They didn't tell him why they were really taking her in. Molly was a little shy when James brought her into their house but within an hour, she and Sean were laughing and playing.

"I can't believe how well she is taking to us," said Susie.

"Unfortunately abused kids often take to anyone who's nice to them," said James. "Plus she's young."

"Isaac seems to love her," observed Reid.

"He's old for his years," said Susie. "He probably had to fend for himself on a few occasions."

"Hopefully, he'll get over that," said James. "Molly will be good for him."

"I think you're right," agreed Susie.

James stayed for a while longer. He promised he would drop by the next day with his wife.

After he left, Susie and Reid looked at each other and laughed.

"What the hell happened to our lives?" asked Reid.

"I think we were blessed," said Susie.

"God, I hope this works," said Reid. "The kids need us."

"Well we wanted kids, right? Now we have them!" exclaimed Susie throwing her hands up into the air.

"Are you still thinking about Elaine?" asked Reid.

"Not so much," said Susie. "She's her own worst enemy and Sean can't be one of her casualties. He never asks about her."

"I guess that's good," said Reid. "Why don't we take the kids for a walk?"

"Great idea," said Susie.

Sean and Molly were excited about going outside. It was beautiful out. Sean insisted on pushing Molly in the stroller. He was very happy to have a sister. Molly acted like she had always been part of the family.

Susie and Reid never imagined they would be kidnapping kids and be fugitives of the law. They knew how deep they were in. They knew they could go to prison. They also knew that the kids would fall through the cracks and maybe even die if they didn't commit their lives to them. They were now part of "the group" as James called it. They believed him when he said they were safe. The group had been operating for over twenty years. During that time no one went to prison. Some came close to being caught but there were so many connections in the system that the group could take care of any close calls.

CHAPTER 41

Kelly Lehman arrived at the meeting. There were about thirty people present. There were drinks and a little food. They met in a conference room in a building owned by a member of the group. Most people thought they were meeting to discuss what charities they would give to this year. Kelly spotted the Governor talking to Jay and walked over.

"Hey guys," said Kelly.

"Hey, Doc," said Jay.

"I hear you have an important agenda item," said the Governor.

"I do," said Kelly.

"I also heard everything went smoothly at the farm," said the Governor.

"Piece of cake," said Kelly.

A voice boomed across the room telling everyone to sit. The meetings were very organized. The head of this group, Marcia Hale, was a pediatrician from an adjoining town. She called the meeting to order. The group went over the minutes of the last meeting and started with the first agenda item. Most of the agenda was a review of the latest cases and introductions of new members. The group discussed its finances and beneficiaries. Updates on national issues were reviewed and then Kelly's name was announced.

"Kelly, I hear you have some concerns about a child," said Maria.

"Yes, it actually involves a father and child," said Kelly.

Kelly proceeded to tell them about Bobby and Chloe. Some of the members looked ambivalent right away because they knew Chloe's grandparents. The grandparents knew nothing of the group but some of the members traveled in the same social circles. One member brought this up.

"If we re-locate the father and child, Ashley's parents will have a team of investigators looking for them and they won't stop until they're found. This could jeopardize the group," Doug explained.

"I understand that," said Kelly. "We have to do something. That child will have no parents if the mother gets custody of her. She's drunk all of the time and never takes care of the baby. She hires nannies for everything and her parents enable the shit out of her," explained Kelly.

"They're pretty big names," said another member.

"You all know that if Chloe goes with her mother, the grandparents will just hire nannies to take care of her. Bobby will have restricted visits. None of this is fair to that child. I can't believe you're more concerned about the grandparents than the baby," said Kelly with a disgusted tone.

"Does anyone have any suggestions?" asked Marcia, trying to calm things down.

Jay raised his hand.

"We could eliminate Ashley," he said without hesitation.

Members of the group shifted uncomfortably in their chairs wondering what Jay meant when he used the word "eliminate". The group had not ordered a parental extermination in thirty years. Of course, there was always speculation that Governor Danner ordered a hit on her brother-in-law when she was in office but that was just speculation.

Kelly looked at Jay. He was serious. The room buzzed with opinions.

"Look," said Jay. "Everyone knows Ashley has a drinking problem and a drug problem. She's in and out of the news all of the time. We could easily slip something into a drink and she would just fall asleep and never wake up. No one will be surprised that she overdosed. It's not like we haven't done it before."

Jay looked around the room and saw a lot of agreeable faces. He wondered if the Doyen was at this meeting. Supposedly the Doyen attended all meetings but no one really knew who it was. Jay knew even if the majority of the group agreed to killing Ashley, the Doyen made the final decision.

"Jay, you know how we feel about killing, except for pedophiles, of course," said Marcia.

"We also know that Bobby won't get custody of Chloe unless Ashley is gone. Bobby's sister is even thinking about killing her. I had to convince her not to today," said Kelly.

"We can't let the sister do it. We don't want Chloe growing up knowing her aunt killed her mother. That's too much for a child to deal with," said Marcia.

"I think we should drug her," said a voice in the back of the room.

Everyone turned to see one of the newest members. He was a police officer from Stoughton.

"For those of you who forgot, my name is Scott. I have had run-ins with Ashley a few times. She's a piece of trash. I know where she goes and with who. When she's out on the weekends, she always stays at the Ritz in Boston. We could easily get to her with no one knowing."

"She always has people with her," said Kelly. "Her sister-in-law told me that."

"Well, we'll have to find a way to get her into her room alone after she parties," said Scott. "I'm sure she'll be out this weekend."

"We need to vote on this," said Marcia. "This is a serious deviation from our work but it certainly lends itself to some consideration. All in favor of terminating Ashley please raise your hands."

Kelly looked around the room as she raised her hand. All hands were up. Meeting adjourned.

CHAPTER 42

Blades was a little surprised that Dr. Lehman examined Sean. He last saw the doctor at the hospital where the newborn disappeared. He wondered if she saw Sean before or after that. He would have to go see her. First, he had to speak to Elaine again. He called Clare to tell her he might be later than expected. She was so accommodating regarding his work. She never complained about his hours. If she had to work and he was running late, she called her mother or Theresa. It was all about family to all of them.

Blades knocked on Elaine's door. There was no answer. He knocked again and yelled her name. He heard some movement. He tried the door and it was unlocked. He let himself in. Elaine was passed out on the couch. Unfortunately Blades was getting used to hearing moans from drug- infested apartments. Colin wasn't there. Blades walked over to Elaine and shook her shoulder.

"Wake-up, Elaine. It's Blades."

Elaine moaned again and tried to open her eyes.

"Elaine, it's Blades. I have questions for you!"

Elaine turned over and went back to sleep. Blades knew she was stoned out of her mind. He was disgusted. He looked around the apartment and took in the mess. It looked like a pigsty. There was trash all over the place. He walked into what he guessed was Sean's room. There was a cot and a plastic bin. That was it. No toys, no curtains, and nothing on the walls. He looked in the bin and deduced that this is where Sean kept his clothes. The bin held a few things. Blades walked out of Sean's room and into Elaine's room. There were ashtrays and empty pizza boxes. The bed looked like it had never been made. The sheets were filthy. Blades' stomach turned.

Blades walked back out to the living room. He looked at Elaine passed out on the couch. He decided to call the social worker in charge of Sean's case. First, he called the department and asked for backup in case she woke up but also so she couldn't accuse him of anything. He wanted to collect and tag all of the drug paraphernalia and arrest Elaine. He took pictures of each room and all of the filth. While he waited for backup, Colin arrived.

"Who the fuck are you?" asked Colin.

"Detective Blades," said Blades as he turned toward Colin.

"Oh, sorry about the language. What's up?" asked Colin.

"What's up is that Elaine was supposed to answer some questions about Sean and she opted to get stoned instead," Blades remarked.

"She's just tired," said Colin dismissing Blades' comments.

"Nice try but I have the meth pipe and its contents," said Blades as he held up the items.

"Really? For all I know you planted that stuff," accused Colin.

"Yeah, Colin. I spent my day looking for a semi-filled meth pipe so I could put it on the coffee table while Elaine slept," responded Blades sarcastically.

Blades saw the rage cross Colin's eyes.

"You have no right to search my place. Where's your warrant?" asked Colin.

"I don't need a warrant. I had an appointment. This is not your place. The door was open and I heard someone moaning. I let myself in to make sure everyone was okay. Clearly, they're not," said Blades.

"I'm going to sue your ass!" yelled Colin.

"Shut it, Colin or I'll arrest *you* for drug possession," warned Blades.

Colin walked over to Elaine and shook her.

"Wake up you stupid bitch!" he demanded.

"Back off, Colin. Leave her alone," warned Blades.

Blades walked toward Colin. Just then Colin decided to take a swing at Blades. Blades ducked and then drove his fist into Colin's right cheek. Colin went down just as backup arrived.

Two officers came into the apartment and saw the scuffle. Colin was picking himself off the floor when one of the officers told him to stay down and put his hands behind his head. Colin stood up and lunged toward the officer. The officer landed a punch into Colin's stomach. He then grabbed Colin's hands and put them behind him. Colin was handcuffed and steered toward the door while trying to catch his breath.

"You okay, Blades?" asked the second officer.

"I'm fine. Take that asshole to booking. Read him his rights and charge him with assaulting two officers and drug possession," Blades instructed.

Colin tried to speak but he had the wind knocked out of him. The officers took him out of the apartment. Blades called for an ambulance in case Elaine needed one. While he waited, he called the social worker and filled her in on the latest interaction with Elaine and Colin.

"I'm calling to tell you what just transpired but also to file a 51A. I know there's already a case open but I want this information on record. These two shouldn't be raising a child," said Blades.

"Duly noted," said Jordan with a smile.

Blades couldn't see the social worker smiling at the end of the line but could sense that she was pleased. At least this social worker had the sense to know bad parents when she saw them.

"I hope Elaine and Colin never get to see that boy again," said Blades. "Hopefully when we find him he'll be placed in a good foster home until everything gets straightened out."

If we find them, thought Jordan.

CHAPTER 43

Mary woke up from a very restless sleep. She had seen Bobby and Chloe last night. Ashley was out as usual. Bobby was more distressed than ever because his in-laws had been pressuring him to not fight Ashley for custody. They actually offered him a substantial sum of money if he would leave quietly. He reacted in disgust and turned them down. Mary reassured him that she would have a new lawyer for him any day now. She left his house feeling like they were losing the battle.

Mary tossed and turned thinking about killing Ashley. She had a gun; a legal one and would shoot Ashley in a heartbeat. Her only hesitation was that Bobby might not fully understand what she would do for him so he could have Chloe. She thought about what Dr. Lehman said about Chloe knowing her aunt killed her mother. Mary knew that was a price she might have to pay but didn't want Chloe to be raised by nannies and a drunken slut mother.

Mary got out of bed and made her way to the coffee pot. The phone rang. Mary looked at the caller ID and saw that it was Bobby. She tried to sound cheerful.

"Hey bud, what's up?" asked Mary.

"Ashley's dead," said Bobby in an almost robotic voice.

Mary wasn't sure this was even Bobby.

"Bobby, is this you?" asked Mary.

"Yes. Ashley is dead," said Bobby again with no emotion.

"What do you mean?" How did she die?" asked Mary.

"She overdosed in the bathtub at the Ritz," said Bobby.

"What the hell!" exclaimed Mary.

"The police are here. Can you come over and help with Chloe? Ashley's parents are on their way, too," Bobby explained.

"Of course I'll come. Why are Ashley's parents coming? I hope they don't think they're taking Chloe anywhere," declared Mary.

"No, they're more concerned about damage control. They don't want the press to know their daughter overdosed," explained Bobby with disgust.

"So, they don't even care that she's dead," stated Mary.

"I don't know. I can't believe she's dead," whispered Bobby.

"Well, I'm glad she's dead. She was an evil witch," stated Mary.

"Okay, Mary, just come over," replied Bobby in a tired voice.

Mary hung up the phone. She couldn't believe the bitch was dead. She called work and told them there was a death in the family. The clerk offered her sympathy and Mary pretended to be sad. Then she called Dr. Lehman and left a message saying Bobby wouldn't need that lawyer after all.

Mary danced all of the way to her bedroom to get dressed. She had never been so happy. Good riddance, Ashley, she thought. Chloe would have a happy life after all.

An hour later, Mary arrived at Bobby's the same time Ashley's parents arrived. Mary let herself into the house, followed by Ashley's parents. Mary didn't bother extending any condolences to them because they knew Mary hated their daughter. They quietly entered Bobby's home. Mary hugged Bobby and then held Chloe close to her. Chloe smiled at Mary.

Ashley's parents pretended to be upset about their daughter's death. They hugged Bobby and touched Chloe. Mary made no move to release Chloe. She left the room. She could hear the parents talking to Bobby, telling him not to mention Ashley's drinking and philandering. The conversation continued for a few minutes and voices were raised at times. Finally, Bobby told them to get out of the house. Ashley's parents didn't expect that. Bobby stared at them until they left. They would make the funeral arrangements, of course.

Mary found Bobby again.

"You, okay?" asked Mary.

"Yes, I'm fine, just in shock," said Bobby.

"I know. I didn't even expect this," said Mary.

"Her parents are more concerned about their image than the fact that their daughter is dead. They offered to make all of the arrangements and write the obituary," Bobby told Mary.

"Oh, I can't wait to read that," said Mary. "It will be littered with bullshit."

"I'm just glad there'll be no more fighting and Chloe is too young to be traumatized," said Bobby.

"Well I, for one, am thrilled," said Mary.

"I get it, Mary but you can't say that out loud in front of people, especially Chloe," explained Bobby.

"I know, I know. I just can't believe the timing," said Mary shaking her head.

"Let's just get through the funeral," said Bobby quietly.

"Did Ashley's parents say anything about taking Chloe?" asked Mary.

"They just said they would always be there for her. They

have a trust fund set up for her but they also know I will inherit Ashley's money. They were fine but kept asking me to at least look sad in public," said Bobby.

"What did you say?" asked Mary.

"I said I am sad and then told them to get out. They didn't even realize that I was sad because they are so pathetic," Bobby replied.

Mary shook her head and walked back into the kitchen with little Chloe. She kissed Chloe on the head and whispered, "No one is taking you."

CHAPTER 44

Kelly Lehman watched the news coverage of Ashley Wright's death. The reporter described the death as an accidental overdose. Perfect, thought Kelly. She knew what really happened, though.

The group had Ashley followed last night. As always, Ashley got trashed at a club. She then took an entourage of sorts back to the bar at the Ritz. As Ashley's new friends continued drinking, a bellboy passed the bartender a note. The note was for Ashley Wright. There was a special surprise waiting in her room.

The bartender called Ashley over and showed her the note. Ashley squealed in delight. She told her group of friends that she would be right back and reminded the bartender that all of the drinks were on her. Ashley staggered to the elevator and went up to her room. She tried to straighten up by fixing her long blonde hair and adjusting her clothes in a way to reveal as much tits and ass as possible. She wasn't sure what was waiting for her but she wanted to be prepared. She entered the room expecting to see something but instead saw a very handsome young man.

Ashley threw herself gleefully at the handsome man. He laughed and gently pushed her away from him. Ashley was a beautiful woman. She had a striking resemblance to Marilyn Monroe. The man understood why other men couldn't resist her. She was advertising her assets by wearing a skintight black dress.

"Where did you come from, handsome?" slurred Ashley.

"I'm a surprise from a close friend," he replied.

"Was it Sheila? That fucker. She knows what I like," said Ashley laughing.

"It wasn't Sheila and I can't say who it was. We can have some fun if you want but how about we start with a bubble bath?" suggested the man.

"That's fine with me," said Ashley as she sashayed to the bathroom. She stumbled a few times so the man decided to help.

The handsome man propelled Ashley to the bathroom. There was a beautiful bubble bath waiting for her. There were two flutes of champagne. Ashley immediately started to undress. The handsome man watched her as she did. She really was a beautiful woman but he knew she was pure evil. The man found her pocketbook and as expected, she had prescriptions for Klonopin and Ambien. He had his own stash as well in case she didn't have hers on her. He took two pills from each bottle.

Ashley was naked and trying to get into the tub without falling. The handsome man helped her.

"Be careful sweetie," he cautioned.

"Get your clothes off and dive in, baby," said Ashley as she tugged on his shirt.

"I will, I will," promised the man.

"What's your name, baby?" asked Ashley.

"It doesn't matter," replied the handsome man.

"You're right, is doesn't!" laughed Ashley.

"I have another surprise for you, Ashley," said the man.

"Do tell!" ordered Ashley splashing around like a child.

"Do you trust me?" asked the man.

"Of course I do," said Ashley.

"Okay, I'm going to take some pills. They'll keep me going all night if you know what I mean but you have to take some, too," said the man.

"Anything for you, lover," Ashley slurred as she gently touched his face.

Ashley extended her palm to the man and accepted the pills. She popped them in her mouth and took a big gulp of champagne. She was very drunk already.

The handsome man took four pills, too, but they were tic-tacs. Ashley was too drunk to notice. The man took off his shirt and dropped it to the floor. Ashley giggled. The man smiled and suggested they take more pills so the night would never end. Ashley just laughed and chugged down four more pills. The last four pills were Oxycontin. The man had brought those pills.

Ashley told him to hurry up. The man told her he had to go to the bedroom first. He just rounded the corner and stood there. He watched as Ashley drank more champagne and finally became really drowsy. He watched as she tried to hold her head up and then tried to speak. She could do neither. He watched her as she sank below the water line and drowned. It only took a few minutes. He picked up his shirt and wiped down everything he touched and left the room.

Meanwhile, a driver waited for the handsome man. He got into the passenger seat. She looked at the handsome man and smiled. She knew Ashley was dead.

"I thought helping to kill her would bother me more than it does," said Dr. Lehman.

"I thought watching her drown would bother me," said Jay. "But it didn't."

CHAPTER 45

Susie and Reid settled in quite nicely in their new community. Molly completely took to them. The little town welcomed the new family with open arms. Reid was a full-time EMT/firefighter at this point and Susie worked half time at the elementary school. James' wife watched Molly every morning. Sean was blossoming in school.

Susie sometimes worried that Sean never asked about Elaine. She saw the news detailing her arrest. She and Colin were both in jail. They would have lost Sean for sure and he would have been placed in a foster home and then probably given back to Elaine. James told Susie that Elaine would still have a chance to keep Sean if she sobered up. He had seen so many cases where the parents were given too many chances at the expense of a child. This so-called biological love was often tainted. Too many people believed in the sanctity of the family.

Susie agreed with James. She was well over second -guessing herself. Why would she ever let Sean spend one night in foster care? Reid was very comfortable with their decision to take in Sean and Molly. Molly was crazy about Reid. They settled in like they had always lived in that little town. At times,

Reid and Susie missed their friends but they had made new ones. They were very close with James and his wife.

Susie was busy in the kitchen when she heard Molly stirring from her nap. She went to Molly's room. Molly held out her arms to Susie.

"Mama," she said. Susie's heart melted. It did every time she heard that word. She picked up Molly and hugged her tightly. After she changed her diaper, she fixed a snack for Molly.

"Isaac will be home any minute!"

"I'ic, I'ic," squealed Molly.

Susie laughed at Molly's attempt to say her brother's name. They headed outside to wait for his bus. Reid would be home in a couple of hours and they were all heading over to James' for a barbeque. James' daughter loved Molly and Isaac.

The bus stopped at the end of the driveway and Sean hurried off. He ran to Susie and Molly and hugged both of them.

"How was school?" asked Susie.

"It was great," said Sean. "We drew pictures of our families today."

Susie panicked for a minute.

"Wow, can I see the picture?" asked Susie enthusiastically.

Sean pulled the picture out of his backpack and passed it to Susie.

Susie stared at what looked like a mom and dad and two kids. There was a dog in the picture, too.

"This is wonderful!" exclaimed Susie.

"That's you, Mom and that's Dad," said Sean as he pointed to the adults.

"That's Molly," said Susie as she pointed to the baby. "Hey, we don't have a dog!"

"I know but maybe we can someday," said Sean with an irresistible smile.

"I'm sure we will," said Susie.

"I love you, Mom," said Sean as he squeezed her hand. "I'll never tell."

Susie's eyes filled with tears as she reacted to those words. She hugged Sean tightly. She knew what he meant. This was the first time he mentioned their circumstances since they moved to Nebraska.

"I love you more," said Susie.

"We all love Molly," exclaimed Sean as he tickled Molly's belly.

"We sure do. Hey, let's play outside for a while until Dad gets home. Then we're going to Uncle James' house," said Susie.

"Awesome!" yelled Sean.

CHAPTER 46

Blades was tired and grumpy as he drove home. He loved his work and he hated it, too. He loved catching the bad guys and seeing the system work. He hated seeing the victims, especially children. Some parents just disgusted him. He honestly believed parenting classes should be mandatory as soon as someone became pregnant. Parents should have to take classes about what it means to be a good parent before they become parents. There are plenty of parenting classes available after a child is born but sometimes that's too late. Blades didn't believe the classes would solve all problems but he did believe the classes would make a bit of difference and he would take all that he could get. There was nothing worse than seeing an abused kid who had no control over his life. This country needed to focus on preventative strategies regarding children instead of reactive ones.

Blades pulled into the driveway and then into the garage. He turned off the engine and sat in his car for a minute. He loved coming home. He was tired, though. He just wanted to relax tonight. It was Friday and he had the weekend off or so he hoped. He started to get out of the car and saw the boys running into the garage toward him.

"Dad, Dad, hurry up! We're going to Aunt Theresa's, remember?"

"I did remember," Blades lied.

He was always happy to see Eric and Tyler. They were always happy to see him. He wasn't used to their unconditional love. Sometimes it overwhelmed him in a good way. He always told Clare they were all in the honeymoon phase. Soon the boys would be teenagers and then maybe they wouldn't always be so happy to see him. Whatever the case, Blades was glad for what he had now.

The boys pulled Blades out of the car and into the house. Clare was standing at the counter laughing.

"I tried to stop them, Dana," said Clare laughingly.

Blades laughed. He gave Clare a big kiss.

"Don't ever stop them, Clare. I love it," Blades said genuinely.

They stood there arm in arm. Blades loved the smell of Clare. He kissed her again.

"Okay, you guys are so gross. Let's go to Theresa's!" said Eric.

"Give Dad a minute," said Clare. "He just got home."

"It's okay," said Blades. "I'll go up and change."

Blades headed upstairs to change. He forgot they were going to Theresa's. Clare and Theresa took turns hosting Baldies' pizza night and it was Theresa's turn this week. Harper was home for the weekend and the boys really wanted to see her. The grandmothers would be there, too. Blades loved these nights especially if he wasn't called in. He smiled as he changed and thought about all of the nights he had come home to an empty house. He loved this kind of noise. He finished changing and hurried downstairs. The boys were waiting impatiently.

"I think I'll take a nap, first," teased Blades.

"No, Dad! Come on," said Tyler.

"Just kidding. Let's go," laughed Blades.

They headed to the garage to get into the car.

"Sorry Dana. You're probably tired. You know you can stay home," said Clare.

"I wouldn't miss these nights for the world. Besides, Theresa has a Sam Adams and a frosty mug waiting for me," said Blades.

"Oh, really? How do you know that?" asked Clare with a grin.

Blades pulled out his cell phone and showed Clare the picture Theresa just sent to him. It was a bottle of Sam Adams and a frosty mug.

Clare laughed. Leave it to Theresa. Theresa adored Blades. They all loved these nights because pretty soon they might not have these nights. The kids would go off to college sooner than they thought.

Blades and the rest of the family pulled into Theresa's driveway. There were a lot of cars there already. The kids rushed out of the car and ran to the front door. They didn't bother knocking. Blades and Clare could hear the loud voices before they reached the door. Theresa was waiting for them at the door.

"Come on in, you lovebirds," said Theresa. "I hope you're hungry because besides pizza, our mothers made wings, salads, chicken fingers, and dessert."

"Oh boy," said Clare. "That's what happens when you invite them."

Theresa laughed.

"We'd be in big trouble if we didn't. Kelsey, Marie, Raffie, Harry, and Austin are here, too."

"Wow," said Clare. "Where's Emily?"

"She might come later but she has a big project due on Monday," explained Theresa.

Emily was their "adopted" daughter. The family had known her for a long time and she was now in graduate school where Theresa taught.

"I hope she comes. We haven't seen her since the wedding," said Clare.

"All I know is that I'm starving and want that good-looking beer that was in the picture you sent, Theresa," declared Blades.

"It's ready and waiting," Theresa replied and she directed them into the kitchen.

Everyone greeted one another. Blades got a big hug from Harper and even bigger ones from the grandmothers.

"We made some extra food, Dana. We know how hard you've been working trying to find those kids," said Nana Catherine.

"I'll never turn down food from you lovely ladies," replied Blades.

"Oh stop," said Grandma Peg as she playfully hit Blades on the arm.

"You sit down and we'll make a plate for you," said Nana Catherine.

"Oh my God," said Clare. "You don't do that for me."

"Now Clare, you know he has had a rough few days," stated Grandma Peg.

"What happened to your feminist ways?" asked Clare.

"This has nothing to do with feminism. It's about food," said Grandma Peg.

"Oh, sure," said Clare as she winked at Blades. "Don't get used to it, Dana," she said as she walked past him.

Blades laughed and let the mothers fuss over him. He

needed a night of fun. He didn't want to think about the missing kids and abusive parents. Blades said hello to Harper's friends and made his way to Jake, who was also having a beer.

"Noisy enough for you?" asked Jake as they clinked mugs.

"I'm not used to it but I love it. Beats going home to an empty house," said Blades.

"So true," said Jake.

"How's work?" asked Blades.

"I actually love it. I love the students. They're challenging but worth it," said Jake.

"I'm glad things worked out, Jake," said Blades with a genuine smile.

"Me, too," said Jake returning the smile.

Blades patted Jake on the back. Sometimes Blades wasn't sure how to read Jake but he thought of him as a friend. They were family now. Blades didn't want to think about what Jake had been accused of. Thankfully the rumor that he may have killed several people was dropped quickly. The cases were still open but no one was really working on them. No one was pressuring them to work on them either. The so-called victims were scumbags. Scumbags were at the bottom of the priority pile. In a crazy way, Blades didn't feel weird about Jake. He would never really know for sure if he killed all of those men. Jake stuck to the story that the swim coach made him sick and he couldn't control his anger. He claimed he sort of snapped. He did his time and now the subject never came up.

"Hey, let's get some pizza before the kids eat all of it," said Jake.

"Great plan," said Blades as they walked into the kitchen.

As Blades wolfed down some buffalo chicken pizza, little Cedric was taken from his home.

CHAPTER 47

Reilly was a bit nervous about interviewing the Police Chief. She waited for about ten minutes in the waiting room until she was called in.

"Nice to meet you Reilly," said Chief Conor.

"Thanks for seeing me," replied Reilly.

The Chief held the door for Reilly to enter his office and then closed it behind him. He told Reilly to have a seat.

"Now, what can I do for you, Reilly?" asked the Chief.

"Well, I'm interested in the cases involving all of those alleged rapists two years ago," explained Reilly.

"Oh, what is it you want to know?" asked the Chief.

"For starters, are there any new leads?" asked Reilly.

"The cases are still open and there really have been no leads," said the Chief.

"Is there an active detective working on the cases? I'm only asking because I never hear about the cases anymore," explained Reilly as she took notes.

"There's always someone working on open cases. My detectives have been chasing leads and talking to people since the first murder but we really have reached a dead end," explained the Chief.

"Are these cases a priority?" asked Reilly boldly.

"All of our cases are priorities," replied the Chief.

"What I meant was do you think these cases aren't considered as important as others given what the men probably did?" asked Reilly.

"It's never been said aloud but I can imagine the detectives investigating aren't losing sleep over the cases but I won't say we're not trying to find the killer or killers," replied the Chief.

"Okay, I get it. What about that professor who attacked the swim coach? Could he be the killer? I mean why did he assault that coach? Was he ever suspected of being a serial killer?" asked Reilly.

"We thought about that and investigated the possibility but there was no evidence linking him to the men. I really think he just assaulted the swim coach and he did his time," said the Chief.

"Do you think he would talk to me?" asked Reilly.

The Chief smiled at Reilly's question. She was bold and determined.

"I don't know if he would talk to you. I'm guessing he wouldn't as he probably wants to put it all behind him," replied the Chief.

"Isn't he the brother-in-law of one of the detectives investigating those killings?" asked Reilly even though she knew the answer.

The Chief was getting uncomfortable with Reilly's questions. He tried to steer her away from the topic.

"Yes, he is and that detective was pulled off the cases for obvious reasons," replied the Chief.

"Hmm, maybe I should speak with Detective Blades," surmised Reilly.

"You can speak with whoever you want but I doubt you'll

get anywhere especially with Detective Blades. He's a very private man and since he believes his brother-in-law had nothing to do with those killings, he won't have anything to say," guaranteed the Chief.

"Okay, but it doesn't hurt to ask. Thank you very much for your time, Chief Conor," Reilly said sincerely.

"You're very welcome. I wish I could have been more helpful," said the Chief.

"Oh, you were. I think I'll try to talk to Detective Blades and his brother-in-law. I'm interested in their perception of characterizing the alleged rapists as victims. That's basically what my story is about," explained Reilly.

"Well, good luck to you," said Chief Conor.

Reilly gathered her things and left the office. She was heading back to her office at the newspaper headquarters.

As soon as the Chief was sure Reilly left the station, he picked up the phone.

"I just had a reporter here from the Boston Globe asking a lot of questions about the dead rapists. She also intends to try and talk to Blades and his brother-in-law," said the Chief.

"What's her name?" asked the voice at the other end.

"Reilly Simonsen."

"Oh, okay. Let's see what happens. If we try to stop her, it'll look suspicious. She won't get far with Detective Blades and Jake won't talk to her."

"You're right. I guess I was getting a bit spooked. No one has asked about those cases in a long time," explained the Chief.

"I'll keep an eye on her. Don't worry about it."

"Okay, thanks," said the Chief.

The Doyen hung up the phone. Miss Simonsen wouldn't get far in her so-called investigation and the Doyen knew exactly how she would stop her.

CHAPTER 48

Cedric was three years old. He lived with his grandmother because his mother was a drug and alcohol addict and Cedric's father was in prison. His grandmother had legal custody of him. She also had a drinking problem. Cedric was left alone on many occasions when his grandmother would go out to get more liquor. She would put a movie on for him and leave. Cedric was three going on twenty. He was used to his grandmother leaving and often had to fend for himself.

The group had people everywhere including Cedric's building. Cedric lived on the third floor and so did a group member named, Marquez. Marquez checked on Cedric often. He saw him quite a bit when he went out with his grandmother. Marquez also knew his grandmother left him alone. He reported this pattern to the group and was anxious to make a move. They had a couple waiting to adopt a child in Portland, Oregon. Cedric would be perfect for them. The group told Marquez to lay low but pay close attention.

Marquez walked toward Cedric's apartment and put his ear to the door. He could hear a movie but no voices. Usually he heard the grandmother who was mostly drunk. She would remind Cedric how lucky he was that she took him in. She would make him thank her. She was mean when she drank but never hit Cedric as far as Marquez knew.

Marquez knocked on the door. He heard little feet coming to the door. Cedric asked who was at the door and Marquez told him.

"Is your grandma home, Cedric?"

"She went to get beer," he replied in a monotone voice.

"Can you open the door?" asked Marquez.

Cedric knew Marquez and trusted him. Marquez was incredibly kind to Cedric. Marquez sometimes played with Cedric when the grandmother took him outside. The grandmother usually took advantage of Marquez and left to do what she called errands. Marquez didn't mind because he could spend time alone with Cedric and try to figure out his situation. Marquez actually moved into the complex long before Cedric was born. He kept an eye on many families. At times he notified the members who were social workers or police officers when he was concerned about a child. This was the first time he would have to help take a child.

Cedric opened the door and let Marquez in. The place was in fair shape. Cedric smiled when he saw Marquez.

"Grandma's out again, huh?" asked Marquez.

"Yes," said Cedric with no expression.

Marquez knew not to ask how long she was gone because Cedric was too young to tell him. He was a beautiful little boy. His grandmother always dressed him nice and he was always clean. He rarely smiled which was what broke Marquez's heart. Marquez, an African-American himself, didn't want to see another black child fall through the cracks.

Marquez looked at Cedric and smiled. Marquez knew Cedric's grandmother would be gone for several hours. Whenever she left, Marquez waited ten minutes and checked on Cedric. Even though Cedric was only three he knew not to touch anything in the kitchen. Marquez talked at length to him about not opening the door to strangers. Cedric's grandmother usually left him during the evenings. Marquez thought she knew he came over when she was gone but she never said anything.

"You, hungry?" asked Marquez.

"Yeah," said Cedric.

"Do you want to go get something to eat?" asked Marquez.

"Okay," replied Cedric.

Marquez looked for a jacket for Cedric. He found one and helped Cedric put it on. Cedric put his arms up to Marquez. Marquez picked him up and they left. Cedric would be safe forever now but he didn't know it. Marquez made a phone call to confirm the pick-up. Cedric was considered an emergency so laying low had to be put on pause. After he dropped Cedric off at the chosen site, he would go back to the apartment and act as if he knew nothing.

CHAPTER 49

Blades laughed all night. They had a great time at Theresa's as usual. They stayed late enough for the boys to fall asleep on the couch. As they gathered the kids to leave, Blades' phone rang.

"Shit," said Blades.

"If you have to go, you have to go," said Clare.

"Hello," said Blades as he smiled back at Clare.

Blades listened carefully to the person at the end of the phone. He told the caller he would be right in. Jake knew what was going on and offered to drive Clare and the boys home.

"Are you sure, Jake?"

"Absolutely," replied Jake.

"Thanks. I'm sorry Clare. I know you wanted us to have a peaceful night," said Blades.

"It's okay, Dana. I'll put the boys to bed and wait up for you," promised Clare.

Blades smiled and gave Clare a kiss and a hug. Clare and Jake headed out to Jake's car.

"He's got his hands full with these kidnappings," said Jake.

"I know, and it's wearing him out," said Clare.

"I'm sure he'll get to the bottom of this soon," Jake reassured her.

Blades went straight to the apartment complex on Mission Hill. He found a parking spot and headed into the apartment building from where a boy was taken. All he knew was that the boy was three and lived with his grandmother. The grandmother left the boy alone and when she returned, he was gone. This section of the city was sad. People struggled to live here; they struggled to eat. Those who got out were either dead or never looked back. Even though Mission Hill was populated, it was abandoned.

Blades was a firm believer that people found themselves in poverty because society was failing them. People who blamed poverty on the poor were ignorant. He wasn't one to think the government should totally subsidize the poor but he did believe that the people who lived here had to face numerous obstacles to make better lives. It wasn't about an individual working hard and getting rich. That was a misleading American value. A lot of people work hard and remain poor. Blades believed that the majority of American people really believed they live in a free country where everyone had the same chances to make it. As long as people were poor, abused, and abandoned, no one was free.

Blades didn't think the U.S. was a democratic country. If that were the case, there wouldn't be such a gap between the rich and poor. The richest of the rich were oblivious or apathetic to the plight of the majority of the population. It disgusted Blades that there were hungry people in the richest country in the world. It disgusted Blades that the education system was failing the poor and families had to pay for a quality education. It made him sick to his stomach to think that parents have to put their kids in a lottery to get the chance to go to a good school. The richest country in the world really should be ashamed.

Blades looked around at this neighborhood and felt sorry for its residents. It didn't have to be this way but it was. Right now he had to find a little boy. Solving the world's problems would have to wait, Blades thought wryly. Blades made his way to the third floor where the boy lived. There were several police officers already there. He entered the apartment and saw what he thought was the grandmother sitting on the couch. She was drunk. She was young for a grandmother. She was maybe thirty-five and very attractive. She had an uncanny resemblance to Diana Ross.

"I'm Detective Blades," he said.

"I'm Eleanor Graves," the grandmother responded with a slur.

"I assume you're Cedric's grandmother," said Blades.

"Yes," replied Eleanor, trying her best to sound sober, a tactic that usually confirmed someone was drunk.

"So, tell me what happened," said Blades.

"I stepped out for one minute to borrow something from my neighbor and when I came back Cedric was gone," explained Eleanor.

"So, you're telling me you were just down the hall?" asked Blades.

"Yes," replied Eleanor.

"According to the clerk at the liquor store, you went there several hours ago," Blades stated.

"I wasn't gone long," snapped Eleanor.

"A neighbor told the police that you were gone at least an hour and you often leave Cedric alone," said Blades.

Eleanor started to cry.

"I was forced to take Cedric. His parents are useless. I have to have a life, too, you know," whined Eleanor.

"Why didn't you give Cedric up for adoption?" asked Blades.

"Because people would think I was horrible," explained Eleanor.

"They don't think you are now?" asked Blades rhetorically.

Eleanor just shook her head.

"You have a drinking problem, don't you, Eleanor?" asked Blades.

"I can quit any time I want," proclaimed Eleanor.

"You might want to now because you're in serious trouble for losing Cedric," said Blades.

Eleanor continued to cry.

"Do you have any recent pictures of Cedric?" asked Blades.

"No, just baby ones," replied Eleanor.

"You have no current pictures of your grandson?" asked Blades incredulously.

"Stop judging me!" yelled Eleanor.

"Fine, Eleanor. You're under arrest. We'll try to find someone who has a picture of Cedric. Stand up," Blades demanded.

As Blades handcuffed Eleanor, he asked her more questions.

"Eleanor, do you think your daughter took Cedric?" asked Blades.

Eleanor laughed.

"She has no interest in her boy. I don't even know where she is," Eleanor claimed.

"She never comes to see her son?" asked Blades.

"Never. Sometimes she calls for money but that's it," replied Eleanor.

"Do you give her any?" asked Blades.

"No. She's on her own. She has a serious drug problem. She'll do anything for drugs," explained Eleanor.

"Any ideas about where she might be?" asked Blades.

"The only place I can think of is this crack house in Dorchester," suggested Eleanor.

Eleanor gave Blades the address. Two officers read Eleanor her rights and escorted her out of the apartment.

Blades asked a couple of officers to see if any neighbors had pictures or could describe Cedric. He walked around looking for any signs of a break-in but saw nothing. Cedric probably opened the door considering he was only three. Blades now knew the grandmother left Cedric alone a lot and for long periods of time. One neighbor told him she would see Eleanor going out at around ten at night when Cedric was sleeping and return after midnight, sometimes with a man. Blades wondered why the neighbor didn't call the police.

"Why didn't you call the police?" asked Blades.

"I knew Cedric was sleeping. You don't understand this place. If I called the police, I might get hurt," explained the neighbor.

"How so?" asked Blades.

"There are gangs here who don't like to see the police. Plus, Cedric's father was a gang member before he went to prison. I don't want anything to do with his family," said the neighbor.

"You couldn't make an anonymous phone call?" asked Blades.

"Nothing is anonymous here. Look at the place. People are afraid to go to work and back. Cedric's grandmother is mean, especially when she's drunk. She threatens people all of the time. If anyone messes with her she'll tell the gang," said the neighbor.

"Any possibility the gang took Cedric?" asked Blades.

"I doubt it but all you would have to do is ask Cedric's father. He might tell you," suggested the neighbor.

Blades talked to a few more neighbors and didn't get much information. He sent an officer to Walpole to speak to Cedric's father. He then headed to the crack house in Dorchester with some backup. Blades didn't want to wait until morning because they didn't want to lose track of Cedric.

CHAPTER 50

Marquez took Cedric to Bridget's house after they ate. Cedric was quiet on the ride. They didn't have to drive far since Bridget lived in Quincy. She rented one half of a two family house. She worked a lot at the local hospital and barely knew her neighbors. It was getting dark when Marquez arrived. He parked down the street a bit and he and Cedric walked to Bridget's.

Bridget was very excited to see Cedric. She was great with kids. Cedric was shy at first but very soon he was sitting on her lap eating ice cream. Bridget had gathered toys for Cedric. Cedric could barely finish his ice cream because he was so excited about the toys. He didn't mention his grandmother once. This was not unusual with abused kids. Kids as young as one could put walls up after long periods of abuse and neglect.

Marquez could see that Cedric was getting tired. Bridget filled the tub with warm, soapy water and gave Cedric a bath. She dressed him in new superman pajamas. Cedric loved them.

"Am I going back to Grandma's?" asked Cedric.

"I thought maybe you and Marquez could have a sleepover at my house," said Bridget.

"What about my grandma?" asked Cedric.

"Well, she's out right now, isn't she?" asked Bridget.

"Yeah," replied Cedric.

"Do you want to go back to the apartment, Cedric?" asked Bridget.

"No," said Cedric abruptly. "Is Marquez staying here?" he asked.

"He might be," replied Bridget.

"Can he sleep in the room with me?" asked Cedric.

"Of course he can. Are you afraid Cedric?" asked Bridget worriedly.

"I don't like when people come in at night," said Cedric.

"What do you mean?" asked Bridget softly.

"Sometimes Grandma takes men in the house at night and they sound scary," replied Cedric.

"Have any of the men hurt you, Cedric?" asked Bridget.

"No. I just don't like their sound," explained Cedric.

"I understand," said Bridget.

Marquez took in the whole scene. Bridget was so good with kids and it was pretty clear Cedric loved her already.

"I don't like living there. Grandma leaves me alone," Cedric shared.

"I'm sorry to hear that," said Bridget very sincerely.

"Can I stay here?" asked Cedric.

"You can stay here tonight and maybe tomorrow we can find a nice happy place for you to stay. How does that sound?" asked Bridget.

"Okay," said Cedric with a smile.

Bridget knew a three year old couldn't understand what she was saying but it was pretty clear that Cedric didn't like his home. There was very little light left in that boy's eyes. Bridget wanted to make sure he could turn into a happy little boy. She looked at Cedric and saw that he was falling asleep. She carried him into the spare bedroom and tucked him in.

"Would you like me to read you a story?" asked Bridget.

"Yeah. Do you have the moon book?" asked Cedric.

"Do you mean *Goodnight Moon*?" confirmed Bridget.

"Yes, I love that story. Marquez reads that to me," said Cedric.

"Would you like Marquez to read it tonight?" asked Bridget.

"No, I want you to. I like your sound," said Cedric, smiling up at Bridget.

Bridget's heart melted when Cedric said this. He liked her voice. She started to read the book and was barely finished before Cedric fell asleep. She kissed his head and joined Marquez in the living room.

"How's Cedric? Does he want me to read to him?" asked Marquez.

"He's asleep and he wanted me to read to him. He likes my sound," said Bridget in a teasing voice.

"Oh, really?" asked Marquez.

"That's right!" said Bridget laughing.

"Peter is taking him to Portland tomorrow. Do you think he'll be upset?" asked Marquez.

"Well, you know him better than I do, Marquez. What do you think?" asked Bridget.

"I think he might be a bit scared but he'll adjust," replied Marquez.

"How about I go with Cedric and Peter?" suggested Bridget.

Bridget had never asked to accompany a child to a new home. Marquez felt something else was going on.

"Bridget, you can't get attached to Cedric. I can already tell you are," warned Marquez.

"We can't send him with strangers, Marquez, and you can't go," she stated. "You want to send him with people he doesn't know like the strangers that go into his grandmother's at night? He's three years old for God's sake," said Bridget raising her voice.

"Okay, calm down. I'll look into it. Let me talk to Kelly. Why don't you get some sleep?" suggested Marquez softly.

"Alright. By the way, Cedric wants you to sleep with him," added Bridget who had calmed down.

"Okay, I will. Now go to bed." Marquez smiled at Bridget.

They liked each other more than friends. Everyone who knew them knew that. Marquez wanted desperately to ask Bridget out on a real date. She was strikingly beautiful with mocha skin and a long lean body. She was also very smart. Marquez didn't know a lot about Bridget other than her role in the group. She never mentioned family. Marquez grew up very comfortably in Milton. His parents were both lawyers and had belonged to the group for many years. Marquez was literally tall, dark, and handsome. His smile lit up the room when he walked in.

Marquez watched Bridget go into her room. He phoned Kelly Lehman to give her the information on Cedric.

"Well, you know you can't go with him, Marquez, because it will look strange if you suddenly left your apartment," said the doctor after Marquez gave her the update.

"What do you think about Bridget going?" asked Dr. Lehman. "Is she insisting on going because she is getting attached to him?"

"She's not insisting. She just thinks Cedric should go with one of us so he won't be scared. Everyone leaves him, remember," said Marquez.

"Okay, send Bridget but tell her she only has a few days because she has to go back to work," ordered the doctor.

"Okay, good night, Kelly," said Marquez.

"Good night, Marquez. Good work," she responded.

"Thanks. Oh, is someone looking for Cedric's mother?" asked Marquez.

"Yes. We have people on it. We're going to try to get to her before the police do. She needs to be sterilized. So does Cedric's father. A correction's officer is going to take care of that since we have a nurse in Walpole from the group," said Kelly.

"Sounds good. Talk soon," said Marquez as he ended the call.

Marquez went into Bridget's room. Bridget was sitting up in bed reading.

"I just spoke with Kelly and she said you could travel with Cedric," said Marquez.

"That's great. I think that'll be easier for him," said Bridget in a brightened mood.

"You're leaving tomorrow so get some sleep. You can pack in the morning. Cedric has to get out of the state before there is a full on search for him," said Marquez.

"You know him better than I do. Do you think he'll really adjust quickly to the couple in Portland?" asked Bridget.

"They were thoroughly checked out and they seem perfect. Their families have been part of the group for ten years now," said Marquez assuredly.

"Everyone seems to abandon Cedric. When we take him to Portland and then leave, don't you think he'll be scared?" asked Bridget.

"I don't know. Unfortunately he's used to being abandoned. Kids are very resilient, Bridget," said Marquez.

"Fine, Marquez. I just want to be sure," said Bridget in an agitated tone.

"He'll be fine. I have to go back to my apartment now. Kelly thinks I should be there so the police will just think I'm a normal resident. I'll see you in the morning," said Marquez.

"You're supposed to sleep with Cedric," said Bridget.

" I know but Kelly said the police will be suspicious if I don't go back," he replied. "He'll be perfectly fine sleeping with you because he clearly likes you already," teased Marquez.

"Okay, if he wakes up I'll deal with it," assured Bridget.

Marquez left the apartment. He had a weird feeling about Bridget. He had known her for many years and this was the first time she displayed this level of concern for a child. He told himself she would be fine. He arrived at his apartment and noticed the police cars right away. He went up to the third floor and started to unlock his door.

"Excuse me, sir," said Detective Blades.

"Yes," said Marquez turning towards Blades.

"I'm Detective Blades. You're Marquez Martins?" asked Blades.

"Yes, is something wrong?" asked Marquez.

"A boy named Cedric is missing. He lived right across the hall. We're asking everyone on the floor if they knew him or could shed some light on the situation," explained Blades.

"I know who he is but barely interacted with him," replied Marquez.

"Did you ever see him alone?" asked Blades.

"No, never. I saw him with his grandmother outside sometimes," added Marquez.

"Did you speak with the grandmother ever?" asked Blades.

"Just the normal chit chat," explained Marquez.

"Did you ever notice anyone else going into the apartment?" asked Blades.

"Occasionally, but nothing made me think there would be trouble," replied Marquez.

"Okay, thanks. If you remember anything else, please call me," Blades instructed.

Blades gave his card to Marquez.

"Okay, I will," promised Marquez.

"Oh, do you mind if we search your apartment?" asked Blades as Marquez started to open his door.

"For what?" asked a somewhat surprised Marquez.

"Anything that might connect to Cedric," explained Blades.

"He's never been in my apartment," replied Marquez.

"Then you won't mind if we search it," quipped Blades.

"Of course, come right in," agreed Marquez.

Blades and several other officers did a thorough search of Marquez's apartment. They found nothing connecting Cedric to Marquez.

"Thank you, Mr. Martins," said Blades politely.

"Anything to help. Have a good night. I hope Cedric's okay," added Marquez.

"Good night," said Blades.

Marquez locked his apartment door. Thankfully he had never taken Cedric inside his apartment. It was late and he was tired. He fell asleep as soon as his head hit the pillow.

CHAPTER 51

Susie and the kids headed over to James' house. Reid would meet them after work. Molly and Sean were very excited. They both loved James' daughter, Jill. By the time they arrived, a small crowd had gathered. Sean ran straight to Jill and Molly started to squirm her way out of Susie's arms. Susie let her down and she ran to Sean and Jill.

"Hi Paige!" yelled Penny

Susie forgot her new name for a moment but James nudged her as he walked by.

"Hi Penny," said Susie. "Thanks for having us."

"Of course. Come and meet some people," said Penny.

Susie recognized a few people from town. Penny introduced her to a lot of people at the party. As she was talking to one woman, Molly ran to her.

"Mama, come," said Molly.

"Where are we going?" asked Susie.

"Swing," said Molly as she pointed in the direction of the swing set.

"Oh my goodness she's so cute!" said the woman standing next to Susie.

"Thank you. She's a real sweetie," said Susie proudly.

"What's her name?" asked the woman. "Mine's Judy, by the way."

"This is Molly," said Susie.

"Hi Molly," said Judy.

Molly smiled at Judy and pulled Susie's hand to make her go to the swing.

"One minute, Molly," said Susie laughing at her impatience.

Susie bent down and picked her up.

"She looks familiar," said Judy as she stared intently at Molly.

Susie's heart skipped a beat. She braced herself for a possible problem.

"Hey, Barbara! Come here. Molly looks like someone. Maybe you'll recognize her," beckoned Judy.

Susie started to walk toward the swing set.

"Wait," yelled Judy as she gently touched Susie's arm.

Barbara walked over to Susie and Molly. She looked at Molly and then Susie and back to Molly.

"She does look like someone," said Barbara.

"I know. It's driving me crazy," said Judy.

"Oh, my God," said Barbara.

Susie started sweating. She was terrified. They recognized Molly from the news.

"What?" asked Judy.

"Molly looks just like Betty's granddaughter," said Barbara.

"That's it!" said Judy.

"Who's Betty?" asked Susie.

"Oh, she's on our bowling team. Sometimes she brings her granddaughter. Molly looks just like her," explained Judy.

"Oh, wow," said Susie. "Okay, we're going to swing a bit."

Susie walked away with her heart pounding out of her

chest. Reid had just arrived and was talking to James. He saw the look on Susie's face and walked over to her.

"Hi, honey. What's the matter?" asked Reid,

"Nothing. I thought Penny's friends recognized Molly. I panicked," explained Susie.

"Okay, okay. They didn't recognize her, right?" asked Reid.

"No, it was a false alarm," said Susie with obvious relief.

"Let's just enjoy the party, Paige," said Reid.

Reid took over pushing Molly. Sean ran over to say hi to Reid. Everything seemed okay. Susie tried to relax but she was a bit paranoid. She reminded herself to watch the news later to see if Sean's name came up. James walked over to tell them that it was time to eat. Reid relayed Susie's scare.

"Don't worry, Paige. I promise it'll get easier. No one will find you guys. You're safe," promised James.

"How do you know for sure?" asked Susie.

"No one knows anything for sure but the group is always one step ahead of every situation. We'll know if anyone is getting suspicious. There are other people in town in the same situation as you," said James.

"Are they here?" asked Susie.

"That's not important and it's better that you don't know. Just try to relax," James suggested gently.

"Okay, thanks James" said Susie warmly.

"Let's eat!" declared Reid.

CHAPTER 52

Blades headed home. There were no leads on Cedric. He would pick up where he left off in the morning. He also planned to see Dr. Lehman since she had treated Sean at the clinic where she volunteered. He still wondered why she didn't mention that she saw him.

Blades let himself in the house and sure enough Clare had waited up for him.

"Hi honey," she said.

"Hi. You didn't have to wait up," said Blades as he kissed her.

"I wanted to," Clare said with a smile. "Do you want some peppermint tea or something?"

"I would love some, thanks," replied Blades.

"Oh, our mothers sent over tons of food in case you were hungry," said Clare wryly.

"God, I love your mothers!" exclaimed Blades.

"They are quite a pair," said Clare. "I'll grab a plate for you."

"I can get it, Clare. You don't have to wait on me," said Blades.

"I know but you always wait on me when I come home from a late shift," Clare reminded him.

"Alright. I'm too tired to argue," agreed Blades.

"Were you working the case about the latest missing boy?" asked Clare.

"Yes and we have no leads as usual. The grandmother left him alone quite a bit. Anyone could have taken him. No one would tell us much because they were afraid of gang retaliation," said Blades wearily.

"Gang retaliation?" asked Clare.

"Yeah, Cedric's father belongs to the local gang but he's in prison," explained Blades.

"What are your thoughts?" asked Clare.

"I'm still thinking. Too many kids have been missing the last few months. I'm starting to think it's not a coincidence," Blades surmised.

"You think one person is taking the kids?" asked Clare.

"I'm not sure. They all have open cases on them and terrible parents. I know I told you that already. It sounds farfetched but I can't shake the feeling that's something strange is going on. This same pattern existed in California a few years ago and not one kid was located," said Blades.

"Do you think maybe relatives took the kids?" asked Clare.

"Maybe, but four in a few months is a lot of kids when you think about it," said Blades.

"I guess. How can people just disappear?" asked Clare.

"It happens. I just hope the kids are with people who won't hurt them," said Blades.

"So, you don't think it's a stranger taking the kids?" asked Clare.

"Most kids are kidnapped by people they know. That doesn't always mean they'll be okay but sometimes it's a little comforting. We're pretty sure the little boy named Sean was taken by his aunt. Her sister is a drug addict and her sister's boyfriend is a drug addict and an asshole," added Blades.

"Are you guys still looking for Sean?" asked Clare.

"Of course. I will say he's probably safe and probably better cared for but it's still kidnapping," replied Blades.

"True. Why didn't the aunt just file for custody?" asked Clare.

"Because the system sucks and tries to keep all of these abused kids with their biological parents. The system is delusional enough to believe that abusive parents need time to rehabilitate themselves. The kids don't seem to be a priority and Sean's aunt probably figured that out," explained Blades.

"The director is under a lot of fire, lately," said Clare.

"For good reason. He needs to do a better job with those under him. Too many kids fall through the cracks and even die," stated Blades.

"So, you're saying that Sean's aunt would not get custody of him even though his mother is not capable of caring for him?" asked Clare.

"Wow, you're asking a lot of questions," laughed Blades.

"Anything involving children bothers me," said Clare.

"Well, to answer your question, it's still a gamble and she knows it," said Blades.

"Then why can't you just leave well enough alone?" asked Clare sincerely.

"You know I can't do that, Clare. Let's just say we're focusing more on the baby who was taken from the hospital, the little girl from her parents' front yard and Cedric," replied Blades.

Clare smiled. Blades knew Sean was better off with his aunt. He just wouldn't say out loud that they weren't actively searching for him. At least that's what she thought.

"Eat up," she said. "You need your sleep."

"I need a lot of things," said Blades with a smirk.

"Meet you in the bedroom, Dana," laughed Clare.

CHAPTER 53

Blades woke up the next morning feeling rested. It was Saturday so he wasn't sure if Dr. Lehman was at the hospital or not. He could hear the boys downstairs. He got out of bed and headed downstairs.

"Good morning everyone," he said.

"Hey, dad," said the boys.

"Morning, Dana," said Clare.

Blades kissed the top of the boys' heads and then kissed Clare.

"What smells so good?' he asked.

"Mom's famous French toast," said Tyler.

"Well I hope I didn't miss it," said Blades.

"There's plenty," said Clare. "Do you want bacon with it?"

"I sure do," replied Blades.

"Dad, are you taking us to basketball?" asked Eric.

"Of course, I am. Mom must need a break from you two hooligans," laughed Blades.

Eric and Tyler laughed and told Blades they would be outside shooting baskets. Blades put a basketball hoop up for them and they were obsessed with it.

"If you're tired, I can take them, Dana," offered Clare.

"Absolutely not. I love taking them. You can come along if you want," replied Blades.

"I'll pass. I have had enough of you men," teased Clare. "I need a shopping day."

Blades groaned.

"Is Theresa going with you?" asked Blades.

"Yes, and Harper," added Clare.

"Oh God, I better dip into our retirement funds," teased Blades.

"Very funny. I'll restrain myself," said Clare.

"I'm sure you will," said Blades sarcastically.

Blades didn't care what Clare bought or spent. They both made great money and they both were very happy. Clare liked spending time with Theresa and Harper more than she liked shopping. Even though the boys were no trouble, they were very active. Blades knew Clare needed a break. She had raised them on her own until Blades came around. At first, it was very difficult for Clare to leave them with anyone but Theresa or her mothers. As much as the boys loved Blades, Clare wasn't used to leaving them with a man. Gradually, she came around and realized how much it benefited the boys to spend time with Blades when she wasn't around. The boys liked their own time with Blades.

Blades finished his coffee, took a quick shower, and headed outside to get the boys. Clare was still getting ready to leave.

"I'm heading out, Clare. We'll be back in a few hours," Blades told her.

"Okay, I'm not sure when I'll be back but will stay in touch," said Clare.

Blades kissed Clare.

"Have a great time and don't feel obligated to buy me anything," Blades said.

Clare started to laugh. Blades loved when she bought anything for him. He was like a kid at Christmas every time she bought him something.

"Oh, I won't feel too pressured," she laughed.

Blades headed outside. He thought he would hear the boys but heard nothing. He immediately tensed up. Something was wrong. When he stepped outside he saw a man talking to the boys. The boys looked scared and uncomfortable.

"What's going on?" asked Blades in a very firm voice as he walked quickly toward the boys.

The man looked at him and Blades filled with rage. It was Dennis, Clare's ex-husband.

"Go into the house, boys," demanded Blades.

"We're okay, Dad," said Eric.

"Go into the house," Blades said again without looking at them. He stared straight into Dennis 'eyes with a look that could kill.

Eric and Tyler hurried into the house. They had never seen Blades angry.

As soon as the boys entered the house, Blades spoke.

"What the fuck do you think you're doing, Dennis?" asked Blades.

"I just wanted to see them," said Dennis slyly.

"For what?" asked Blades, still fuming.

"They're my sons. I miss them," said Dennis.

"You lost that right, remember? You signed the papers, you piece of shit," Blades reminded him.

"I made a mistake," declared Dennis.

"Well that's too bad. Go to confession because you're not getting near those kids," Blades said with a warning.

"I'm going back to court. I want to be part of their lives," announced Dennis.

"Go right ahead. You'll never win. I saved the tape, Dennis. I'll play it in court. I'm sure the judge will think you should get the father of the year award," replied Blades sarcastically.

"You'll just hurt the boys, Blades if you attack my reputation," warned Dennis.

"Oh, now you're concerned? The boys want nothing to do with you," claimed Blades. "And by the way, your reputation is one of an asshole."

"They don't know me. I've changed. Every kid wants their real father," reasoned Dennis.

Blades knew what Dennis was doing. He was trying to provoke Blades but it wouldn't work.

"Did you ask the boys if they wanted to see you?" asked Blades.

"I did and they said they would think about it," replied Dennis.

"That's called being polite. They learned that from Clare. You won't be seeing them, Dennis. When they're fourteen they can decide if they want to see you but for now, you'll stay away from them," warned Blades.

"Or what?" said Dennis in a menacing voice.

"Watch yourself, Dennis. Get the hell out of here or I'll call the police," Blades replied.

"You wouldn't do that in front of the boys, Blades," said Dennis.

"Watch me," said Blades.

Clare came out of the house with a look of fear on her face.

"Dana, it's time to go," she said.

Clare didn't look at Dennis.

"I'm coming. Tell the boys to get in the car," replied Blades.

"Hi, Clare," said Dennis with an evil smirk.

Clare's expression changed from fear to more fear.

"Get the hell out of my driveway," demanded Clare through clenched teeth.

"Whoa, no need to get hysterical. I just wanted to see my boys," added Dennis.

"You don't have any boys. You now have 45 seconds to leave before I call the police and get a restraining order," warned Clare.

Dennis saw that Clare was serious. She took her cell phone out of her purse.

"Okay, I'm leaving but I will see those boys," declared Dennis.

"Over my dead body," said Clare.

Blades walked over to Clare.

"It's okay, Clare. I got it," said Blades softly.

"You don't know what he is capable of, Dana," explained Clare.

"I'll take care of it, Clare," Blades repeated.

"Well, you two have a great day," said Dennis as he left the driveway.

When he was finally gone, Clare started shaking uncontrollably. Blades hugged her tightly.

"He won't ever get to them, Clare. I promise," said Blades.

"He's evil. You don't understand. He doesn't want to see them. He wants me to suffer," said Clare.

The boys got out of the car and walked towards Clare and Blades.

"Mom, I didn't know that was our father, I mean Dennis," said Eric.

"It's okay. You haven't seen him in a long time," said Clare.

"What did he say to you, Eric?" asked Blades.

"He just told us he was our Dad and wanted to get to know us," replied Eric.

"How do you feel about that? Be honest," said Blades.

"I didn't feel anything," said Tyler. "He's kind of creepy."

"Your mom and I don't think it's a good idea for you boys to see him. He has some problems," explained Blades.

"What problems?" asked Eric.

"Adult problems," said Blades.

"When you're a few years older you can decide if you want to see him but your father and I will be part of that decision," said Clare. "Your father, meaning Dana."

"I knew what you meant, Mom," said Eric.

"I don't ever want you to feel like you have to choose between me and Dennis," said Blades. "It's just not a good idea for you guys to be around him right now."

"We know," said Tyler. "We know what he did."

"What do you mean?" asked Clare nervously.

"We know he walked away from us," said Eric. "We'll be fine. We have you and our real Dad."

Blades couldn't believe how mature Tyler and Eric were. He loved those boys and would never let Dennis near them. He walked towards them and hugged them both.

"Let's go to basketball, guys," said Blades.

The boys jumped back into the car. Blades looked at Clare.

"Go shopping, Clare and try not to think about him. I'll take care of it," Blades promised.

"Don't do anything crazy, Dana. We need you," replied Clare.

"I won't. I promise. Now shop until you drop," said Blades.

Clare hugged Dana for a long time. Blades squeezed her closer.

"Clare, I promise he won't be back," whispered Blades.

"Okay," said Clare. She wiped her eyes and looked at Blades. She touched his arm and turned to go.

"I love you, Clare," said Blades.

Clare turned around.

"I love you, too, Dana. More than you ever know."

Blades watched her as she got into her car. He wanted to kill Dennis. He was more worried about Clare than the boys. Dennis did a real job on her. Blades wondered if he did more than she told him. He would find out. He got into the car with the boys. They were fooling around as if nothing happened. They headed to basketball practice.

CHAPTER 54

Marquez knocked on Bridget's door. He was right on time. There was no answer. He knocked again. Still no answer. He let himself into Bridget's apartment with the key she gave him a while ago. He called Bridget's name. There was no response. He looked through the entire apartment but Bridget and Cedric were not there. He saw the note on the kitchen table and before he even read it, he knew Bridget ran.

Bridget left a brief message. She took Cedric because she didn't believe he would adjust to two strangers. She ended the note with two words: "I'm sorry."

Marquez wasn't sure what to do. Just then his phone rang.

"Hi, Marquez," said Kelly Lehman. "I'm just checking in."

"We have a problem," said Marquez.

"What is it?" asked Kelly.

"Bridget left with Cedric," replied Marquez.

"What happened? I thought this was under control," asked Kelly.

"So did I but she didn't want Cedric to go with some strangers according to the note she left" replied Marquez.

"Where do you think she went?" asked Kelly.

"I'm not sure. Anywhere. She knows the system and she's knows how to disappear," said Marquez glumly.

"She also knows we won't call the police," added Kelly.

"I know. What do you want me to do?" asked Marquez.

"Nothing, yet. Wait a day or so and see if she gets in touch with you. She may change her mind about Cedric," suggested Kelly.

"I don't think she will," said Marquez.

"Let's just hope she doesn't blow the roof off the group," replied Kelly.

"I wouldn't worry about that. If she exposes us, she loses, too," said Marquez.

"Okay. We'll sit on this for now. The group doesn't have to know just yet so keep it quiet," instructed Kelly. "At least we know Cedric is safe."

Marquez ended the call and looked around the apartment. He didn't bother trying to call Bridget because he already knew she would have a burn phone. He didn't expect this. Bridget did sometimes get attached but she was always happy when the group placed a child with good people. What happened this time? Marquez knew Cedric would be safe but this made the situation more complicated.

Marquez's phone rang. Nothing came up on the caller ID.

"Hello," said Marquez.

"Hi Marquez," said Bridget softly.

"Bridget, what are you doing?" asked Marquez patiently.

"I'm taking care of Cedric," she replied.

"What happened to the plan?" asked Marquez.

"The plan would never work. He needs to trust someone. He woke up during the night and was terrified. He was looking for you, Marquez. I told him you had a family emergency and then he asked if he could sleep with me. I took him in bed with me and he clung to me like he was afraid I would leave him. I'm not leaving him, Marquez," Bridget stated firmly.

"Bridget, the couple in Oregon is great people. They'll take care of Cedric and love him," assured Marquez.

"I'm done, Marquez. I'm done watching kids being passed around. I know we're doing the right thing in the long run but I just can't leave Cedric. There's something about him I can't leave alone," replied Bridget.

"Where are you, Bridget?" asked Marquez.

"You know I'm not going to tell you and you won't be able to find out using my phone," said Bridget.

"I know. I don't know what to say, Bridget," Marquez replied.

"You don't have to say anything. Just trust me," stated Bridget.

"I'll never see you again," said Marquez sadly.

"I'll be in touch, Marquez. You'll see me again," reassured Bridget.

"Promise?" asked Marquez.

"I promise," said Bridget and Marquez could hear the smile in her voice.

Bridget ended the call. She looked at Cedric and smiled.

"Are you ready?" she asked.

"Yup," said Cedric.

"We're going on a big plane," Bridget reminded him.

"Yay!" yelled Cedric.

Bridget took Cedric's hand and headed to her gate. No one would notice them. They were both African American and looked like any mother and child. Bridget had an old passport with an old name. She counted on the fact that the attendant wouldn't ask for I.D. for Cedric, who was now Caden. They sailed through security and boarded the plane. They were headed to California.

CHAPTER 55

Kelly Lehman had just finished convincing a priest to write a suicide note confessing his crimes. He was sent to her from Texas. Another group member, Paul, was with her. It didn't take long for the priest to decide to write a note and swallow a deadly pill combination. For a second, Lehman thought he was actually sorry for his sins. It didn't matter. Either way he would die. He was older and on the brink of retirement. He had molested boys in a small town in Texas for too many years to count. Most of them were men now and had families of their own. Many were alcoholics as a result of the abuse. Some were married, most not. Several had come forward with the news that Fr. Neilson abused them when they were altar boys. It didn't take long for the priest to deny it or for the group to be notified. The police were gathering evidence when Fr. Neilson was taken by the group.

Dr. Lehman and Paul had transported Fr. Neilson to a remote graveyard. Lehman informed the priest in the car that he could die peacefully or die in pain. After he wrote the note detailing his transgressions, he accepted the pills. He said nothing. The priest fell asleep in about ten minutes and died shortly after. Paul threw the priest over his shoulder and walked to the nearest gravestone. He then laid the priest down, put the note next to him and walked away with Dr. Lehman. They drove away in silence. The newspapers would have a field day about a priest who committed suicide in a graveyard.

Dr. Lehman told Paul she was heading back to the hospital when she dropped him off at his apartment. She was surprised to see Detective Blades when she got there.

"Hello, Detective Blades," greeted Dr. Lehman.

"Hi, Dr. Lehman. I was looking for you," Blades said.

"What can I do for you?" asked Dr. Lehman.

"I understand that you treated a boy several months ago who is missing now. His name is Sean Craven. You saw him at the clinic where you volunteer," stated Blades.

"I see a lot of boys, Detective Blades," replied Dr. Lehman apathetically.

"I'm sure you do but this boy is missing," replied Blades.

"I know who he is. Why are you asking me about him?" asked Dr. Lehman.

"You were one of the last people to see him," Blades informed her.

"What makes you think that?" asked Dr. Lehman.

"Because the police officers who came to the clinic to speak to Sean told me," replied Blades.

"How can I help?" she replied.

"Why did you see Sean?" asked Blades.

"His aunt and uncle brought him in because they thought he might have been abused," replied Dr. Lehman.

"Was he abused?" asked Blades.

"I would say so. He had a lot of old bruises on him and some new ones. There was not much I could do about the bruises but I did call DCF," explained Dr. Lehman.

"I know. The police talked to them and then Sean and his aunt and uncle disappeared. Where did they go?" asked Blades.

"All I know is that they stepped outside and I assumed they were following the officers. Apparently the officers thought they were with me. The officers didn't say much about the aunt and uncle leaving. I had the aunt's cell phone number and I gave it to the police. I guess we all assumed Sean was safe with his aunt and uncle," said Dr. Lehman confidently.

"You knew a social worker was on her way to the clinic," Blades retorted.

"No, I didn't. When the police officers stepped outside, I assumed they had it under control. I didn't know until much later that the boy was actually taken. I gave a statement a long time ago," explained Dr. Lehman.

"I realize that but I don't understand how a couple could drive away without the officers knowing," said Blades.

"Like I said, the officers probably thought they were still with me," Dr. Lehman repeated.

"I find it very interesting that you were one of the last people to see Sean and you were also at the hospital when that newborn disappeared," Blades remarked.

"I don't find it that interesting at all. I perform surgeries here all of the time," said Dr. Lehman with a little chuckle.

"Something doesn't feel right. Something is up and I think you're involved," declared Blades.

"That's preposterous," said Kelly. "Involved in what?"

"I'm not sure yet but my gut tells me there's something not right," said Blades.

"I don't know what else to tell you," replied Dr. Lehman.

"I'll be talking to you again, Dr. Lehman," warned Blades.

Dr. Lehman watched Blades walk away. She wasn't in the

least bit nervous about his questions because there was no way he could connect her to any disappearances.

Blades headed back to the house. Clare was home from shopping and it looked like she had a great time.

"Hi, Clare. Looks like you had fun," Blades said as he observed the many shopping bags.

"We did. It was just what I needed. I told Theresa about Dennis showing up and she thinks we should get a restraining order or a lawyer," said Clare.

"That's not necessary, Clare. I'll take care of it," promised Blades.

"Dana, Dennis will file for custody or visitation. He's a lawyer. He knows what to do," Clare said with a nervous tone.

"So do I, Clare," Blades reassured her.

"He's evil, Dana. He tortured us when we were married. He played head games with me constantly. He locked us out of the house in the dead of winter. We had no coats or shoes and had to walk to the neighbors and asked for help. He'll stop at nothing. We have to legally stop him," demanded Clare.

"We did, Clare. I legally adopted the boys. He signed the papers, too," Blades reminded her.

"It doesn't matter, Dana. He'll try to torture me for the rest of my life unless he's stopped permanently. If he thinks his law license might be revoked, he might back off. That's why I think we should go to court first and get a restraining order," suggested Clare.

"Okay. Let's do that first thing Monday morning. We'll start there and see what happens," agreed Blades trying to both appease and calm Clare.

"Good. Now let's enjoy the rest of the weekend," said Clare with a somewhat forced smile.

"Where are the boys?" asked Blades.

"They're at Steven's house for a couple of hours," replied Clare.

"Oh, so we're alone?" asked Blades with a twinkle in his eyes.

"Yes," laughed Clare as she left the room.

The next morning Clare felt a lot better about dealing with Dennis. Clare left as the boys and Blades slept. She had a busy day as a trauma nurse. During her lunch hour she was joined by Audrey. Audrey worked trauma as well and was a great friend. They talked about their kids for a few minutes. Clare decided to confide in Audrey about Dennis. Audrey knew Dennis because she and Clare had been friends for a long time. Audrey was disgusted but not surprised when Clare relayed her story.

"You need a lawyer, Clare," said Audrey.

"I know. We're going to court first thing in the morning and getting a restraining order," agreed Clare.

"We both know that won't stop Dennis from harassing you," stated Audrey.

"It's a start. He'll stay away from us for a while," said Clare somewhat confidently.

"Not for long. You know damn well he'll try to get custody or visitation, Clare," warned Audrey.

"I'll know more tomorrow, Audrey," said Clare with a smile.

"What time are you going?" asked Audrey.

"About nine. Why?" replied Clare.

"Just curious. I have a lawyer friend I could call," offered Audrey.

"I think we'll go alone this time because Dennis won't be there. He has no idea that we're going to court," said Clare.

"Okay, but let me know if you change your mind," said Audrey.

"I will. Thanks, Audrey," said Clare gratefully.

"I have to run to the bathroom before we head back. See you out front," replied Audrey.

"Okay," said Clare.

Audrey left the break room and headed to the bathroom. She checked to see if the bathroom was empty and then made a phone call.

"Hi, Dr. Lehman. I want to run something by you," said Audrey.

"Go ahead," replied the doctor.

Audrey filled the doctor in on her friend Clare's situation.

"Who's the new father, so to speak?" asked Dr. Lehman.

"A Detective Dana Blades," replied Audrey.

"Really?" said Dr. Lehman, sounding very intrigued.

"What's up?" asked Audrey. "Do you know him?"

"A bit. I'm just surprised Clare's ex-husband is messing with a police officer," said Dr. Lehman.

"Dennis is a lawyer," said Audrey.

"That explains it," replied Dr. Lehman.

"Can you help?" asked Audrey.

"I believe I can. Don't say anything to Clare. I'll get back to you," instructed Dr. Lehman.

"Okay, thanks," said Audrey as she ended the call.

Audrey headed back to the front desk. She loved being part of the group.

CHAPTER 56

Reilly left messages with Detective Blades and Jake to call her. She explained who she was and told them about the story she was writing.

Reilly heard Aunt Loretta singing in the kitchen. She was baking cookies. She was an incredible cook and baker. Reilly could smell the ginger snaps. She decided to work from home today. She had gathered all of the newspaper articles on the rapists' cases. She was able to get her hands on some legal papers as well. There wasn't much connecting Jake to the killings and Detective Blades had not commented too much to any reporters.

Reilly was busy typing away when Aunt Loretta walked into the room. She had tea and cookies for Reilly.

"Aunt Loretta, you don't have to serve me," laughed Reilly.

"Of course I do, dear. Pretty soon you'll move out and get your own place," replied Aunt Loretta.

"Are you trying to tell me something?" laughed Reilly.

"No, not at all! I hope you never move out but I expect you will at some point," replied her aunt.

"Well, I have no plans to do that any time soon!" reassured Reilly.

"Good to know, dear. Now what are you writing about?" asked Aunt Loretta.

"Do you remember the cases involving those alleged rapists getting killed?" asked Reilly.

"Yes, I do. I'm glad they're dead," proclaimed Aunt Loretta.

"A lot of people are but I am interested in why we haven't heard much about them in a while. I don't think the police see them as victims. I'm also interested in why that professor attacked the swim coach," said Reilly.

"Now, Reilly. Those men weren't victims. They were rapists. No one cares about them. Why do you want to reopen old wounds?" asked Aunt Loretta.

"I don't know for sure but I think there's something beneath all of this. Hopefully I'll get to talk to Detective Blades and get his take," replied Reilly.

"Well maybe you should stick to just focusing on more current cases. I don't think you'll make any fans if you present those men as victims," suggested her aunt.

"Maybe you're right but I want to talk to the detective and the professor first before I decide that," replied Reilly.

"Alright dear, just be careful," said Aunt Loretta.

" I will, Aunt Loretta. Don't worry," Audrey replied.

Reilly thought about what Aunt Loretta said. She was probably right but Reilly really wanted to talk to the professor and the detective. It wouldn't hurt and then she would move on. The killings were definitely vigilante based. Reilly agreed the men were horrible human beings but she felt strongly about the system treating everyone fairly. Reilly decided to re-read the article about the professor that the Globe did while he was in jail. He was only there for six months. Reilly thought this was interesting because Jake was a first time offender. Usually first time offenders don't get six months. Maybe she was over thinking the whole story.

CHAPTER 57

The searches continued for the missing children. The newborn from Kelly Lehman's hospital just vanished. There were absolutely no leads. The baby's father didn't even ask for her anymore. He was too busy getting high.

Elaine and Colin were released from jail with strict orders to go to parenting classes and AA. They stayed sober for about two months. Elaine stopped calling the social worker because she continued to get her checks and keep the apartment. She convinced herself that Sean was better off with Susie. As long as Sean was missing, she could keep the apartment and keep getting a monthly check. Colin worked construction from time to time to pay for their drug habits. Jordan, the social worker, stopped visiting Elaine because there was nothing she could do. There was no boy to check on.

Jordan had seen a lot. She saw kids fall through the cracks. She saw the system failing them. That's why she joined the group. She wanted to save children. She had helped so many kids escape abusive situations by arranging adoptions, filing false reports, and kidnapping a few. She loved her work. She had kids of her own and knew how important it was to raise them in a healthy environment.

Jordan was well aware that some of these kids were often perceived as disposable and powerless. That's why she joined the group. They needed a voice and they needed protection. They needed to know someone cared. She got a big kick out of the social workers fresh out of college and trying to save the world. They had no idea what the world was really like. She knew most meant well but the system needed to be revamped. As much as they pushed to reunite "broken" families, Jordan pushed back reminding them that reuniting a family wasn't in the child's best interest in many cases.

Jordan heard about Bridget taking that little boy. She smiled at the thought. She liked Bridget and trusted that she knew what she was doing. She knew that the higher-ups in the group weren't happy but there wasn't much they could do. It had been a long time since they had a runner. The group never located the last one as far as Jordan knew.

CHAPTER 58

Clare and Blades were just about to leave the house when there was a knock on the door.

Blades opened the front door and saw a stranger with a manila envelope.

"What can I do for you?" asked Blades.

"This is a subpoena for Clare Lane to appear in court regarding a custody issue," said the man.

"Are you kidding me?" asked Blades.

"No, sir. Is she home?" asked the man.

Blades hesitated and then yelled to Clare.

Clare came to the door and was asked to identify herself. She did. The stranger handed her the envelope. She opened it and almost fainted.

Blades slammed the door in the stranger's face.

"I told you he would pull something," said Clare as she read the order.

"We're still going to court, Clare. This is going to be cleared up this morning," Blades promised.

"I hate that man!" screamed Clare. "He's the reason Tyler wet the bed for seven years."

"Let's go, Clare. Everything will be fine. Don't let him see you worked up. He'll get off on it," instructed Blades although he knew that was easier said than done.

Blades and Clare drove to the courthouse in silence and walked in hand in hand. Clare had calmed down on the way there. They spoke with the clerk and signed several forms. They entered the courtroom and waited to be called. Blades was sure they could get a restraining order. He had the recording as well if he needed to use it. The judge would hear what Dennis said about the boys.

Clare couldn't keep still once she got into the courtroom. Blades kept telling her everything would be okay. He wondered what else Dennis did to her. He wanted to kill that prick.

A man tapped Blades on the shoulder.

"Excuse me. Are you Dana Blades? Is this Clare Lane?" he asked.

"Yes, why?" asked Blades suspiciously.

"I'm here to represent you," said the man.

"Represent us for what?" asked Blades, clearly confused.

"I'm here to make sure Dennis never sees the boys again," the man said matter of factly.

"Who sent you?" asked Blades with a surprised look on his face.

"An acquaintance. Oh, we're up next," replied the man hurriedly.

The judge called Clare's name. As Clare got up, Dennis walked in. Clare turned as white as a ghost. Dennis smiled at Dana and Clare.

"How the hell did he know we would be here?" asked Blades.

"I told him," said the lawyer.

"What the hell is going on?" asked a bewildered Blades.

"Trust me," said the lawyer as if Blades had a choice.

The judge called all parties forward.

Dennis explained that he wanted visitation with his boys. He decided to represent himself. That was no surprise. The lawyer representing Clare and Dana spoke first.

"Good morning, your honor. We're here to request a restraining order against Dennis Clark. Clare Lane and Dana Blades are also here to defend their legal right as parents of Eric and Tyler Blades. We understand that Mr. Clark has had Mrs. Lane subpoenaed for another court date. We would like to take care of that issue as well today," stated the lawyer.

Dennis scowled at the mention of the boys' new last name.

"And you, Mr. Clark. What are you here for?" asked the judge.

"I'm here to retain my rights as Eric and Tyler Clark's father. I was under great duress when I signed the papers giving Dana Blades the opportunity to adopt my boys," explained Dennis while looking pitiful.

"I see. We'll start with Ms. Lane," instructed the judge.

"Good morning, Ms. Lane. Tell me why you're here," said the judge to Clare.

Clare spoke very well. She was so angry that she was no longer intimidated by Dennis. She told the judge about her marriage and the abuse inflicted on her and the boys. She told the judge that Dennis walked away so he wouldn't have to pay child support. She told her how Dennis recently tried to blackmail her for money to pay off his gambling debts or he wouldn't sign the adoption papers.

The judge listened carefully. She turned to Dennis.

"What's your story?" asked the judge.

Dennis told an incredible story about how he turned his life around. He told the judge that he was getting help for his minor gambling problem. He told the judge that Blades assaulted him in his office and forced him to sign the adoption papers.

Clare's lawyer objected.

"He's not on trial, Attorney Francis," said the judge. "You can't object."

"Sorry your honor but we have a tape that we would like you to hear," said the lawyer.

Blades leaned towards the lawyer.

"How did you know I have a tape?" asked Blades.

"I'll tell you later. Give me the tape," instructed Attorney Francis.

Blades handed the attorney the tape. He played it for the judge. Clare cringed as she listened to Dennis trying to sell her sons. When the tape ended, the judge turned to Dennis.

"What do you have to say for yourself now, Mr. Clark?" asked the judge, clearly disgusted.

"That's not the entire tape. Detective Blades erased the part where I begged him to let me see my boys. He suggested the pay off," lied Dennis.

"You know I can have the tape examined, don't you Mr. Clark?" asked the judge with raised eyebrows.

Dennis didn't answer.

"I have a right to see my boys," he claimed.

"How old are your boys, Mr. Clark? When are their birthdays?" asked the judge.

"What? I don't know. You're confusing me," replied Dennis.

"You don't know your own kids' birthdays?" asked the judge.

"A lot of fathers don't remember birthdays," replied Dennis.

"Their birthdays are August 18th and May 30th," said Blades. "Eric will be 13 in May and Tyler will be 11 in August."

Dennis glared at Blades with a look that could kill.

"How long have you known the boys, Detective Blades?" asked the judge.

"About a year and a half," replied Blades.

"I see. Impressive," commented the judge.

"I knew that, your honor. I'm nervous. I'm afraid I'll never see my boys again," declared Dennis.

"Don't be nervous, Mr. Clark. I will end your misery," replied the judge.

Clare's stomach turned. The judge was going to let Dennis see the boys. She clutched Blades' sleeve.

Dennis smiled at the judge. It was an evil victory smile. The judge smiled back and turned to Clare and Blades.

"Ms. Lane and Detective Blades," she started.

"Yes, your honor," whispered Clare.

"You are hereby granted a restraining order against one Dennis Clark," determined the judge.

"What!" screamed Dennis.

"Order in this court!" demanded the judge. She turned to Clare and Blades again.

"You're also awarded full, legal custody of Tyler and Eric Blades. Their adoption by Dana Blades is recognized as legal and binding," added the judge.

Clare almost screamed in delight.

"Mr. Clark, you are to stay away from Ms. Lane, Detective Blades, and their sons, Eric and Tyler. You'll be arrested if you go within one mile of them. You cannot contact them under any circumstances, in any way," instructed the judge. "Do you understand?"

"This is illegal!" screamed Dennis.

"Be careful, Mr. Clark or I will order you to pay the child support you haven't paid in 10 years," warned the judge.

"I want to see my sons," demanded Dennis.

"No you don't. You want to torture your ex-wife. I read your file, Mr. Clark. If you don't want your firm to hear that tape or read the closed file, I suggest you get on with your life. Case dismissed," said the judge as she banged her gavel.

Dennis stormed out of the courtroom. Clare and Dana hugged and shook the lawyer's hand.

"So, who are you?" asked Blades.

"Stanley Francis. Clare's friend Audrey called me and I was happy to help," explained the lawyer.

"Thank you so much," said Clare. "Here I'll give you our information so you can bill us."

"I have your information and this one is one the house," said the lawyer.

"Are you from the Francis and Jones firm?" asked Dana.

"Yes, I am," he stated.

"Wow, Clare, Audrey has friends in high places," commented Blades.

"Thank you again. Mr. Francis," said Clare.

"Any time," replied the lawyer.

Stanley Francis looked up at the judge.

"We thank you, your honor," he said.

"Of course. I wish you all the best," replied the judge.

Blades and Clare also thanked the judge. They turned to leave.

"Have a great day, you two," said Stanley.

Blades and Clare walked towards the exit. Things went better than they ever expected. They were still confused about the lawyer and how he knew they had the tape. Blades suddenly realized he left the tape with the judge. He told Clare he would be right back. He walked into the courtroom and stopped short. The judge and Stanley were chatting. They looked like they knew each other very well. They laughed and hugged.

"Excuse me," said Blades.

The judge and Stanley looked up and tried to regain some sense of seriousness.

"Yes?" asked the judge.

"I would like the tape back," said Blades.

"Of course," said the judge as she passed it to him.

"Thank you. Do you two know each other?" asked Blades.

"Yes," said Stanley. "We go way back."

"I wanted to ask, you something, Mr. Francis," said Blades.

"Okay," answered the attorney.

"How did you get Dennis to come to court and how did you know I taped my conversation with him?"

"I called him and told him you and your wife were coming and requesting a restraining order," replied the lawyer. "He was dumb enough to tell me about the tape believing I could somehow have it suppressed or destroyed."

"Why would you tell him we would be in court?" asked Blades.

"I assumed Clare would want this ordeal over with given what Audrey shared with me. I called Dennis under the pretense that I was helping him get one step ahead of you," he explained.

"I see," said Blades. "Well played."

"Detective Blades," said the judge. "You know that this could drag on for months. Clare would have to wait another ten days for a permanent restraining order if Attorney Francis had not contacted Mr. Clark. That's a long time to wait and face someone as unpredictable as Dennis Clark, considering what he put Clare and the boys through."

"I owed Audrey a favor and she said you guys were great people," explained the lawyer.

"Well, we appreciate everything. It was very kind of you to help," said Blades.

Blades looked at them suspiciously. Something was off. He said good-bye and caught up with Clare.

CHAPTER 59

Kelly Lehman finished talking to Audrey on the phone. Audrey told her that everything went well in court. Kelly was happy about that for a number of reasons. She was glad the boys would be raised by great parents and she did something nice for Detective Blades. She might need a favor at some point in her life. She switched her thoughts to Bridget. She hadn't expected Bridget to run. The group never had a problem with her before. Part of Kelly understood. Bridget had been working for the group for a long time. She was a valuable asset. Kelly wondered what made her run. She must have seen something in that little boy. Members of the group would discuss it at the meeting but Kelly was sure they would never hear from Bridget again.

Things were quiet right now but anything could happen at any moment. There were several missing kids in the area and of course all over the country. She knew they had to lay low because there were too many high profile cases right now. That didn't mean Kelly wouldn't be called to go elsewhere to help children. She often travelled all over the country and to Canada under the guise of medical conferences or volunteer work and did some "consulting" regarding troubled kids. She thought about little Sean, Ivy, and Deirdre who all had different names now. She knew they were safe and their parents would never see them again. She was also pretty sure the parents had stopped asking about them.

Kelly knew that the children's disappearances had to be investigated. What bothered her is that all of a sudden there is immense concern about the children's safety. There was barely any concern when they were in the hands of their parents, who abused them. The system kept returning the kids to their parents. From her perspective, there was little concern for the kids and too much for the parents. Although Kelly knew what the group did was illegal, she did not believe it was wrong.

Dr. Lehman believed that sometimes tradition fails children. They become objects and commodities. They literally have no control over who they have for parents and little to no control over how they are treated. They either stay with their parents when they are abused or they live in foster care unless they have safe relatives who will care for them. Nothing is 100 percent ideal because in all cases children lose. There are not enough good foster homes in the country and even when children are placed in great foster homes, the goal is to return them to their parents. Just last week a baby had died in a foster home and the police were still investigating. If children are placed with relatives, the abusers still may get access to them. There were of course many cases where children were placed permanently with relatives but sometimes that involved kidnapping the children.

Kelly was just about to shut off the television when she saw who she thought was Sean's mother's boyfriend on the news. It was Colin, pleading for the safe return of Sean. This was strange. Why did he care? He was an asshole. Elaine stood next to him looking like shit. Kelly wished she could tell them that they would never see Sean again but they were probably more concerned about their welfare check. She still wondered why they were back on television pleading for Sean's return.

CHAPTER 60

Blades decided to tell Clare about what he saw at the courtroom as soon as they got home. He couldn't shake the feeling that something was off.

"Clare, I meant to tell you something after I went back into the courtroom for the tape," Blades said.

"Okay," said Clare as she looked at his serious face.

"I saw Stanley Francis and the judge laughing and hugging each other," said Blades.

"What's wrong with that? A lot of lawyers are friends with judges," replied Clare.

"I know but something felt weird about it. Why would a big name lawyer just suddenly show up and help us?" asked Blades.

"He's a friend of Audrey's. I'm not surprised she called him," replied Clare.

"Alright, maybe I'm over thinking this," said Blades as he threw his hands in the air.

"Look, Dana, we've been through a lot in the last few days. Dennis definitely threw us off. I'm just thankful we had a judge who shut him down completely. He's out of our lives or he goes to jail," said Clare with relief.

"I guess," said Blades.

"Let's just enjoy the rest of the day," suggested Clare.

"You're right," said Blades.

"I have to work the night shift tonight so I'm going to take a nap," said Clare.

"I'll get the boys from school after basketball practice. I'm going to head into the office and work on some stuff until then," replied Blades.

"Alright, I'll see you later," said Clare.

Blades left the house and went back to his office. He still thought the interaction between the judge and lawyer was strange. For now, though, he had to focus on the missing kids in his jurisdiction. He wanted to talk to Bridget again about the missing newborn. Maybe she remembered something since their last talk.

Blades read over the case files for the hundredth time. The kids he was trying to find had been gone for several months now. Every day that went by made the search for the kids harder. Blades looked at the videotape again from the hospital. He watched again as Bridget carried the newborn out of her mother's room and then returned the baby about twenty minutes later. Blades reviewed the video again. Why was Bridget carrying the baby? Why didn't she wheel the baby out the room? Blades watched as Bridget returned the baby. The baby's head was not visible. Bridget carried a blue and white striped bundle. Blades looked at the video again. When Bridget left with the baby, he could see the top of the baby's head. She wore a pink hat and was wrapped in a white and pink striped blanket. When Bridget returned with the baby, there was no hat and there was a different blanket.

Blades sat up straight. Bridget didn't return with the baby. She returned with a bundle that looked like a baby. The blankets were different. Of course, Bridget could say she had to change blankets but where was the hat? Blades decided to find Bridget right away. He didn't want to call ahead and give her any reason to avoid him. He was about to leave but decided to check his phone messages. There was a message from someone from the Boston Globe who wanted to ask him some questions about the rape cases he investigated a few years ago.

Blades listened to the message a couple of times. He wondered why a reporter wanted to dredge this stuff up? He decided to just call her back and tell her he was pulled off those cases.

Reilly answered after the first ring.

"Hello", she said. "Reilly Simonsen speaking."

"Hi Miss Simonsen, this is Detective Blades. I'm returning your call."

"Oh, thanks for calling," said Reilly excitedly.

"I understand you have some questions about some old cases. I'm sorry I can't help you. I was pulled off those cases you mentioned," explained Blades.

"I know but I wanted to get your take on what happened," said Reilly.

"Well I'm not exactly sure what happened. We just reached a dead end," said Blades.

"Do you think those men are just not seen as victims?" asked Reilly.

"It may be part of it but I can't speak for other detectives. Most of us want to finish cases. I'm sure the public isn't pushing us to catch the killer but we still do our jobs," said Blades.

Blades was getting uncomfortable with the conversation.

"I get what you're saying but doesn't that make the system very selective? I mean no one seems to be concerned about the dead rapists," asked Reilly.

"The system has always been selective. It's called plea bargaining and discretion," replied Blades, getting irritated.

"I just find it interesting that the men aren't mentioned anymore. No one seems to care. Your brother-in-law isn't mentioned anymore, either," commented Reilly.

Blades didn't like where this was going.

"I'm not about to discuss my brother-in-law with you, Miss Simonsen, except to say he had nothing to do with those men's deaths" replied Blades.

"Do you know that for sure?" asked Reilly.

Blades was starting to dislike this woman.

"Look, I have nothing else to give you. I'm off the case," said Blades, clearly impatient.

"Do you think your brother-in-law would talk to me?" asked Reilly.

"About what?" asked Blades incredulously.

"About why he assaulted the swim coach," replied Reilly.

"You know as well as I do what the news reported," Blades said.

"Is that the whole story?" asked Reilly.

"Okay, Miss Simonsen, you are clearly new at this. Most people would have hung up on long ago. I'm not discussing Jake but I can't stop you from contacting him. Have fun getting by his wife," replied Blades.

Blades hung up. He shook his head. That reporter just burned a lot of bridges but he did like her spunk. He gathered his things and left the station. He arrived at Bridget's home thirty minutes later. He knocked on her door. No answer. He waited a few seconds and knocked again. Maybe she was working, thought Blades. He turned to leave as a neighbor stepped out of her apartment.

"Are you looking for Bridget?" asked the neighbor.

"Yes, do you know her?" Blades asked after he identified himself.

"I know her but not well. She works a lot. I haven't seen her in several days which is odd," said the neighbor.

"Why is it odd?" asked Blades.

"Every other time she went away, she would ask me to collect her mail. She didn't this time but I collected it anyway," explained the neighbor.

"How many days do you think she's been gone?" asked Blades.

"At least three," said the neighbor.

"Okay, thank you very much," replied Blades.

"Is she in trouble?" asked the neighbor.

"Oh, no, not at all. I just have some questions about an incident at the hospital," said Blades.

"Oh, wow. I hope she's okay," the neighbor replied.

"Me, too. Thank you for your time," said Blades with a smile.

Blades left. He decided to go to the hospital. He got back into his car and drove straight there. He walked into the maternity ward and went straight to the main desk.

"Hi, I'm Detective Blades. I'm looking for Bridget Janney," he said to the nurse.

"Oh, she doesn't work here anymore," said the nurse behind the desk.

"Really? When did she leave?" This surprised Blades.

"A few days ago. She just called and said she was moving and she had a family emergency," replied the nurse.

"Did she say where she was going?" asked Blades.

"No, and when I tried to call her back a few hours later her phone was no longer active," said the nurse.

"Okay, thank you," answered Blades now believing Bridget was involved with the missing newborn.

Blades really thought he was on to something. Bridget suddenly moved and switched phones. What was she running from? But why did she leave now? There was no way she would know about his suspicions. Blades decided to look for Dr. Lehman. Maybe she knew something.

CHAPTER 61

Susie and Reid decided to have a birthday party for Sean. He had never had one. They weren't surprised. His date of birth had to be changed when they agreed to take him. In fact Susie, Reid, and Molly all had new birth dates. It was weird and a little difficult to get used to. Sean was very excited about his party anyway. He and Susie picked out superman invitations and invited everyone in his class to come. Susie also invited their closest friends in the community.

The day of the party arrived and Sean was over the moon. He helped Susie decorate the kitchen and also the back yard. Reid was busy keeping Molly entertained. They hoped she would take a nap before the party started. Sean didn't know what to do with himself. He kept running around the house.

"Slow down, big guy!" said Susie. "You have to save some energy for the party."

"I will but I'm so excited. I've never had a party before!" proclaimed Sean.

Susie smiled at Sean even though he broke her heart. He was five years old and never even had a birthday cake. She and Reid always sent presents to him or brought them when they visited. Susie never realized how awful his living situation was.

She didn't think about Elaine much anymore. When she did she just wondered if she missed Sean. Almost on cue, James walked into the kitchen.

"Hey, happy birthday, birthday boy!" yelled James.

"Uncle James!" screamed Sean as he hugged his legs.

"You must be excited," said James.

"I am!" yelled Sean.

"Can you go outside with your dad for a few minutes?" asked James.

"Sure, but don't touch the cake!" said Sean with a giggle.

James laughed and promised he wouldn't. Sean knew he had a major sweet tooth.

"What's up?" asked Susie.

"It's about Elaine," said James hesitantly.

"What about her? Is she okay?" asked Susie.

"There's no easy way to say this, Paige," started James.

"Oh my God, she overdosed, didn't she?" asked Susie.

"Yes" James replied.

Susie grabbed the edge of the counter and held on. Her knuckles turned white from the grip. Her heart was beating so fast she could barely breathe. She always feared this would happen but was still not prepared.

"What?" asked Susie.

"I'm sorry, Paige. Elaine and Colin got high and passed out. Elaine choked on her vomit," explained James.

"Oh my God! Oh my God! What am I supposed to do?" asked Susie.

"Nothing. You can't go back. It's too risky," warned James.

"This is all my fault," said Susie.

"No, it isn't. Elaine chose to live the way she lived," James responded.

"Where is he now?" asked Susie referring to Colin.

"He's in custody but he'll get out. He's not being blamed for the overdose," said James.

"What's going to happen to Elaine? Who will bury her? Who will be at her funeral? What am I supposed to tell Sean?" asked Susie.

"It's Isaac, Paige," said James.

"You know what I mean! Why did you have to tell me this today of all days?" asked a distraught Susie.

"You would have seen it on the news," said James quietly.

"You're right, I'm sorry," said Susie.

"I'm so sorry, Paige," said James.

"She'll be buried with no one there. She was my sister." Susie started to cry.

"I'll go to Boston and make sure everything is taken care of," said James as he put his hands on her shoulders.

"People will wonder who you are," worried Susie.

"I'll say I was a friend. No one will ask questions," James assured her.

"We don't have the money to bury her," said Susie sadly.

"The group already took care of that. She has a beautiful coffin and will have a beautiful headstone," promised James.

"Why would the group do that?" asked a surprised Susie.

"Because she's dead. She's no longer a threat and also so you won't torture yourself," replied James.

"Maybe someday I can visit her grave," said Susie tentatively.

"Maybe. Sawyer knows about Elaine. He's trying to keep Molly and Isaac preoccupied. I'm leaving for Boston tomorrow," added James.

"Thank you, James. Thanks for everything. I'm actually glad we're having a party for Isaac. It will take my mind off Elaine for a bit. Part of me actually expected this. She was a train wreck," said a calmer Susie.

"I'll come and see you as soon as I get back. Let's enjoy the party," said James.

"Should I tell Isaac about Elaine at some point?" asked Susie.

"Not now. Not at this age and not if he is not asking about her," instructed James.

"Okay, I get it," said Susie.

"I'll make sure Elaine is treated well," said James gently.

Susie headed outside. Reid looked up as she came outside. She was trying hard not to cry as she hurried into Reid's arms.

"It's okay. Everything will be okay," said Reid as he hugged her.

"I know but I feel terrible. Elaine died a horrible death," said Susie.

"I know and I'm sorry. I wish it didn't have to be this way. Think about what would have happened if Sean was there. We're doing the right thing," said Reid as he wiped her eyes with his thumb.

"I know. It's just hard," said Susie.

"Look at him. He's so happy. Look at Molly. She's so happy. This is right. We're right. I'm sorry about Elaine but she would never make sure Sean was okay," Reid reminded Susie.

"You're right." Susie took a deep breath. "James is going to make sure she's fine."

"He will," said Reid assuredly.

Susie looked at Reid.

"Let's get this party started," said Susie with some effort.

Reid smiled and kissed Susie's nose.

CHAPTER 62

Kelly Lehman opened the door to the clinic. Flu season was coming and the clinic had to be fully stocked. There would be hundreds of men, women and children wanting shots. Clinics all over the country and in Canada were preparing for flu season. Dr. Lehman was in charge of one of hundreds of clinics. They were all special clinics run by the group. Some people would get flu shots but most would get shots that would make them infertile or sterile. The group made sure of this every year. Letters were sent out about two weeks before the free flu shots were offered. The letters went to people from all races, classes, and sexual backgrounds. The recipients were invited to specific clinics to get free flu shots and a gift card. The gift card got them in there. The group tried to sterilize as many people as possible.

Dr. Lehman thought the advertised free flu shots were a brilliant cover for the group. Thousands of people would be sterilized without suspecting anything. Those invited included people who had kids, people who had kids taken from them, and people who wanted to have kids but shouldn't. Of course many people came who weren't considered threats to children but they got actual flu shots.

Dr. Lehman waited for her staff to arrive at the clinic. Most of the staff didn't know they were sterilizing people. One or two belonged to the group. Dr. Lehman knew that about 20,000 people died each year from the flu but that was nothing compared to how many children were abused or how many children died at the hands of their caretakers. Not giving actual flu shots was a chance the group took. It didn't care if these particular people got the flu.

Dr. Lehman was early. There wouldn't be people coming for a couple of hours. She busied herself in the enormous medical cabinet, getting things ready. She was lost in thought when she thought she heard someone come in. She was sure she locked the front door. She walked around the corner and was about to ask who was there when she was punched in the face.

Dr. Lehman went down. She had no time to react and literally saw stars for a few seconds. She shook her head and looked up. She could barely focus but realized the assailant was a man. She tried to get up. The man kicked her back down. She was terrified and confused. When she finally cleared her head, she sat up a bit on the ceramic floor. She looked at the man and realized who it was. It was Colin, the guy she saw on the news. Why was he at the clinic?

Before she could ask any questions, he spoke.

"You fucking bitch doctor. You took my girlfriend's kid," said Colin as he glared at her.

"What are you talking about?" asked Kelly. She was very confused.

"Sean! Don't play dumb with me. You treated him at this clinic. I heard the police talking about it. You helped him get away. Thanks to you, we lost everything!" Colin yelled.

"I didn't take him. I just treated him," said Kelly in a

desperate voice. She had a bad feeling this guy would think nothing of killing her.

"You ruined our lives! Elaine couldn't deal with not having that brat around. She got high every chance she could and died!" said Colin with venom in his voice.

"What happened?" asked Kelly as she tried to remain calm.

"You know what happened. She choked on her fuckin' vomit!" yelled Colin.

"I'm so sorry," said Kelly using a very sincere tone. "How can I help?"

"How can you help?" asked Colin incredulously. "You're the problem and you're going to pay!"

Kelly was trying not to panic. Colin was unreasonably angry and clearly high. Her cell phone was in her left lab coat pocket. If she could just reach her hand in, she could try to call someone. The problem was that Colin didn't take his eyes off her.

"How did you get in here?" asked Kelly, trying to distract him.

"I jimmied the lock. Not a very tight place for a drug den," commented Colin.

Kelly looked at Colin again.

"Look, I can give you whatever you want. Then you can leave and I won't report this," said Kelly.

Colin laughed. "Oh, you're going to give me what I want alright and it isn't just drugs."

Colin had an evil sneer on his face. Kelly knew what he meant and the look in his eyes confirmed it.

"Get up," Colin said in an angry voice.

"Please don't hurt me," implored Kelly.

As she struggled to get up, she stuck her hand in her pocket and pressed the last number that she called or the last number of a call she received. She wasn't sure what would happen. She just let it ring. She wasn't going down easy. She was going to fight.

Colin pulled her to her feet. He was well over six feet and well built for a druggie.

"Take your doctor's coat off," demanded Colin.

"Please, don't hurt me," cried Kelly. She could hear someone answering the call she pressed so she spoke louder.

"Why did you come to my clinic?" Kelly purposely asked this question again to alert the caller of her whereabouts.

"What are you talking about?" asked Colin. "You fucked up my life! Take your fucking coat off!"

Kelly did what she was told but worried the caller didn't hear her and she worried Colin would hear her phone even though it was on vibrate. She dropped her lab coat on the examination table.

"Listen, I can give you whatever drugs you want. I have Percocet, Vicodin, all kinds of stuff. Please just let me get them and you can leave." Kelly was trying hard to stall.

Colin removed his jacket. Kelly thought she was going to get sick. Colin inched toward her and she tried to make a run for it. She pushed Colin as hard as she could but she couldn't get by him.

"Don't you fucking move, bitch," said Colin as he grabbed a handful of her hair on the back of her head.

"Please, Colin," Kelly said.

"Shut the fuck up!" he yelled.

Then Colin realized she knew his name.

"How do you know my name, bitch?" he asked.

"I guess I did see you on the news. I forgot. I'm sorry," whispered Kelly.

Colin smiled an evil smiled and grabbed Kelly's face. He squeezed hard.

Kelly froze. She tried hard to put that wall up. Colin grabbed her pants and started to rip them off. Kelly fought back some more but he grabbed her by the throat with one hand and continued to try and yank her pants down with the other. He squeezed her throat. Kelly continued to try to get him off her. She tried to bite him. She tried to scratch his face but she felt herself passing out. She swiped one last time and suddenly Colin backed away. His eyes were wide with terror and confusion.

When Colin dropped to the floor, Kelly saw a huge knife sticking out of his back. When she looked up, she saw Jay. She moved away from Colin in a state of shock. She pulled one side of her pants up and collapsed on Jay. She was sobbing uncontrollably. Jay squeezed her tight and tried to comfort her.

"It's over, Kelly. He can't hurt you," said Jay gently.

Kelly just kept crying and held tightly onto Jay. Her whole childhood flashed before her. This wouldn't be the first time someone had tried to rape her. She was starting to hyperventilate. She had never let someone get to her like this before but it was time to let go.

Jay made her sit down and put her head between her knees. He rubbed her back gently as she tried to calm down.

"Kelly," said Jay. "The police are coming. I called them on my way here. He can't hurt you."

"Is he dead?" asked Kelly as she picked her head up.

"Yes," said Jay. "He's dead."

"He was going to rape me, Jay."

"I know, Kelly. I'm so sorry."

"Why did you come here?" asked Kelly as she leaned back to look at Jay.

"You called me and I could hear everything. I knew you were in trouble and I was on my way to the clinic anyway," Jay replied.

Kelly started to cry again.

"I can't stay in this room with him," she said as she tried to get up.

Jay was about to answer when the police burst in.

"Is everything okay?' asked officer Kilroy as he ran into the back room.

"It is now," said Jay and pointed to the dead body. Jay helped Kelly stand up and they left the room.

"Okay, let's sit over there and tell me what happened," said Officer Kilroy. "There's an ambulance coming, too."

Kelly held onto Jay as she recounted the attack. She told the officer she didn't know the man but he broke into her clinic. She told the officer that she pressed the button on her cell and Jay came. She told the officer Jay stopped Colin from raping her.

The detective nodded sympathetically.

"You need to get your jaw looked at, Dr. Lehman. Is that where he punched you?" asked Officer Kilroy.

"Yes," whispered Kelly. "I don't need to be looked at. I'm fine."

"Just let them look, Kelly," said Jay. "I'll stay here."

Kelly held on to Jay's hand for dear life and agreed to stay.

Jay was seething inside. He couldn't shake the image of Colin attempting to rape Kelly. He was glad he killed him. He wanted to kick the shit out of Colin's dead body but he knew he had to stay calm for Kelly.

The paramedics looked Kelly over and cleared her medically. One paramedic cautioned Jay that she might be going in a little shock.

"I'll keep an eye on her," said Jay. "And I'll stay with her as long as she wants."

Kelly looked up at Jay with a surprised and thankful look.

"Thank you, Jay," said Kelly softly.

Kelly wasn't used to depending on anyone. She considered herself to be very independent but at this moment she needed someone and Jay was the perfect someone. She liked that she needed him because sometimes she didn't feel like being so tough. Colin had terrified her. Kelly was about to ask Jay a question when Blades walked in.

"Dr. Lehman, I heard what happened. I'm so sorry. Are you okay?" asked Blades in a very sympathetic tone.

"Yes, thank you, Detective Blades. Jay is definitely my hero," said Kelly affectionately.

"Yes, I heard," said Blades as he looked at Jay with respect.

Blades turned to Jay and introduced himself.

"Jay, could I ask you a few questions?" asked Blades.

"I'd rather not leave Kelly, Detective Blades," replied Jay.

"We can talk here. I have questions for Dr. Lehman, too," replied Blades.

"Please call me Kelly, Detective Blades," replied Kelly.

"Okay, as long as you call me Blades."

"It's a deal," said Kelly with a weak smile.

Kelly told Blades what happened in great detail. She ended her story with Jay saving her. Jay confirmed what happened when he walked in.

Blades was satisfied with their accounts.

"Sounds like self defense to me," said Blades. "Listen, why don't you guys go home? You don't have to come to the station. If I have any other questions, I know where to find you," said Blades.

"Thank you very much," said Jay. "I would like to take Kelly home now."

"What about the flu shots?" asked Kelly, "I forgot all about them."

"The clinic can't open today, Kelly," explained Blades. "It's a crime scene. Can the patients be directed elsewhere?"

Before Kelly could answer, Jay spoke.

"I'll make a call and get someone else to come and direct the patients to another clinic," said Jay.

Blades seemed puzzled by that.

"Who would you call? Do you work here, too?" asked Blades.

Jay quickly rebounded after he realized he said too much.

"I volunteer here sometimes," said Jay. "Kelly can tell me who to call and I'll make the call."

"Sounds good," said Blades. "We'll be here for a while."

After Jay made the call, he helped Kelly up and with his arm around her they left the clinic. There were reporters outside by now and they rushed toward them. Jay held them off and they walked silently to his car. He helped Kelly into the passenger side of the car and then got in the driver's side. Kelly was quiet. Jay worried she was going into shock.

"Are you okay, Kelly? I mean as much as you can be?" asked Jay.

Kelly patted Jay's hand.

"I'll be okay," she answered.

"I'll stay as long as you want me to," said Jay.

"I want you to stay," replied Kelly.

They drove toward Kelly's house and Jay would not let go of her hand.

CHAPTER 63

Reilly was so mad at herself. She knew she had been pushy with Detective Blades. She got caught up in becoming a tough investigative reporter. She would have to work on that. Detective Blades would probably never speak to her again and he was right when he said Jake wouldn't talk to her.

Aunt Loretta walked into the room.

"What's wrong, Reilly?" asked her aunt sensing the tension.

"I blew my first story," said Reilly, clearly disappointed.

Reilly told her aunt about her conversation with Detective Blades. Her aunt was very sympathetic.

"Reilly, as long as you learned something, it's okay. Maybe you should move on to another story," she suggested.

"You're right. I shouldn't have pushed so hard and I should've known no one would talk to me," agreed Reilly.

"There are plenty of things to write about," said Aunt Loretta hopefully.

"Thanks, Aunt Loretta. I'll have to think about it," replied Reilly in a defeated voice.

"You'll be fine, dear. You're smart and ambitious. Just try to have some patience," advised her aunt.

"I will," said Reilly with a small smile.

Aunt Loretta left the room. Reilly surfed around the Internet for a while and finally decided on a new story. She would look into the missing children cases. She had been following the cases a little but needed to catch up. She knew one of the missing kid's mother overdosed and died. This was all over the news. Her newspaper wrote about the death but Reilly thought it would be interesting to see if there was some kind of pattern with the missing kids' parents. So many kids were missing or abused right here in Boston. It felt like an epidemic to Reilly.

Reilly read the detailed story again. Elaine Craven would be buried in a few days. Her obituary was somewhat short but did include her final resting place. Reilly decided to go because she wanted to see who attended the service. She knew she wouldn't be able to ask any questions but thought the funeral might be insightful.

On top of this there were three more child deaths to deal with. Three kids had died in the last two weeks. All three were killed by their parents. A four year old was beaten to death by his mother because she thought he was gay. Her boyfriend was also charged. A two week old and a four week old had died as well. The parents in both cases were charged with murder. Reilly couldn't believe this was happening so frequently.

Reilly read that social workers had failed to check in with these families. On one occasion the police were called regarding possible harm to the four week old. A letter was faxed to the police and it was misplaced. In the meantime the baby died. The authorities were still waiting for the official causes of death for both babies. Reilly became sick to her stomach thinking about those helpless kids.

Reilly read that the Governor called for the head of DCF to resign. Reilly knew this was a Band-Aid move. It wasn't the commissioner's fault that the kids were killed. One person could not micro-manage such a huge system. Hundreds of people worked for DCF. All of them were accountable in some way. Reilly believed too many people turn their heads or stop caring. More people had to be held accountable. The whole system stunk. But it wasn't just a systemic problem; it was a societal problem. This had been a bad week for so many people. On top of the missing kids, a dead priest had been discovered in a graveyard. He had committed suicide after he confessed to molesting a lot of boys.

Reilly was intrigued by all of it. She decided to research more information on Elaine Craven. Then she would gather more information on the priest.

CHAPTER 64

Kelly fell asleep almost immediately after she showered and climbed into her bed. Jay had a cup of tea waiting for her before she nodded off. He promised to sit with her until she fell asleep and then he would sleep on the couch.

Kelly woke up screaming three hours after she fell asleep. Jay wasn't sure what she was yelling but ran into her room. He grabbed her shoulders and tried to calm her.

"Kelly, Kelly. Wake up. You're safe. I'm here!" said Jay.

Kelly was wide-eyed and looking around. She finally focused on Jay.

"Jay, Jay! He's coming to get me!" yelled Kelly.

"No one is coming to get you, Kelly! Colin is dead!" Jay said urgently.

Kelly continued to look around the room with a crazed look on her face.

"Butch is coming!" screamed Kelly.

"Who's Butch?" asked Jay.

Kelly seemed to snap out of her semi-asleep state. She looked at Jay.

"Who?" she asked.

"Who's Butch?" asked Jay.

Kelly looked shocked again.

"Who told you about Butch?" she asked.

"You were screaming that Butch was going to get you," Jay informed her.

Kelly put her face in her hands and sighed deeply.

"Butch was my foster father and he tried to rape me when I was fifteen," said Kelly quietly as she stared into space.

"Oh, I'm so sorry, Kelly," said Jay gently.

"It's okay," replied Kelly. "I'm fine now."

"You don't have to be brave all of the time, Kelly. You should talk about stuff that bothers you," said Jay softly.

"I know but sometimes it's hard reliving that stuff," said Kelly quietly.

"What happened to Butch?" asked Jay.

"My foster brother killed him," whispered Kelly.

"Oh my God. Where's your brother?" asked Jay.

"He lives in Canada now. He didn't get into any trouble because he was protecting me. A family from Canada took him in. We stay in touch and I see him when I go to Canada," said Kelly.

"I'd like to meet him someday," said Jay.

"That would be nice," said Kelly trying to smile.

"You should get some rest, Kelly," suggested Jay.

"Will you stay in here?" asked Kelly.

"Sure. I'll sleep on the chair," Jay offered.

"No, here," said Kelly as she pointed to the bed.

Jay was pleasantly surprised.

"If that's what you want," answered Jay.

"It is," said Kelly.

Jay stayed in his jeans and t-shirt and climbed into bed with Kelly. She put her head on his shoulder as he wrapped one arm around her. Kelly breathed deeply and let release a very calm breath.

"I'm fine now," she whispered.

Jay smiled and kissed the top of her head.

"I won't leave," he promised. But Kelly was already asleep.

Kelly woke up with a start the next morning and looked at a sleeping Jay. He was gorgeous. She knew she was in love with him and had been for a long time. It was very difficult for her to trust anyone, especially men. Despite that, she hoped that Jay felt the same way. She crawled quietly out of bed and went into the bathroom. She washed up and decided to make Jay breakfast in bed. She turned on the television in the kitchen as she puttered around.

The news was covering the multiple deaths of children. The Governor tried to keep it quiet until he could find out how the kids died and why they were not being monitored properly. Kelly's heart broke for those babies but her fervor to protect kids grew exponentially. These deaths proved that children needed protection from their parents and society. She lamented the fact that children were born to people who had no business having them. She was even angrier that these parents were allowed to take these babies home even though DCF knew they had serious problems. If parents have to be monitored after they have a baby, they shouldn't have the baby.

Kelly's passion for helping children was a saving grace in her life. She smiled at the thought of Jay in her bed. She made coffee and bagels and carried them on a tray into her bedroom. Jay was just waking up and smiled at Kelly.

"Wow, breakfast in bed," he said with a bigger smile.

"Well, you are my hero," declared Kelly.

"I was glad to help," said Jay with an obvious look of love on his face.

"Would you like your coffee?" asked Kelly.

Jay kept looking at Kelly. Kelly blushed and put her head down. When she picked it back up Jay was taking the tray from her. He put it on the nightstand next to him. When he turned around, Kelly was already climbing back into bed. She reached for him and breakfast took a distant second place.

CHAPTER 65

Blades watched as people began to gather at the cemetery for Elaine's burial service.

There weren't very many people attending. Blades could tell that most were friends but not necessarily close friends. They were probably drug friends, thought Blades cynically. He wasn't sad for Elaine. She was probably better off. Blades hated to think like that. He was sorry she died the way she did but she was headed for the grave. Ironically, Colin was headed to another graveyard.

Blades listened as the minister read a few passages from the Bible. He looked over the crowd very closely. He noticed one man standing off to the side a bit. He didn't look like he fit in and he wasn't talking to anyone. Blades decided to watch him. The man basically stood there with his hands in his pockets. When the service was over he hurriedly left the cemetery. Blades decided to follow him but then noticed a reporter heading towards him.

"Detective Blades?" she asked.

"Yes?" answered Blades.

"I'm Reilly Simonsen and before you say anything I want to apologize for my stupidity on the phone."

"Reilly Simonsen, huh? I guess it's nice to put a face to the name," said Blades half teasingly.

Blades saw how young Reilly was and understood her initial amateur approach. He softened a bit.

"I really am sorry," said Reilly sincerely.

"It's okay. I admire your spunk. I would love to talk but I have to run," explained Blades as he walked faster.

"Where are you going? Are you on a case?" asked Reilly, a little too anxiously.

"I'm always on a case, Reilly," said Blades halfheartedly.

"Can I tag along?" she asked.

"Why not?" said Blades. "Follow me. I'll give you some tips on making friends with police officers so you can write an objective article if that's even possible."

"Alright!" said Reilly excitedly. "Should I drive with you?"

"No, but you can follow me," said Blades.

"Okay, what are we looking at?" asked Reilly.

"I'm following a guy I like for a crime I'm investigating," explained Blades.

"Can you give me any more information?" asked Reilly.

"Not yet, Reilly. You'll have to trust me," said Blades with a smile.

Blades watched as the stranger got into his car. Reilly followed his stare. Blades noticed that the man had a rental car. Blades hopped into his car to follow him. Reilly did the same. They followed the man as he left the cemetery. After some time it appeared that the man was going to the airport. Blades kept a safe distance behind and Reilly followed Blades.

The man took the exit to the airport and Blades followed suit. The man drove straight to the rental drop-off. Blades parked nearby and watched as the man went through the motions of returning the car. Blades motioned to Reilly to stay in her car. The stranger finished up and headed into the airport. Blades waited a few minutes and then followed. Reilly sat impatiently in her car as Blades again motioned her to stay put. The man seemed to be in a hurry. Blades stayed behind him in the airport. This was an easy task since it was so crowded. He noticed the man didn't have any luggage, not even a carry-on.

The man walked up to a JetBlue counter and checked in. He then walked to the nearest Starbucks and bought a coffee. Blades casually walked up to the JetBlue counter and asked where the next flight was going. He pretended that he was confused about where to check in. The clerk informed him that people were now checking in to fly to Lincoln Airport in Nebraska. Interesting, thought Blades. He couldn't suddenly buy a ticket and go there. He had a feeling that this man was somehow connected to Elaine's sister. He decided to go back to the rental car counter and ask for the man's name.

Blades walked by the man again and tried to memorize his face. He then went to the rental car counter and asked the clerk if she would give him the name of the man who had recently returned a Toyota Corolla. The clerk told Blades she couldn't share that information. Blades pulled out his badge and told her it was official police business. The clerk hesitated but gave Blades the man's name, James Coughlin. Blades immediately called the station to get an address for James. A few minutes later Blades was told that James Coughlin lived in Wahoo City, Nebraska. Blades headed to his car and then remembered Reilly. He walked toward her car and she rolled down the window.

"What's happening?" asked Reilly.

"Just a hunch," replied Blades.

"Can you tell me more?" asked Reilly eagerly.

"No but I promise you'll be the first one I share anything with," said Blades.

"Are you teasing me, Detective Blades? I'm serious about my reporting," declared Reilly.

"I know you are, Reilly and I'm not teasing. Like I said, I admire your spunk and I have good vibes about you. Call me in a few days and hopefully I will have something."

CHAPTER 66

The Doyen thought about Bridget. Bridget definitely had a thing for Marquez so it was quite possible he knew where she was. The Doyen wasn't worried, though. Marquez's parents were very prominent members of the group so there would be no issues with Marquez. He could be trusted. They all assumed that Marquez would leave to be with Bridget. The Doyen wasn't in the least worried about Bridget exposing the group. Bridget and Cedric probably had new names by now. Eventually, Cedric's grandmother would stop asking about him.

The Doyen often thought about Cedric's grandmother adopting Cedric. She probably had good intentions initially but soon realized taking care of a toddler was a big job. The Doyen had issues with adoption in general. When the Doyen thought about Americans and Canadians adopting children from other countries, the Doyen wanted to scream. There were so many kids who needed to be adopted in the United States but Americans didn't want baggage. They wanted a kid "from scratch." The adoption process might be a bit complicated here but not for a minute did the Doyen believe prospective parents who claimed the system took too long to free children for adoption. That was bullshit. It took just as long to adopt from other countries. These parents would pay tens of thousands of dollars to buy a baby from China, Ethiopia, Ecuador, and other countries. Sure kids in these countries needed help but kids in the U.S. needed help, too. It was disgraceful.

Celebrities made the Doyen equally disgusted. Adopting black babies outside of the United States was practically a fashion statement. Of course, the Doyen had nothing against adopting black babies. In fact, the group put great emphasis on adopting African American babies for the right reasons. Celebrities are honored for their humanitarian work out side of the country. Cameras follow them everywhere recording their every move. When the day is over, the celebrities bid adieu to the needy and return to their mansions. Celebrities even build schools for children in other countries and actually neglect the poor excuse for education here in the United States. It blew the Doyen's mind. The world seemed so superficial at times.

Right now the Doyen had to think of ways to keep the group protected. There was a pedophile about to be killed at Walpole. He had abused over thirty children, one as young as eight weeks. He offered to get castrated in exchange for lifetime protective custody. He would get castrated alright but not the way he imagined and then he would bleed to death.

CHAPTER 67

Blades arrived in Nebraska. He had James' address and was eager to sift through the little town of Wahoo. He rented a car at the airport but decided to walk around the center of town before he drove to James' house. He had to think about what he would say to James. He could simply ask him why he was at Elaine's burial and study his reaction. He didn't think he would get far but he told Clare he would be gone for the night.

Wahoo was very nice. It was quaint. People were very friendly. Blades had lunch at a small diner and then decided to head to James' house. He lived about ten minutes from the center of town. The town was very clean and it was evident that people took pride in their properties. After sightseeing briefly, Blades headed to James' house with the help of his GPS. Blades pulled up in front of James' house and just sat in the car. There wasn't much activity there. He had James' license number and car description in case he saw his car while visiting Wahoo. James didn't seem to be home so Blades decided to drive around a bit.

Blades thought it was probably a long shot if he found out anything about Elaine or her sister. He was sure no one would admit to anything. He turned into what he thought was a relatively new development. He drove slowly around not really knowing what he expected to find. After about fifteen minutes, he thought he spotted James' car. He slowed down to take a closer look. It was James. He was outside talking to a couple that seemed to be playing with a young boy. Blades' heart skipped a beat. He decided to stop and check things out.

James saw Blades walking toward them and knew immediately that he looked official. He mouthed to Susie and Reid to stay calm.

"Hello, may I help you with something?" asked James.

"Hi, I'm Detective Dana Blades from Massachusetts. I'm here to ask you a few questions about a funeral you attended in Boston."

"Oh," said James. "Why do you have questions? I was just paying my respects to an old friend."

"You were friends with Elaine?" asked Blades.

"Yes, we were friends but didn't really stay in touch. I read about her death in the paper," James replied.

"Do you know her family?" asked Blades as he looked at the couple.

"No, just Elaine," said James.

"We're looking for her sister. We think she took Elaine's son," explained Blades. He looked at the couple again to see if they would react. They didn't.

"Oh, that's awful," said James.

While James and Blades talked Susie thought she was going to throw up. Sean kept playing catch with Reid. Detective Blades turned to Susie,

"And you are?" he asked.

"I'm Paige. We're friends with James," said Susie nervously.

"Have you lived here long?" asked Blades.

"Yes, about five years now," she lied.

"Where did you come from?" asked Blades.

Susie was not ready for that question. She was also thinking about Molly who was napping. She prayed she stayed asleep.

"We came from California," said Reid as he joined the conversation. "What's this about?"

"I'm just checking out some possible leads on a missing boy," Blades replied.

"I see," said Reid.

Just then Sean yelled to Reid.

"Come on, Dad. I want to keep playing!" he said.

"Okay, I'll be right there," Reid yelled back.

"Where was the boy from?" asked Reid.

"The Boston area," said Blades as he stared at Sean.

"Why would you come here?" asked Susie.

"Just a hunch, I guess," said Blades.

"We haven't seen anyone new around here," said Reid.

Sean decided to join the group. Blades watched as he ran toward them. He threw himself at Susie and gave her a big hug. Blades knew for sure he was Elaine's son. He was a perfect match to the photo he had. He watched as Reid also received a big hug. Sean was very happy.

"Hi, there," said Blades. "What's your name?"

Susie stiffened.

"Isaac. What's yours?"

"Detective Blades."

"Oh, I want to be a police officer too when I grow up or a fire fighter like my Dad," said Sean.

Blades looked at this happy family and this healthy and safe boy.

"Well I think that's a great idea, Isaac. You seem to be a very happy boy!" declared Blades.

Blades looked at Susie and Reid. He knew that taking Sean from them would be a terrible mistake and a terrible ordeal for Sean to go through.

"Well, sorry to bother you guys," said Blades to the group as he turned to go.

"No bother at all," said Susie.

Blades looked directly at Susie.

"It looks like I reached a dead end here. I'll have to go back to Boston with no news of the missing boy. I won't be back to waste any more of your time. You have a great little boy there," said Blades with obvious sincerity.

Susie understood what Blades was saying. He knew who they were and he knew Isaac was Sean. He was walking away from them. He would leave them alone.

Blades shook hands with James.

"Sorry again about your friend, James," said Blades.

"Thanks. Sadly, she's probably better off," replied James.

Susie put her head down. Sean wrapped his arms around her neck.

"You okay, Mom?" asked Sean

Susie hugged him back.

"I am now," she said.

Blades looked at Susie and smiled.

"Take care," he said and walked away.

Blades got into his car and took one last look at the happy family. He knew what he was doing was illegal. He knew he should arrest Susie and Reid. It felt like the Jake situation again but much less serious. With Jake, he was pulled off the case immediately. He wasn't given any information. He was told Jake would plead guilty to aggravated assault. That was it. In this case, a little boy's safety was involved. If he arrested Susie and Reid, Sean would have to be placed in foster care for a bit of time. Blades didn't see any benefit from that. The boy was clearly happy and loved his new parents.

Blades didn't know who he was anymore. He was losing faith in a system that he devoted his life to. He knew in his heart that kids fell through the cracks everyday and the system wasn't patching those cracks quickly enough. Maybe one day, Sean could use his old name and his aunt and uncle could raise him with no fears of getting in trouble with the law. But now wasn't the time.

Blades headed back towards the airport. He didn't regret the decision he made to leave Sean where he was but he couldn't shake the need to know how they pulled off the disappearance. Obviously Blades found them so it wasn't really a successful disappearance. They had to have had help. Blades couldn't help but think of Dr. Lehman. He had a gut feeling she was somehow involved with all of the child disappearances.

Blades arrived at the airport. His plane would be leaving soon. He decided not to stay the night.

Meanwhile, Susie, Reid, and James were in shock. It was a happy shock but it was still unbelievable.

"Why did he walk away?" asked Susie.

"He probably knew you were Sean's only relative and would get custody of him anyway. Why put a little boy through that process?" said James.

"You're probably right," said Reid.

"I guess we can relax a bit," said Susie.

"Yeah, but not too much. You still have to keep your new identities and go on with your new lives. Blades isn't the only law enforcement agent looking for you. Sean is still listed with missing children and Molly is too," cautioned James.

"True, but I honestly feel a bit better about the whole

thing. If a detective agrees with our decision, it can't be that bad," said Susie.

"Just be glad Molly didn't wake up. It would have been a whole different ball game," said Reid.

CHAPTER 68

Clare was anxiously waiting for Dana's return. She missed him even though he was only gone one night. The boys missed him, too. Clare spoke with him a few times and he sounded like he was making progress with whatever he was doing. He was expected home late afternoon the next day. Clare dropped the boys off at basketball practice and decided to go food shopping until practice was over. Eric and Tyler practiced for about two hours and then called their mom to ask if they could go to a friend's house.

"Hey, Mom. Can Tyler and I go to Dylan's house for a bit? His mother said it was okay."

"I guess so. Your father will be back tomorrow afternoon, by the way" she informed them.

"I know. He called us. We'll only stay for a couple of hours. Can you pick us up later?" asked Eric.

"Okay, let me talk to Dylan's mom," said Clare.

"We're not babies, Mom!" said Eric.

"I know. Just let me do it for me, okay?" asked Clare.

"Fine, here she is," said Eric reluctantly.

Clare confirmed with Dylan's mom that the boys would be at her house for a couple of hours. She would also be there.

Clare decided to shop a little longer and then head home. Her phone rang just as she hung up from Eric. It was Blades.

"Hey honey, I'm coming today but late afternoon. I hit a dead end in Nebraska," said Blades.

"Oh too bad but I'm glad you're coming home sooner. We miss you," replied Clare.

"I miss you guys, too. How are the boys?" asked Blades.

"They're fine. They're at Dylan's for a couple of hours. I won't tell them you're coming back early so you can surprise them," said Clare.

Blades chuckled at the thought that he was a special surprise.

"Okay love, I'll see you soon," said Clare.

Clare figured she would get home around the same time as Dana and then they would both pick up the boys. Meanwhile, the boys continued to play basketball in the park directly across from Dylan's house. Dylan's mother could see them from the step where she was reading. The boys were getting thirsty so Dylan offered to run to his house and get water. He ran across the street yelling to his mother that they needed water. His mother went into the house to get three water bottles. She was gone maybe one minute when she heard Dylan screaming.

"Mom, Eric and Tyler just got into someone's truck!" he yelled.

Monica came running out of the house, dropping the bottles of water.

"What do you mean? Where?" she asked.

"From the park! A man pulled up to talk to them and then they got into the truck," Dylan said nervously.

"Was it Blades?" asked Dylan's mother.

"No. I don't know who it was. I tried calling Eric's phone but he's not answering," replied Dylan.

"Oh, my God. I'll call Clare!" said Monica in a panic.

Dylan's mother ran into her house to get her phone.

CHAPTER 69

Eric and Tyler did in fact get into a truck. As they waited for their water, a man in a grey truck pulled up beside the basketball court. He yelled to the boys.

"Hey, Eric, Tyler, it's me, your dad," said the man.

Eric ran to the truck thinking the man was Blades in someone's truck. As Tyler caught up to Eric, they both realized it wasn't Blades, it was Dennis.

"We're not supposed to talk to you," said Tyler.

"I'm just saying hello. I just wanted to see you guys," said Dennis, trying to sound genuine.

"Come on, Tyler, we have to go," said Eric as he turned Tyler around.

"Wait," said Dennis. "I want to apologize for being such a jerk. Can we go for a quick ride around the park? Just to talk."

"No," said Eric. "Mom's waiting for us."

"I just have a few things to say and then I'll leave you alone. Your mom won't mind," promised Dennis.

"I don't know about that," said Eric nervously. "I'll call Mom."

"So, I guess you two are mama's boys," said Dennis in a sarcastic tone.

"We are not!" yelled Tyler.

"Then let's just talk in the truck," said Dennis.

"Okay," said Eric, reluctantly. He would convince Dennis to leave them all alone, especially his Mom.

The boys got into the truck. Dennis locked the doors and windows and started to drive away.

"What are you doing?" asked Eric.

"Just going for a little drive," Dennis replied.

"We need to get out," replied Eric, realizing he made a big mistake getting into the truck.

"Give me your phone and I'll call your mother and tell her I'll drive you home," said Dennis.

In a panic, Tyler handed Dennis his phone.

Dennis broke it in two and threw it out of the window.

"What are you doing?" screamed Eric.

"I want to talk to you guys with no interruptions. I want to tell you how your mother ruined my life," sneered Dennis.

Tyler started to tear up. Eric squeezed his hand.

"It's okay, Tyler," he said.

"Give me your phone, Eric," demanded Dennis.

"I don't have a phone. You threw the only phone we have out the window," replied Eric.

"Tyler has a phone and you don't?" asked Dennis finding that hard to believe.

"We have to share a phone. Mom gives us that phone when we're out," lied Eric.

"How frugal," said Dennis in a very bitter tone.

"Where are we going?" asked Eric nervously.

"On a little trip," replied Dennis with a smirk on his face.

Eric and Tyler both knew this wasn't good. Eric blamed himself for getting into the truck. But he silently patted himself on the back for lying about his phone. He had a phone in his pocket. It was on vibrate. It also had a feature similar to a GPS. If someone wanted to know where he was or if he lost his phone, all anyone had to do was go on the computer and in seconds, the phone would be located. Eric's battery was fully charged. He was, however, worried about his mother. She would be hysterical when she found out they were gone.

Eric looked at Tyler and winked. Tyler smiled slightly because he knew Eric had a plan and he knew Eric had a phone. Eric had always protected Tyler from their father when they were young. That's one thing he never forgot.

CHAPTER 70

Dylan's mother called Clare.

"Hi Clare. Did you send someone to pick up the boys?" asked Monica clearly shaken.

Clare's heart skipped a beat.

"No, why?" she asked in a panic.

"A man in a grey truck took them and drove away," said Monica.

"Who? What? Oh, my God! Who was it?" asked Clare.

"I don't know. I went into the house to get water for the boys and when I came out, they were driving away. I'm so sorry, Clare," said Monica.

Clare didn't hear what Dylan's mother said. She dropped to her knees and screamed. While sobbing, she called the police and reported the boys being taken. The dispatcher had a hard time understanding her but when he heard the names Eric and Tyler Blades, he knew this was serious.

"Okay, Mrs. Blades, calm down and give me as much information as you can," replied the dispatcher.

Clare repeated what Dylan's mother told her. The police were already on their way to Dylan's to get a more accurate description of the truck. The dispatcher told Clare that Blades was being contacted and asked if he could call anyone for her.

"Yes, Theresa Lane. Call her."

Clare dropped the phone. She sat in stunned silence willing the moment away. Finally, she called Blades.

"He took the boys, Dana," sobbed Clare. "That bastard took our boys."

"I'm almost home, honey. It'll be okay. We'll find them," Blades promised.

Blades was driving well over the speed limit trying to get to Clare. Theresa would probably get there first. He tried to stay focused on the road but he couldn't calm down. He knew who took the boys before the officer told him. He was going to kill Dennis.

Blades arrived at his house and there were already several cars there. He recognized Theresa's. There were several police cars as well. The FBI was even there. Kidnapping was a federal offence but Blades was surprised the FBI were called in so soon. He parked and ran into the house.

Blades saw Clare as soon as he opened the door. She was sitting on the couch staring straight ahead. Theresa was trying to comfort her. Theresa saw Blades and nudged Clare. Clare looked at Blades and started to sob. She tried to walk to him but he got to her first.

"He took them, Dana. He took my babies," cried Clare.

"We'll find them, Clare. I promise. They're smart boys and I don't think Dennis will hurt them," assured Blades.

"You don't know him, Dana. He's cruel. If he hurts my boys, I'll kill him," Clare swore.

Blades held Clare close and kept whispering that he would find them.

"Clare, honey, is there any place you think he might take them?" asked Blades.

"I don't know. I can't think," she replied.

"Clare, try to focus. Does he have a house anywhere else?" asked Blades.

"Yes, yes. He doesn't have a house but one of his partner's does. I know Dennis has a key. The house is in New Hampshire," replied Clare.

Blades told one of the officers to call the partner and get an address. Meanwhile one of the technicians yelled that he had good news.

"We located the truck," yelled Reid.

"Where?" asked Blades.

"It's heading toward New Hampshire," replied Reid.

"How do you know it's them?" asked Clare.

"Because one of your boys left his phone on and we located it. They're moving," replied Reid.

"Good old Eric," laughed Blades.

"We have to go get them!" said Clare urgently.

"We'll contact the New Hampshire police. Do we have the address of the partner's house?" asked Blades.

"Yes, here it is and they're about an hour from it if that's where they're going," said Henry.

Blades turned to Clare.

"I'm going to get the boys, Clare. You're going to stay here with Theresa," Blades ordered.

"No, I'm coming with you, Dana!" demanded Clare.

"No, Clare," said Theresa. "You need to stay here in case the boys call."

"She's right," said Blades. "Jake and Theresa will stay here with you. I'll keep in constant touch, Clare. I'll bring them home."

"If anything happens to them, I'll die," whispered Clare staring straight ahead. "He tried to kill us once before. He locked us in the car and left it running in the garage. He rigged the locks so we couldn't get out. The boys were terrified. I smashed a window with a baseball bat and got us out of the car. Dennis had left a suicide note signed by me because he wanted the life insurance money for his gambling problems. He didn't think we'd get out. Dennis convinced the authorities that I was trying to kill the boys and myself but changed my mind. I was so distraught from the experience, I had a nervous breakdown and Dennis was given temporary custody of the boys for several months until a judge granted joint custody. He mentally tortured the boys when he had them. It took years of therapy for them to feel like they could trust anyone. Dennis and I later divorced and he never asked to see the boys again. No one ever believed that he tried to kill us."

Blades understood now. He understood why Clare was so afraid of Dennis and why she didn't want him around the boys. Blades was seething inside and wanted to kill that motherfucker. He knelt down in front of Clare and looked into her eyes.

"I'll get our boys, Clare. I promise nothing will happen to them. You have to trust me," Blades said.

"I trust you Dana but you don't know what Dennis is capable of," replied Clare with no emotion left.

Theresa interrupted their moment with a question for Blades. She wanted to snap Clare out of her past.

"Blades, what's the address? Leave it with us in case the boys contact us and can confirm it," said Theresa.

Blades repeated the address and Theresa wrote in down.

Blades looked at Clare and his heart broke for her. He kissed her and promised to call her soon. He left the house and was about to get into his own car when the Chief of police motioned him to his car.

"Blades, you're not driving alone. You're too close to the case. Hop in with Captain Froio. That's an order," said the Chief.

Blades looked at the Chief and was about to object when Captain Froio pulled up.

"Get in Blades. We need to go," said Captain Froio.

Captain Froio was a huge guy in perfect shape. He even sported a baldhead that seemed to be the latest fashion among police officers. In Captain Froio's case, it was authentic. He really was bald. He was one of the best detectives Blades knew and very persistent when it came to arresting assholes.

Blades reluctantly slid into the passenger's seat and slammed the door. As he put on his seatbelt, Captain Froio drove away.

"Blades, we'll get him. I promise," declared Captain Froio.

"I just want my kids," said Blades quietly. "Then I'm going to kill that fucker."

CHAPTER 71

Eric told himself to stay calm. If he stayed calm, Tyler wouldn't panic.

"Where are we going?" asked Tyler.

"To a special house. You'll love it. It's a cabin in the woods," replied Dennis.

"Why are you taking us there?" asked Eric.

"So we can spend some time together. Your mother never let me see you after the divorce," Dennis lied.

"That's not what she told us," said Eric. "You didn't want to see us."

"Of course she said that. She's a bitch," replied Dennis with a scowl on his face.

"Hey, don't talk about my mother like that!" yelled Tyler.

Dennis gave Tyler a look that could kill. Eric changed the subject.

"What's the cabin like?" he asked.

"It's right on a lake," said Dennis. "You'll love it."

"Don't you think you should call Mom and tell her we're okay?" asked Eric.

"She'll be fine. She can suffer like she made me suffer for years," sneered Dennis.

"That's not nice, Dennis!" said Tyler.

"I'm your father! Don't ever call me Dennis again!" he yelled.

Tyler put his head down. He was trying hard not to cry.

They finally arrived at the cabin. It was on the lake. Eric prayed that the police would know to track his phone. Of course they would, he thought to himself. Blades would find them. He was sure Blades would come back from wherever he went.

Dennis followed the boys as they walked toward the cabin door. He knew they wouldn't run because they had nowhere to go. They were deep in the woods. He'd keep the boys for a few days to torture Clare. Maybe he could come to some agreement with her about a loan. He knew he would be in trouble with the law but he would play the distressed and maltreated father. He just wanted to clear his debt with Sheldon Hawkes.

As Dennis settled into the cabin, the Chief of police called Blades.

"Blades, we have a group of officers on their way to the cabin. The phone is still on and the location is clear. You need to stand off," the Chief commanded.

"I'm not standing off, Chief. They're my kids!" yelled Blades.

"You're too emotional, Blades. You might do something you'll regret. You can't put yourself in a position to get hurt or arrested," replied the Chief.

Blades took a deep breath. The Chief was right but he was still going to the cabin.

"Fine, Chief but I'm still going. The boys need to see someone they know," reasoned Blades.

"Okay, but you let us do the negotiating and you have to stay out of sight," replied the Chief.

"Fine," agreed Blades reluctantly.

Blades felt a rage that he had never before experienced. He now knew why parents went over the deep end when something happened to their children. He drove with Captain Froio in silence to the cabin. He knew other police and agents would get there before him. The Chief sent six officers to the cabin. The FBI had eight agents and the New Hampshire State Police supplied six troopers. They were well armed.

Meanwhile, Dennis had the boys sit on the couch. He asked them if they were hungry. Even though they were, both declined to eat.

"Come on, guys. Let's make the best of this situation," said Dennis.

"You're going to get into big trouble for taking us," said Tyler.

"Shut up," said Dennis.

Eric intervened again.

"I'm thirsty. Is there anything to drink?" he asked.

"Sure, I'll get you a soda. Do you want one, Tyler?" asked Dennis.

"Sure," he replied.

Eric sat next to Tyler and whispered to him to be calm and not upset Dennis. Tyler agreed by nodding his head. Eric told him his phone was on and Blades would find them. Tyler was relieved.

"What are you guys whispering about?" yelled Dennis.

"Nothing. Just talking about why we haven't seen you in so long," explained Eric.

"Because your mother wouldn't let me see you," replied Dennis.

"That's too bad," said Eric. Eric told Tyler to play along.

"Well, we can catch up now," said Tyler.

As they were catching up on so-called lost time, many officers were making their way into the woods. They were surrounding the cabin. Dennis heard the vehicles come up the driveway.

"What the fuck?" yelled Dennis. "How did they find us?"

Tyler jumped up and tried to run to the door but Dennis grabbed him and threw him onto the couch.

"Which one of you little fucks has the phone?" asked Dennis.

"You took our phone," said Eric. "You must have left your own on."

"Shit, shit, shit!" yelled Dennis.

Just then the boys heard a voice asking Dennis to come out.

"I'm not coming out!" he yelled.

"Then let the boys out so we can talk," replied Henry, the negotiator.

"Do you think I'm stupid?" asked Dennis.

"No, I think you're a reasonable man and will let the boys out," replied Henry.

"Not today. I'm keeping these boys until I get what I asked for," said Dennis firmly.

"What did you ask for?" asked Henry.

"I asked for help to pay off some debts. That's the least Clare can do for me since I signed off my boys to her and her new husband," yelled Dennis sarcastically.

"We can arrange that," promised Henry.

"These boys are not leaving here until the debt is paid," assured Dennis.

"You want us to pay the debt?" asked Henry.

"Yes, I owe Sheldon Hawkes $40,000. As soon as you pay

him, I'll let the brats go. I'd rather go to jail than be tortured or killed by Sheldon," replied Dennis.

"Okay, let me make some calls but I want to speak to both boys," said Henry.

Dennis took the boys to the window and held on to their shirts.

"Speak," he told them.

"We're fine," said Eric.

Blades had arrived and could see the boys in the window. He saw Dennis sneering and holding onto their shirts. Blades was seething with rage. It took every ounce of strength not to get out of the car. Captain Froio remained in the driver's seat. He was given the job of restraining Blades.

"They're fine, Blades. I know this is hard but try to stay calm. We'll get them and we'll get him," promised Captain Froio.

Blades nodded in agreement.

"I'm trying, Captain," he said.

"Blades, we'll get him. Do you understand?" asked Captain Froio.

Blades turned to Captain Froio and realized what he was saying. He wasn't sure how to respond so he stayed quiet trying to decide whether he agreed with what Captain Froio alluded to.

"Call Clare and tell her the boys are okay. They're not hurt," suggested Captain Froio.

"Good idea," agreed Blades.

Blades called Clare and spoke softly. Captain Froio could hear him consoling her and making promises. Captain Froio had known Blades for ten years. He knew how he felt about Clare and the boys. As much as he came to dislike Dennis, he hoped Blades would stay calm.

The negotiator was back on the horn.

"Dennis, we're making headway. We have the money. Who do we contact?" asked Henry.

"You know fucking well who to contact. Contact him now and make arrangements to give him the money and then I'll call him myself," ordered Dennis.

"Okay, talk soon," replied Henry.

Two officers had been in contact with Sheldon Hawkes who agreed to play along. Sheldon might be a bad guy so to speak but he had no respect for people who messed with children.

CHAPTER 72

Chief Conor contacted Officer Scott. He filled him in on the situation.

"Scott, Dennis has the boys in New Hampshire. I want you to go to the cabin and take care of business if you get the opportunity," the Chief instructed.

"You got it, Boss. My pleasure," replied Scott.

"Set it up right, Scott. We want this to be clean and believable," added the Chief.

"No problem," replied Scott.

"The place is surrounded by officers, troopers and FBI. As soon as they clear out, make your move. Hope all goes well," the Chief said.

"Where's Blades?" asked Scott.

"He's with Captain Froio," replied the Chief.

"Okay, good. Captain Froio will keep him calm," said Scott.

The Chief ended his call with Scott and called Dr. Lehman.

"Hey, Doc. I assume you heard the news," said the Chief.

"It's all over the news. Did you find the boys?" asked Dr. Lehman.

"Yes, we think it'll be okay," replied the Chief.

"Blades is a good man, Chief. He loves those boys," said Dr. Lehman.

"I know. Let's hope when this is all over, they can all live peacefully. The Doyen gave orders to make sure this never happens again. I sent Scott to settle things," said the Chief.

"Oh, good. Tell him to make it look legit. The Doyen doesn't like when we're messy and this is not routine for us," added Dr. Lehman.

The Chief and Dr. Lehman were both thinking about how they segued into killing people other than pedophiles. The group would have to hold a serious meeting about these new developments.

CHAPTER 73

Reilly heard about Blades' boys on the news. He must be sick with worry thought Reilly. She called her editor and asked if she could travel to New Hampshire to get first dibs on the story.

"There are reporters there already, Reilly and you're too new," said Rebecca.

"Blades will talk to me, Rebecca," declared Reilly.

"Since when?" asked Rebecca.

"Since yesterday when I saw him at the funeral," replied Reilly with confidence.

"Contact him when this is over and see if he'll talk," suggested Rebecca.

"Fine," agreed Reilly.

Reilly closed her phone and sighed. She really wanted to go to New Hampshire but knew she shouldn't press her luck. The guy holding the boys was their biological father. Reilly decided to search the net for information on Dennis. Her first hit took her to his law firm. Interesting, thought Reilly. It was quite a prestigious law firm. Reilly wondered if they knew about Dennis kidnapping the boys. She decided to call the firm and ask.

The call was picked up by the firm's receptionist. Reilly asked to speak to one of the partners. The receptionist asked who she was.

"My name is Reilly Simonsen from the Boston Globe," said Reilly.

"We're not speaking to the media at this time," declared the receptionist.

Reilly could hear murmuring in the background. A new voice came on the phone.

"This is attorney Vickers. What can we do for you?" he asked.

"I'd like to hear your thoughts about Dennis Clark," stated Reilly excitedly.

"We have one comment for you and that's it," stated Vickers.

"Okay, " said Reilly.

"Dennis Clark no longer works for our firm," said Vickers.

There was a long pause.

"Is that it?" asked Reilly.

"That's it," stated Vickers in a very formal voice.

"But Mr. Vickers," said Reilly.

The call was over. Vickers had hung up. Regardless, Reilly had a little something. She wondered if Dennis would be surprised by his very public dismissal. Reilly started to pen her story. She would also try to keep up with the news so she could talk to Blades.

CHAPTER 74

Sheldon informed Henry he was ready to talk to Dennis.
"Dennis, you're good to go. Call Sheldon," instructed Henry.

"This better not be a joke," said Dennis.

"Sheldon doesn't seem like the joking type," replied Henry.

Dennis made the call. The officers could see him through the window. He was smiling and laughing. Finally he yelled to the negotiator.

"Okay, boys, we're good. Now I want a lawyer," Dennis demanded.

"That wasn't part of the deal, Dennis," replied Henry.

"I'm not walking out of here without a lawyer," said Dennis firmly.

"Send the boys out, Dennis and we'll get you a lawyer," replied Henry.

Dennis laughed again.

"Nice try but not gonna happen," declared Dennis.

Henry told Dennis he would get back to him. He passed on the demand to the agent in charge. He was told to proceed.

"Dennis, we're getting you a lawyer. Send the boys out, now please," implored Henry.

"I'll tell you what. I'll send one out," Dennis bargained.

"We need both boys," said Henry.

"One or none," yelled Dennis.

Before Henry could respond, Dennis pulled Eric off the couch. Henry could see they were arguing. Eric wouldn't leave.

"Sorry boys, Eric won't leave his little brother so they both stay," said Eric.

Blades was hearing every word. He wasn't surprised Eric refused to leave. He looked at Captain Froio. He wanted out of the car but he knew his presence would fuel Dennis' fire. It seemed like an eternity but finally, a lawyer arrived.

"We have your lawyer, Dennis," said Henry.

"Who is it? He better be real," warned Dennis.

"It's a she and she's real," promised Henry.

"Even better. Send her in," said Dennis.

"Send the boys out first," instructed Henry.

"Send in the lawyer or no deal," Dennis retorted.

Henry motioned for Jules to come forward. She was dressed in a professional suit and looked the part even though she was an FBI agent with a black belt in karate. Henry was surprised Dennis didn't ask for the fictitious firm's number. From what he heard, he was cocky and quite the ladies' man. That's why they were sending in Jules.

Jules walked toward the cabin carrying nothing. She smiled at Dennis through the window. He let her in. She promptly told him not to speak any further with the police. Dennis liked her suggestion. She then told him to let the boys go. Dennis hesitated.

"Dennis, I can't help you if you don't keep your end of the deal. We'll think of an angle to play," said Jules. "We can't talk in front of the boys."

"Fine. Get out, you two," ordered Dennis as he motioned the boys to leave.

Eric and Tyler walked toward the cabin door. They opened it and walked out.

"Don't run," said Eric to Tyler. "Stay calm."

The boys walked slowly down the walkway and saw all of the police cars. Two officers ran toward them very fast and scooped them up. They were quickly put in an SUV and knew they were safe.

"Is Blades out there?" asked Dennis. "I don't want any trouble. We're coming out."

"No," lied Henry. "He's not here."

Eric and Tyler were in the SUV giving the officer their account of the kidnapping. They were panicked about calling their mother and kept looking for Blades.

"I have to call, Mom," said Eric. "She's probably really scared right now."

"You two are incredibly brave," said the officer. "Go ahead and call your Mom."

As Eric was about to call his mother, Blades threw open the door. Both boys jumped at him through the door and hugged him tight. Both cried. Blades told them how proud he was of them as they stepped outside of the SUV.

"We knew you'd find us, Dad," said Tyler.

"A lot of people found you," Blades laughed.

"Well we're sure glad to see you," said Eric.

"You have no idea how happy I am to see you guys," said Blades choking on his words.

"I have to call Mom," said Eric.

Blades placed the call telling Clare he had the boys. Both boys talked to her. She cried the entire time. They kept assuring her they were fine. Blades told her to meet them at the hospital.

"Are they hurt?" she asked.

"No, but it's standard procedure to have them cleared. They can make their formal statements there, too," explained Blades.

"Okay, Dana. Don't let them out of your sight," said Clare.

"I won't, Clare. I love you," said Blades.

"I love you, too," replied Clare.

Blades took Eric and Tyler to the last SUV in the driveway. He told the officers to watch the boys.

"Dad, you can't leave us," said Tyler.

"I'm just going to tell the agent we're leaving. I'll be right back," Dana promised.

Blades headed back to the first vehicle. Dennis could see him from the window. He knew the negotiator lied about Blades not being there. He smiled at Blades. Blades didn't smile back. Instead, he just pointed at him, nodded his head and walked back to where the boys were.

Dennis and Jules came out of the house. Dennis had his hands in the air.

"Put your hands down, Dennis," said Jules.

"I don't want them to shoot me," he said.

"They're not going to shoot you so put your hands down," instructed Jules.

Dennis did as Jules said and she promptly knocked him to the ground.

"What the hell?" yelled Dennis.

"You're under arrest, you piece of shit," said Jules. "I suggest you stay quiet."

"You're not a fucking lawyer?" asked Dennis incredulously.

"No, you dolt," answered Jules. "I'm FBI."

Two more officers came to assist Jules even though she didn't need help. Dennis was handcuffed and lifted off the ground. Dennis thought it was odd that he was handcuffed in front of his body but he was no longer a threat. Jules read him his rights. Several officers had their guns pointed at him. Meanwhile Blades was on his way to the hospital with the boys. As much as he hated Dennis, he didn't want the boys to see him arrested. They had gone through enough.

The officers were told to stand down. They lowered their weapons but kept a secure distance from Dennis. Jules headed to her car. Two officers walked behind Dennis and two walked beside him holding his arms. Dennis was thrashing about and the officers had to stop frequently to settle him. He kept screaming for a real lawyer.

Dennis finally settled down and walked toward the cars. Most of the officers were getting into their cars and leaving. Dennis thought that was strange but shook it off. The two officers following him slowed their gait. As he was prodded along by the officers holding him, he felt them loosen their grips.

"You can walk on your own, Dennis," said one of the officers.

"Fine with me," said Dennis.

The two officers who had been holding his arms stepped farther away from Dennis. Dennis became puzzled.

"What the fuck is going on here? Why are you moving away from me?" asked Dennis.

"Shut up, Dennis. Keep walking," said the agent.

Dennis suddenly realized what was happening. They were going to kill him. He lunged toward an agent and tried to grab his gun. The agents had counted on that. He struggled a bit with the agent and all of a sudden a voice was heard yelling "Gun!"

As Dennis tried to spin around, his head exploded.

The officers went down as well but instinctively.

"What the fuck happened?" yelled Henry as he ran toward the officers.

The officers guarding Dennis feigned shock. Dennis was definitely dead. Henry was about to ask the officer how this happened when a voice was heard from within the woods.

"I'm coming out of the woods. I have my hands up. My name is Officer Scott."

Scott walked out of the woods carrying a shotgun.

"Who the hell sent you?" asked Henry.

"Chief sent me to watch from the woods in case you needed extra back-up," stated Scott.

"It was a good shoot," said one of the officers who had been with Dennis. "Dennis was trying to get my gun."

"I saw what happened," confirmed Henry. "I guess you made the right call, Scott."

"I did," agreed Scott. "I'll ride with you and someone can take my car back."

"Smart thinking," said Henry. "You probably shouldn't drive. Sometimes it takes a while for the shock to sink in. It's not easy shooting someone; even assholes."

"Oh, I'm completely fine," said Officer Scott.

Officer Scott walked towards Henry's car and threw his keys to the officer who offered to drive his car back.

Henry caught up and got in the car.

"Nice work, Scott," said Henry. "The Chief will be pleased. So will the Doyen."

CHAPTER 75

Blades sat in the back seat with the boys. Each boy had his head on Blades' shoulders. His phone rang.

"Blades," he answered.

"Dennis is dead, Blades," said the Chief.

"What?" asked Blades.

Captain Froio really meant what he said. Blades tried to figure out how he felt about it. Dennis had put Clare and the boys through hell. Even though he and Clare had legal custody of the boys, Dennis would still be a lingering thought in their heads. So, Blades decided he was glad Dennis was killed. Part of him wished he had shot him himself.

"He's dead. He tried to take a gun from one of the officers and he was taken down by a sharp shooter in the woods," explained the Chief.

"Holy shit," said Blades. "Fill me in at the hospital."

"Okay. How are the boys?" asked the Chief.

"They're tired, but fine," replied Blades.

"See you at the hospital," said the Chief.

Blades finished the call. Eric and Tyler hadn't changed positions. They didn't ask what the phone call was about. A few hours later, they arrived at the hospital. Blades walked in with the boys. They hadn't taken two steps before they saw Clare running towards them.

"Mom!" they yelled.

"Oh my God! Are you okay?" asked Clare as she grabbed both boys.

"We're fine, Mom," said Eric.

Clare hugged them tightly and cried. The boys kept telling her they were okay. Theresa finally walked to them and hugged the boys, too.

"Clare, the doctor wants to check the boys, now," said Theresa.

"I'm going with them," said Clare.

"He's expecting you," said Theresa as she smiled at the boys.

Clare finally looked at Blades and walked into a deep hug.

"Thank you, Dana. Thank you so much," said Clare.

"I wasn't the one who negotiated their return, Clare," said Blades modestly.

"But you were there for them," she replied.

"I wouldn't have missed it," said Blades.

Clare's hug lingered and then she left with the boys. Theresa stood next to Blades.

"What will happen to Dennis?" she asked.

"Dennis is dead, Theresa. He was shot while attempting to shoot one of the officers," replied Blades.

"Oh my God! Do the boys know?" asked Theresa.

"Not yet. I'll have to tell them soon," said Blades.

"Well then, everything really did work out. The boys are safe and the prick is dead," said Theresa.

Blades looked at Theresa and shook his head again.

"I figured you'd say that. I'm going to find the boys," said Blades shaking his head.

"Okay, tell Clare we'll call later," replied Theresa.

"You got it. Theresa, don't make any comments to the reporters out there. Let the Chief handle it," said Blades.

"I can't say one thing? Come on, can't I just tell them that Dennis was a piece of shit?" asked Theresa with a smile.

"No, Theresa, you can't," said Blades as he smiled and shook his head.

Theresa winked at Blades.

"Fine, I'll behave," she promised.

Blades walked into the examination room. Eric and Tyler were laughing and joking around. Clare watched them with a relieved look on her face.

"Clare, can I talk to you for a minute?" asked Blades.

"Sure. I'll be right outside this door, boys," said Clare.

"Okay, Mom. We're fine, though. Stop worrying," replied Eric.

Clare smiled and stepped outside of the room with Blades.

"There's no easy way to say this. Dennis is dead, Clare," Blades said bluntly.

"What? What happened?" asked Clare.

"He tried to take a gun from one of the officers so another officer shot him," explained Blades.

"Oh my God," said Clare. "He's really dead?"

"Yes, he is," said Blades.

"Good. He deserves to die, the prick. I hope he suffered," said Clare in a matter of fact way.

"Clare, you can't say that in front of the boys. They have to process everything. I have to tell them Dennis is dead," replied Blades.

"I'll tell them," said Clare. "I won't be crass about it."

"Just try to be neutral. It will help them heal," suggested Blades.

"You're right, Dana. I just hated him for what he did to us," replied Clare.

"Well he can't do anything anymore," said Blades.

"No, he can't," said Clare quietly.

Clare and Blades went into the room with Eric and Tyler. In hushed tones, they broke the news about Dennis' death. Clare explained that he was really messed up. The boys barely reacted.

"It's kind of sad," said Tyler.

"Yeah," said Eric. "He must have been really unhappy."

Clare was a bit taken aback by their reactions.

"You guys are so great," said Clare.

"We're very proud of you," said Blades. "By the way, Eric, smart move leaving the cell phone on vibrate."

"I'm a lot like my dad," said Eric with a smile and a nudge.

"You sure are," said Blades as he hugged the boys for the hundredth time.

"Boys, the doctor wants to wrap things up and the hospital psychiatrist wants to talk to you," said Clare.

"We're fine, Mom," Tyler said with an exasperated sigh.

"Let's get it over with, Tyler," said Eric.

The doctor came in and Clare and Blades stepped out.

CHAPTER 76

Reilly heard about Dennis' death. She wondered how Blades felt about it and hoped he would talk to her. She decided to wait until the morning to call him. In the meantime, she decided to reacquaint herself with the missing children.

Reilly jotted down what she knew about the missing children. There was a newborn taken from the hospital. She was the daughter of two druggies; one of which is dead. The father gave up the search for his daughter. There was a young boy taken by his aunt; at least that's what the police think. He had been living with his drug-addicted mother and her abusive boyfriend. His mother has since died from choking on her vomit and the boyfriend was stabbed in self defense. A little girl was taken off the street by someone. Her parents were alcoholics who seemed sincere about wanting her back but soon relapsed. Finally, a three-year old boy was taken out of his apartment. His grandmother had a drinking problem and left him alone, only to be taken by a stranger. To top it off, Detective Blades' boys were taken but retrieved unharmed.

Reilly read over her notes a couple of times. It seemed like a lot of kids went missing in a short period of time. Reilly decided to visit the hospital tomorrow and see if anyone would talk to her about the missing newborn. Maybe she would discover something the police missed. She laughed at the thought but figured if she wanted to be a great investigative reporter, she had to investigate. She also had to work on her approach.

Reilly decided to write down the names of people she would like to interview. There were a few social workers mentioned in the newspaper articles as well as a couple of nurses. Reilly didn't think the parents and guardians would talk to her but she might try. She did notice a doctor mentioned a couple of times. Her name was Dr. Kelly Lehman. She worked at the hospital where the newborn was taken and she also worked at the clinic where little Sean was treated. This could be a simple coincidence. As Reilly thought about this she recalled that Dr. Lehman was attacked by the boyfriend of Sean's mother. This was intriguing and perplexing at the same time. Reilly thought there was something here. Dr. Lehman seemed to be a common denominator.

Reilly made a few more notes and decided she needed a break. Her head was spinning. She was tired and excited. She would talk to Detective Blades in the morning, too. She would have a busy day. She decided to have a nice hot shower and spend some time with her aunt.

Aunt Loretta was sitting in the living room when Reilly came downstairs. She was reading something. Reilly was always happy to see her.

"Hi, Aunt Loretta, what are you reading?" she asked.

"Oh, Reilly. I didn't know you were home. How was your day?" asked Aunt Loretta as she hurriedly put the papers away.

"It was good. I think Detective Blades and I will get along just fine. I saw him at the funeral I told you about and we mended fences. He's going to give me an exclusive on the missing children," declared Reilly.

"Oh really?" asked Aunt Loretta with obvious interest. "Does he have good leads on the missing children?"

"No, I don't think so but he's willing to discuss things with me," replied Reilly.

"That's great, dear. I heard about his boys being taken. That was terrible," said Aunt Loretta.

"I know, he must be pissed!" said Reilly.

"Language, Reilly," said Aunt Loretta. "That's unprofessional."

"You're right. Sorry about that," Reilly said as she kissed her aunt's cheek.

"I heard the boys' biological father was killed by a police officer," said Aunt Loretta.

"Really?" asked Reilly in a surprised voice. "That was their father?"

"Well, yes. It was on the news unless I misunderstood," replied her aunt.

"I'll have to check that out," said Reilly.

"Eat first," demanded Aunt Loretta who was always trying to feed people.

"Will do!" replied Reilly.

"What information do you have on the missing children?" asked Aunt Loretta.

"Just preliminary stuff," said Reilly.

"How many are missing?" asked her aunt.

"Well four that I know of. I've never seen you so interested in a case, Aunt Loretta. Do you want to help me investigate?" asked Reilly.

"No, dear. You don't need me. I just wanted to see how much information you have," her aunt replied.

Reilly headed to the kitchen. Aunt Loretta got back to her reading. When Reilly reached the kitchen she decided to look up the article involving Blades' sons. She quickly read a few versions but saw nothing about the dead man being the boys' real father. Aunt Loretta must have been confused thought Reilly. Reilly quickly scarfed down some potatoes and meatloaf and went back into the living room.

"I couldn't find anything on the boys' biological father, Aunt Loretta. Are you sure that's what you heard?" asked Reilly.

"I thought so, dear. Maybe I misunderstood. I know that nice detective adopted them. Maybe I mixed that up," replied Aunt Loretta.

"You probably did because there's nothing about the dead guy being their real father. I'll ask Blades when I talk to him," said Reilly.

Just then the news came on and the rescue of Blades' boys was the top story. Reilly and Aunt Loretta listened intently. The reporter began her presentation of the news by claiming that they just got word the man who kidnapped the boys was their real father.

"Wow, Aunt Loretta, you were right!" said Reilly with a chuckle.

"I should start telling fortunes," laughed Aunt Loretta.

"You're adorable, Aunt Loretta!" said Reilly. "I'm going upstairs to write a bit."

"Alright, dear. Have a good night," replied Aunt Loretta.

Reilly started up the stairs. She smiled at the thought of Aunt Loretta telling fortunes. She loved her to death but she could be flighty.

CHAPTER 77

Kelly Lehman woke up and realized Jay still had his arms around her. She recalled the missed breakfast with a smile on her face. She couldn't believe they finally gave into the chemistry between them. But it was more than chemistry. She loved Jay and Jay loved her. They could be open about it, too.

Kelly gently moved Jay's arms and attempted to get out of bed without waking him up. She was almost off the bed when Jay spoke,

"Hey, where are you going?" he asked.

"I'm going to remake breakfast," said Kelly shyly.

"I thought you did already?" said Jay slyly.

Kelly blushed and playfully hit Jay.

"Stop, Jay. Just because you saved me doesn't mean you can tease me," joked Kelly.

"Well, you did thank me properly," continued Jay.

"Are you hungry or not?" asked Kelly with feigned impatience.

"Oh, I'm hungry," said Jay "but not for food."

"Okay, that's it," retorted Kelly with a deepened blush. "I'm going to shower and head into work."

"You were told to take a few days off," said Jay.

"I need to get back on the saddle," said Kelly with renewed confidence.

"Fine, I'll drop you off," replied Jay, knowing there was no point in trying to keep her home.

"I can drive," said Kelly.

"Of course you can but I want to be the one to drop you off and pick you up," said Jay softly.

Kelly's stomach did a teenage flip.

"I'd like that, Jay," said Kelly. "I'll take a quick shower."

"Do you need someone to wash your back?" asked Jay.

"Don't push it!" answered Kelly and walked away laughing.

Jay lay back down and thought about their morning. He was definitely smitten. They had gone through a lot together lately. Kelly was an amazing doctor and protector of children. He loved everything about her. He jumped out of bed and threw his clothes on. He would shower at his house after he dropped Kelly off.

Jay headed toward the kitchen and flipped on the television. He listened intently as the reporter recapped the kidnapping of two boys. Jay realized the boys were sons of Detective Blades. He yelled to Kelly as she came out of the shower.

"Kelly, did you know about Detective Blades' kids being kidnapped?" asked Jay.

"Yes, I did. Are they okay?" Kelly replied with obvious concern.

"Yeah, they're with their parents now and it looks like their real father was killed in the process. He was the kidnapper," explained Jay.

"Good enough for him," said Kelly.

"I knew that was coming," said Jay.

"Thank God they have Blades," said Kelly.

"I wouldn't want to cross him," said Jay.

"It looks like they are headed to the hospital," said Kelly. "Maybe I'll see them."

"Are you ready to roll?" asked Jay.

"In a minute," replied Kelly as she threw on her clothes.

Several minutes later, Jay handed Kelly a coffee to go and they were on their way.

CHAPTER 78

Blades and Clare walked down the hall. Clare was emotionally exhausted.

"How about I get you a coffee, Clare?" asked Blades.

"That would be great," said Clare. "I'll meet you in the lounge."

Blades walked down the hall toward the cafeteria. As he passed by the nurse's station, he saw Dr. Lehman. He walked to where she stood.

"Dr. Lehman," said Blades. "Funny to see you here. How are you feeling?"

"Oh hi Detective Blades," she responded. "I heard about your boys. Are they okay?"

"Yes, they're fine. The doctor is just checking them over," replied Blades.

"Thank goodness they weren't hurt. I heard their so-called father, Dennis Clark, was killed," said Kelly.

"Yes, he was," said Blades. He watched Dr. Lehman's face. She remained impassive.

"How did you know his name? His identity wasn't released yet," Blades said.

"It was on the news," replied Dr. Lehman.

"Oh, of course. I'm sorry for the questions. I'm just tired," said Blades.

Dennis' name wasn't mentioned on the news but Blades didn't want to spook Dr. Lehman. Something was up.

"As well you should be," stated Dr. Lehman. "And thank you again for being so nice to me when I was assaulted."

"My pleasure, Kelly," said Blades.

"Well, I have to go. Nice to see you Blades," said Kelly sincerely.

"Kelly, do you ever wonder about the two missing kids you were acquainted with?" asked Blades abruptly.

Kelly stopped in her tracks.

"Pardon me," she said with a surprised look on her face.

"You know, Sean and the newborn. Do you ever wonder about them?" asked Blades.

Blades wasn't sure where he was going with this and it was definitely unplanned.

"Of course I wonder about them but I'm busy here. I have faith in the police to find them," responded Kelly.

"I know what's going on, Kelly," said Blades, looking straight at her.

"What do you mean?" she asked.

"I know you're involved in something related to the missing kids," replied Blades.

"That's absurd!" said Dr. Lehman with a laugh.

"I was in Nebraska yesterday," said Blades.

Kelly Lehman looked surprised but didn't flinch.

"Why are you telling me this?" she asked.

"You know why I'm telling you this," said Blades as he locked eyes with her.

"I really don't," she said.

"I found them, Kelly. I found them but I'm leaving them alone," said Blades.

Dr. Lehman looked around her to see if anyone was listening.

"Can you come into my office, Blades?" she asked.

"Lead the way," Blades replied as he motioned for her to go first.

Blades followed her into her office and shut the door.

"I know nothing about anyone in Nebraska," declared Kelly.

"Then why did you want to speak in private?" asked Blades.

"Because you were accusing me of something and I don't want people talking," explained Kelly.

"Nice try. I know you're somehow involved with the missing kids. I'm going to find out exactly what you're doing. You may think it's the right thing to do but it's illegal. I know you're a good person underneath but you're crossing lines," said Blades.

"If that's the case, why are you leaving Nebraska alone?" asked Kelly.

"Because in that case the boy would end up with his aunt anyway. I didn't want to put the boy through anymore trauma. They'll come forward one of these days," replied Blades.

"Well, aren't you breaking the law, Blades?" asked Kelly.

"I didn't positively identify the people in Nebraska, Kelly," he answered coolly.

"That's obstructing justice, Blades," said Kelly.

Blades knew she was baiting him.

"You're obstructing justice, Kelly. There are others involved, too," accused Blades.

"You're getting paranoid, Blades," laughed Kelly.

"You just happen to have connections to every case? You

treated Sean at the clinic. You were in the hospital when the newborn was taken. You know Bridget," he said.

"Like you, Blades, I care about the welfare of children. I took an oath to help people stay or get healthy. Children are the most vulnerable creatures in our world. They're abused on a daily basis and people just keep going through the motions as if everything in the world is fine," said Kelly.

Dr. Lehman was getting angry. Blades decided to use this change in mood to his advantage.

"There's a system in place to help children, Dr. Lehman," declared Blades.

"Now that's funny. The system stinks and you know it. A mother killed her four- year old last week because she thought he was gay! What the fuck, Blades! Family members and teachers stand around like idiots when they know full well children need protection. Social workers focus on re-uniting families. They place abused kids back with their abusers! And don't check on them. How much sense does that make? This society isn't set up to protect children. It's set up to keep families together because the powers to be are delusional enough to believe that as long as you have a family, you're safe. There are people who don't deserve to have kids! There are people who should never have the opportunity to parent! My God, when we discovered the so-called shoe bomber, national security reacted by making everyone take off their shoes at the airport. That was a drastic move. Kids are beaten, raped and killed every day and we do nothing drastic to change this. We react. That's it. We even release pedophiles from prison. There have been no drastic changes!"

"I see you are very passionate about protecting kids," said Blades carefully.

"I'm sick of seeing all of these no good parents coming in

here pretending they don't know what's wrong with their kids. I'm tired of seeing those empty eyes in every kid when they are abused. I'm tired of watching fucking social workers send kids back to their asshole parents or lie about home visits."

"You playing God, Dr. Lehman?" Blades commented.

"I'm doing my job," she replied through clenched teeth.

"You could get in big trouble for what you're doing, Kelly," warned Blades.

"I'm doing my job," she insisted.

"You can't keep up," Blades said.

"I have a lot of assistants, Blades. This isn't an admission of guilt by the way. I just help when I can by treating kids," replied Kelly.

"It runs deep, does it?" asked Blades.

Kelly ignored that question. She knew Blades was getting close but she really hadn't given anything away.

"Do you remember Attorney Francis, Blades?" asked Kelly.

"Of course," said Blades with a confused look. "Why are you asking about him?"

"He volunteered to help you," stated the doctor.

"Clare's friend arranged it," replied Blades.

"He makes over $500 an hour Blades. Why would he volunteer to do something free for someone he never met? Why was the judge so firm with her decision to give you and Clare full custody of the boys? Most judges would at least let the biological father see his kids. Why is Dennis dead? How do you think I knew Dennis' name?" asked Kelly.

Blades felt the color drain from his face.

"What are you saying, Kelly? You had Dennis killed?" asked Blades.

"I didn't have anyone killed, Blades," replied Kelly.

"You know what I mean. You arranged for me to get custody of the boys?" asked Blades.

"Those boys deserve a great father, don't you think?" Kelly replied.

"Did you have Dennis killed, Kelly?" Blades asked again.

"I didn't have anyone killed, Blades," said Kelly calmly.

"I'm going to get to the bottom of this," warned Blades.

"Be careful, Blades. You're in the bottom. You were involved in every custody issue and I believe you threatened Dennis. It looks to me like you were using your position to guarantee custody of the boys. On top of that Dennis happened to get shot in the head. Maybe you had your police officer friends set that up," Kelly remarked.

"That's bullshit and you know it," said Blades angrily.

"I know nothing," declared Kelly.

Blades looked at Kelly intently.

"I'm looking into this," said Blades.

"Go home and enjoy your family, Blades. You have two beautiful sons and an incredible wife. You're a great father. Look all you want. You'll find nothing. I have to go now," said Kelly abruptly.

Blades' head was spinning. He walked back to the lounge to meet Clare. He couldn't believe what he just heard. What the hell was going on?

CHAPTER 79

Blades couldn't stop thinking about what Dr. Lehman said. She was angry. She was evasive. She was smart. She admitted nothing and seemed to cover all bases. The mention of pedophiles intrigued him. There was a priest found in a graveyard recently. He had committed suicide according to the note he left. He confessed to molesting a lot of children. Another pedophile was recently killed at Walpole. He had been castrated and left to bleed to death. Blades didn't want to believe that Dr. Lehman was involved in murder. Maybe she was covering for someone.

Blades thought about other recent unusual deaths. Ashley Walters died at the Ritz a few weeks ago. She had a bad reputation for drinking and using drugs. She was also a bad parent. The missing kids all had bad parents. There was a pattern here. All of the cases involved abused or neglected kids. Pedophiles fit right in since they were the most horrific abusers. Blades was tired and his thinking was foggy. He would look into these cases tomorrow. Right now he wanted to take his family home.

Blades and Clare gathered the boys and went home. Everyone was happy to get into their own beds. Blades practically had to carry the boys to bed but he didn't mind. He and Clare talked for a few minutes and fell asleep. It had been a long and crazy day.

The next morning Blades and Clare talked over coffee. The boys didn't get up until almost noon. They seemed okay. All of their friends were calling them because they had seen them on the news. Blades told Clare he had to go into the office for a bit. She expected this and didn't mind.

Blades went straight to his desk when he arrived at work. He pored over the most recent child disappearances and pedophile deaths. At first there didn't seem to be a connection. He decided to look up cases of missing children nationally. There were thousands of missing kids. That really wasn't unusual. Blades then looked up cases of dead pedophiles across the country. There were a lot of deaths. Some were murdered but a lot of them committed suicide. Many accused or known pedophiles were also missing.

Why did Dr. Lehman mention pedophiles in her rant? Something was going on. Dr. Lehman was too angry, not that she shouldn't be but her level of anger was unusual. Maybe she was abused as a child. She had connections to Bridget, the nurse, who was now missing. She treated Sean at a clinic. She got involved with Blades' custody issues, and she knew Dennis' name before it was released. Now that his head was clear, Blades was even surer that Dr. Lehman was involved in something.

Blades saw that he had a message. It was Reilly, his new ambitious friend. She wanted to know if they could meet. Blades decided to call her back and they made plans to meet for coffee in the afternoon.

CHAPTER 80

Dr. Lehman thought about her conversation with Blades the night before. She knew she got a little angry but believed she didn't technically give anything away. She didn't regret warning Blades to stop snooping. She had the day off and wanted to relax. She noticed she had a message on her cell phone and hoped it wasn't work. She listened as Marquez told her he was safe and had the package. She laughed. Marquez loved being mysterious. He was telling her that he was with Bridget. She was happy for them. Her thoughts went back to Blades. He didn't know she knew Marquez. That would be hard to explain. Blades wasn't stupid but he had no evidence of any crimes.

Dr. Lehman sipped her coffee and turned on the television. Her cell phone rang. It was probably Marquez again.

"Hello," she said.

"Hey Kelly, it's Rita."

"Hi Rita, what's up?" asked Kelly.

"We have an unexpected visitor," said Rita.

"What do you mean?" asked Kelly.

"A guy was sent to us from Florida. He likes to molest little girls," explained Rita.

"It's my day off. Can't Melvin handle this?" asked Kelly.

"Melvin is away. We can hold the guy for a few days at the farm but we need you to take care of him," said Rita.

"Fine. Call me in a few days and I'll let you know when I can come. I need more supplies, anyway," said Kelly.

Dr. Lehman was tired of working right now. She would be fine after a few days rest and then would put another pedophile where he belonged. Since the group wasn't taking children for a while, she knew she would be expected to make as many pedophiles disappear as possible. It didn't bother her but she didn't want to think about it right now. She decided to go for a run. She let Jay know where she was going.

"I could come with you, Kelly," said Jay.

"You don't run," laughed Kelly.

"I know," laughed Jay. "Are you sure you'll be okay?"

"I'll be fine. Thanks for your concern. I'll see you later," said Kelly.

Jay leaned in for a kiss and watched Kelly leave.

Dr. Lehman loved running. She felt re-invigorated every time she ran. She needed the release. Even though she listened to music when she ran, she couldn't help re-hashing her conversation with Blades. He was smart. She wondered how hard he would look into the missing children and dead pedophile cases. She had tried to warn him by mentioning the attorney and the judge but he didn't flinch. He was a stand- up guy. There was really nothing she could hold over his head but she tried.

Kelly's thoughts changed to Jay. She smiled and wondered what would happen with them. She could imagine spending her life with him. They had known each other for years. She decided to tell him about her conversation with Blades and get his take on it.

CHAPTER 81

Marquez and Bridget, who was now Sophia, watched Cedric, now Caden, play in the sand. They sat in their beach chairs and sipped cold drinks. Cedric adapted quite well to his new mother and father. He answered to "Caden" as if he was born with the name. Marquez kept his name because he knew no one was looking for him. Bridget worked part-time as a nurse and Marquez planned to get a job as a teacher where they lived. They had a nice two-bedroom condo that Marquez's parents bought for them. They also had a nice bank account since Marquez's parents were loaded.

Bridget loved that Marquez came to be with her. The only regret was that they couldn't see his family in Massachusetts. His family would have to travel to them. They didn't mind. Marquez figured after a few years, it would be safe to visit Massachusetts. Bridget might even be able to go back after several years since she had a new name and a new look. Cedric would change his looks as he got older. Marquez was pretty confident that Cedric's grandmother wouldn't look for him.

Cedric would be four soon and was very bright. He gained weight and seemed very happy. He loved his friends from pre-school and he loved his teacher. Life was good for him as it should be.

"Hey, Dad, you said you would make a sand castle with me!" he yelled to Marquez.

Marquez smiled at him and turned to Bridget.

"I love being a Dad!" he said with a huge grin.

"I know you do. You're good at it, too!" replied Bridget.

Bridget and Marquez talked to Cedric abut calling them Mom and Dad. Cedric eagerly agreed. He loved having a real mom and dad.

"Well, you're a great mom and I have to say again for the thousandth time, I'm glad you ran with him," declared Marquez.

"Me, too. My heart broke for him. He touched me like no other child ever did. I couldn't leave him," replied Bridget.

"He's happy now and that's all that matters. When are we getting married, by the way?" asked Marquez.

"Now that's a weak proposal if I ever heard one," Bridget commented.

"Oh, how many have you heard?" Marquez asked as he chuckled.

"You know what I mean, Marquez," teased Bridget.

"Mom! Let Dad make a castle with me!" yelled Cedric.

"Go play with your son, Marquez," ordered Bridget.

"I'll be back to question you some more," he teased.

Bridget watched as Marquez and Cedric played together. They were laughing and whispering. She decided to read her book for a few minutes. As she was reading she heard some giggling and looked up to see Cedric.

"Caden, why are you giggling?" she asked with a big smile.

"I found this in the sand and Dad wants to know if it's yours," said Caden, still giggling.

"What is it?" asked Bridget as she leaned forward.

"A ring," said Cedric with a grin.

Bridget leaned forward and took the ring from Cedric. It was a beautiful sapphire with small diamonds on each side.

"You found this?" asked Bridget with a confused look on her face.

"Yeah, Dad said to try it on and see if it fits. He wants you to read this note, too," replied Cedric.

Bridget took the note and opened it. It was obvious that the note was written by Cedric with help from Marquez. Cedric had used a red crayon. The note read, "Please marry my Dad."

Bridget looked up at Cedric and then at Marquez who was now behind Cedric.

"Are you asking me to marry you, Marquez?" asked Bridget nervously.

"Well, you told me my proposal was weak so I thought maybe you would like one from Caden," Marquez remarked.

Bridget stood up and put the ring on. It fit perfectly.

"Of course I will marry you, Marquez!" screamed Bridget as she threw her arms around his neck.

"Hey, what about me?" asked Cedric. "Will you marry me, too?"

Bridget and Marquez started to laugh but then stopped when they saw Cedric's serious face.

"Well, of course I will marry your Dad. I can't marry you because you're my son," said Bridget.

Cedric looked confused but then decided to clap his hands in glee.

"We're getting married," he yelled.

Several other people on the beach looked their way and started clapping. One person offered to take a picture using Marquez's phone. All three smiled brightly.

Bridget kept looking at her ring and then at her two boys.

"It can't get any better than this, Marquez. We have to tell your folks," said Bridget excitedly.

"They already know," said Marquez with a smile.

"Oh, confident were you?" teased Bridget.

"Well, I knew you wouldn't say no to that little guy," he said as he pointed to Cedric.

"Bribery will get you everywhere!" exclaimed Bridget.

"Let's go celebrate with some ice cream," suggested Marquez.

They packed up their beach gear and headed to their favorite ice cream shop. Several beach goers wished them well as they left. It was a happy day. They would have a happy life.

CHAPTER 82

Blades saw Reilly waiting for him at a table. Somethin's Brewin" was busy as usual. Lorraine ran a great café. Her chicken salad with walnuts and cranberries was amazing. Blades decided to have one. After he ordered he sat down with Reilly.

"So, Blades, you had quite a scare lately!" Reilly said.

"Yes, I sure did but the boys are fine," replied Blades.

"The culprit was their biological father!" exclaimed Reilly.

"Are you interviewing me, Reilly?" asked Blades with a smirk.

"I wasn't but I will!" laughed Reilly.

"Are you writing a piece on that story?" asked Blades.

"I will be if you want to share your thoughts!" replied Reilly.

"Okay, you need a good first story, so I'll agree that you can write about it but only what I tell you," said Blades.

"Okay, okay," said Reilly excitedly.

Blades laughed at Reilly's enthusiasm and began to talk.

"Eric and Tyler were duped into getting in their biological father's truck. He took them to a cabin in New Hampshire against their will. Eric was smart enough to leave his phone on so we were able to locate the boys. We negotiated a rescue and Dennis got killed. The End."

"That's it?" asked Reilly.

"That's it. That's the exclusive. I'm a man of few words," claimed Blades.

"How are the boys now?" asked Reilly.

"They're fine. Like nothing happened," stated Blades.

"How did they react to their father's death?" asked Reilly.

"Persistent, aren't you?" laughed Blades.

"Well, yes. I have to probe," said Reilly.

"The boys actually felt sorry for him," said Blades.

"Wow, that's amazing," said Reilly.

"They are amazing and get their kindness from their mother, Clare," said Blades.

"What was Dennis like?" asked Reilly.

"I'm going to really end it here, Reilly. I don't want to dredge up bad memories for the boys or Clare," stated Blades.

"I understand. Thank you for answering my questions," said Reilly with a huge smile.

"I like you, Reilly. You're good at this and sincere," said Blades.

"Thanks! On another note and off the record, what do you think about all of these missing children?" asked Reilly.

"Well, we're investigating the kidnappings and have some leads that I can't share with you right now," said Blades.

"I find it weird that their parents stopped looking for them, at least publicly," said Reilly.

"Well, their parents have problems and their kids aren't priorities," said Blades.

"That's so sad," said Reilly. "I'm lucky to have my Aunt Loretta," said Reilly.

"Where are your parents?" asked Blades.

"My Mom died of breast cancer when I was six. I don't know who my father is because Mom was artificially inseminated," explained Reilly.

"Sorry to hear about your Mom," said Blades.

"Thanks. I miss her but I am so fortunate to have my aunt," replied Reilly.

"Do you have any other relatives?" asked Blades.

"I have an aunt who lives in California. I see her now and then. Aunt Loretta is really my great aunt and my mother named her in her will as my guardian," explained Reilly.

"That's great, Reilly. Do you ever wonder who your biological father is?" asked Blades.

"Sometimes," said Reilly. "I'm really not that interested."

"Just curious," said Blades.

"Speaking of family, I have to meet Aunt Loretta in half an hour. Thanks for meeting me, Blades," said Reilly.

"My pleasure. Can you send me a copy of the article before you publish it?" asked Blades.

Reilly was surprised by the request but acquiesced.

"Sure, Blades, as long as I remain your go-to reporter," replied Reilly.

"Deal, " said Blades. "As long as you stay sincere."

"I will. Thanks again," said Reilly.

CHAPTER 83

Blades couldn't shake his suspicions of Dr. Lehman and believed she was somehow involved in the missing children's cases and maybe even involved in the killing of many known and unknown pedophiles. Blades knew he couldn't question Bridget any further because she was gone. There were absolutely no leads as to where she might have gone. He did, however, want to speak to Cedric's grandmother again. He gathered some notes and headed to Mission Hill.

Blades arrived at the apartment complex where Cedric had lived. He went directly to Eleanor's apartment door and knocked. There was no response at first. Finally, Cedric's grandmother answered the door.

"Is that you, Detective Blades?" she asked with a noticeable slur in her voice.

"Yes. How are you, Mrs. Graves?" asked Blades.

"I'm not so good. I miss my boy," said Eleanor.

"I'm sorry we haven't found him yet. Do you have any family or friends you can lean on?" asked Blades.

"No, and I don't want any. I'm going to stay in my apartment until Cedric comes home," she said.

"You have to get sober," said Blades.

"I can stop drinking any time I want," declared Eleanor.

"Well, when we find Cedric, you won't be getting him back unless you clean up your act," said Blades.

Eleanor Graves started to cry.

"It's all my fault. I should never have left him," she said.

"We're working hard to find him but you have to get clean," said Blades again.

"I know," replied Eleanor.

"Now, do you want me to call someone for you?" asked Blades.

"No, I'll call my sister. Bye, Detective Blades," said Eleanor.

Cedric's grandmother shut her door. Blades shook his head. She was drunk. Even if they found Cedric, she would never get custody of him. What a mess. Blades headed home but halfway there he decided to swing by Dr. Lehman's house. He soon realized that no one was home.

CHAPTER 84

Dr. Lehman looked at her latest task. He was pathetic. He was probably forty some years old. He had been arrested for molesting his niece. Apparently he had done so for many years until she finally told her teacher. He had molested her friends as well. Shockingly, he was let out on bail. He was supposed to be under house arrest but two members of the group dismantled the ankle bracelet and took him to the farmhouse. As far as the authorities knew in Florida, he was still in his house. The ankle bracelet was on his kitchen table. The group assumed the authorities would think he removed the bracelet himself and ran.

A member of the group worked with one of the girls' fathers. He told the group member that he wanted to kill Earl Basker. His little girl hung out with Earl's niece and apparently Earl molested them on several occasions. The group member, whose name was Ben, listened to his heart breaking story every day. Ben informed the group of Earl's misdeeds and the group gave him the green light to put him down.

Earl lay on the bed with his eyes closed. He felt like he was in a nightmare. He heard the door open and locked eyes with a tall, very attractive woman. She smiled at him. Maybe he could convince her to let him go.

"Hello, Earl," said Dr. Lehman.

"Please let me explain. I didn't touch those girls," whined Earl.

"Really? Well those girls say otherwise and gave very detailed information that most eight year olds would not be capable of doing. You're a pig," replied Kelly.

"Please let me go. I'm being put on trial. Let the system deal with me. I won't say anything about being here," promised Earl.

"Just like you told the little girls not to say anything? You like secrets it seems. Those little girls were so brave despite your vicious deeds. You'll never touch another child. Now, do you want to commit suicide or take the needle?" asked Kelly.

"What do you mean?" Earl asked with terrified eyes. He thought the guys who kidnapped him were kidding about committing suicide.

"You can write a note detailing what you did and then finish the note by stating you took your own life. Or, I can give you a paralyzing shot and finish you off with a lethal dose of what we call, "justice juice," explained Kelly.

"Who are we?" asked Earl.

"We're a group of people who believe children are treasures and should be treasured. We protect them and save them from vermin like you," replied Kelly.

"I'm not writing a note. I'm innocent!" declared Earl.

"Fine with me," said Dr. Lehman as she grabbed Earl's arm. She quickly gave a shot of puffer fish venom into his vein.

Earl's body went stiff. He looked at Dr. Lehman with terrified eyes. She didn't flinch.

"How are you feeling? You scared? I hope so because what you're feeling is exactly what those girls felt as you violated them. They'll take years to get over what you did. I'm doing you a favor. You only have to be afraid for a few minutes. Then you'll die. Your demise is your gift to society," said Kelly.

Dr. Lehman watched Earl for another minute then plunged the antidote into Earl's arm. He gasped for air. He was so terrified he couldn't speak for several seconds.

"Please let me go. I'll turn myself in," Earl cried.

"That's very noble of you," said Dr. Lehman with a sarcastic tone. "But we both know you'll eventually get out of prison and there's no cure for your diseased mind."

"Please, I'm sorry. I won't touch another kid," Earl swore.

Dr. Lehman smirked. "I know you won't. In fact, I can guarantee it."

Before he uttered another word, Dr. Lehman gave him part one of a three part series of shots. She finished with the remaining two shots and watched as the light left his eyes. She packed up and walked out of the room.

"He's all yours, boys. Make sure he gets cremated tonight."

CHAPTER 85

Blades headed back to his office to look at his files again. He arrived at the station and headed to the Chief's office.

"Chief, can I ask you something?" asked Blades.

"Of course, Blades. What's up?"

"I had a conversation with Dr. Lehman the night my boys were being checked out at the hospital," Blades began.

"Yes, how are they?" asked the Chief.

"They're fine, thanks. They don't seem to be affected at all by the incident," replied Blades.

"Good. What about Dr. Lehman?" asked the Chief.

"She asked me about the boys and then about Dennis' death. She knew he was the boys' biological father but we didn't release that information or his name right away. How would she know that?"

The Chief had to think fast.

"I believe it was mentioned on the news," replied the Chief.

"I went through every news report, verbal and written. That information wasn't there when Dr. Lehman mentioned it to me. Something is going on with her. She's connected to a lot of the missing kids' cases and she even made a remark about pedophiles deserving to die. There are quite a few pedophiles missing across the country. I checked. There are also a lot of dead ones. I also saw Dr. Lehman with one of the nurses we questioned about the missing newborn and she treated the missing four year old at a clinic," said Blades.

"She's a doctor. She's bound to be seen at clinics and hospitals. She also probably found out about Dennis in the hospital," replied the Chief.

"It doesn't feel right. I think I have enough concern to get a search warrant for her house," said Blades.

"Now that's jumping the gun, Blades. We have to be careful about accusing a reputable citizen of these misdeeds," warned the Chief.

"I'm not accusing, I'm searching," said Blades.

"Get some actual evidence and we'll go from there," said the Chief.

"Fine, I'll try but I am sure she's involved in something," said Blades.

Blades left the Chief's office feeling unsettled. The Chief seemed to go out of his way to protect Dr. Lehman. Maybe it was because she was a well-known doctor. Blades decided to swing by her house again and talk to her. He arrived there thirty minutes later. She wasn't home. He headed to the hospital to speak with her but not before looking up the make, model, and license plate of her car. He had an idea.

CHAPTER 86

Dr. Lehman answered her phone. The Chief called and relayed to her what Blades had shared with him.

"Blades can't connect me with anything, Chief," she assured him.

"Just lay low, Kelly. Don't be seen with anyone connected to the missing kids," said the Chief.

"Fine, but you're being paranoid," she said.

"Just wait it out," repeated the Chief.

"Okay, okay," said Kelly.

Dr. Lehman sighed a heavy sigh. The Chief was a worrywart. Her phone rang again.

"What now?" she asked thinking it was the Chief again.

"Hey Doc, it's Jay. We have a situation," he said.

"Hi Jay. What's the situation?" asked Kelly.

"We have a local pedophile in our custody, so to speak," said Jay.

"What do you mean by local?" asked Kelly.

"He's the guy from New Hampshire accused of molesting all of those boys in junior high," explained Jay.

"Why do you have him?" asked Kelly.

"One of our spotters in New Hampshire got word that one

of the fathers of the boys who got molested was going to kill him. Really kill him. We don't want a parent going to prison for that," said Jay.

"No, we don't. What do you want me to do?" asked Kelly.

"He's at the farmhouse," said Jay.

"He's at the farmhouse?" asked Kelly incredulously.

"Yes, we didn't have a choice," explained Jay.

"I just spoke with the Chief and he asked me to lay low. Apparently Detective Blades is asking a lot of questions," said Kelly.

"I can't get in touch with any of our other medical people," said Jay. "I don't think helping with this matter will expose anything," declared Jay.

"Okay. Will he agree to suicide?" asked Kelly.

"Not yet. He's begging us to let him go and says he'll turn himself in," replied Jay.

"Alright I'll be there in the morning. I have to do rounds first. You should stay at the farmhouse," said Kelly.

"I will," said Jay.

CHAPTER 87

Blades decided not to find Dr. Lehman. Instead, he planted a GPS under her car while it was parked at the hospital. He was going to monitor her for a while. He would remove it in a few days. He went home after planting the device and had a nice dinner with Clare and the boys. While the boys were busy with their homework, he opened his laptop so he could check on Dr. Lehman.

Dr. Lehman was on the move and it looked like she was heading south. She was probably going home thought Blades. As Blades saw that she was going home, he decided to check on her in the morning.

The next morning Blades watched as she drove past Quincy and headed towards Brockton, going south on route twenty-four. He decided on a whim to follow her. He told Clare he had to check on something and might be a while.

Blades hopped in his car and drove towards Brockton. He kept his laptop open on the passenger's seat. He followed Dr. Lehman as she turned onto route 495 and take an exit leading to Rochester. He stayed as far behind her as he could. She eventually drove down a long driveway or road. Blades stopped as he got closer and pulled into a field beside the road.

He waited about fifteen minutes and got out of his car. He walked down what turned out to be a driveway. There was a farmhouse at the end of the driveway with a few lights on. He walked behind the farmhouse to see if he could possibly get a look inside of the house. He couldn't see anything but he heard several voices.

"What's it going to be Dan? Suicide or justice juice?" asked Kelly.

"You'll never get away with this," warned Dan.

"Look you piece of shit, one of the fathers of your victims was going to shoot you. We're doing you a favor. You can write a suicide note and then take these pills. I would even be willing to slit your wrists for you or I can give you an injection" replied Kelly.

"I told you I would turn myself in," insisted Dan.

"And I told you I didn't care," said Kelly.

"It's a mortal sin to commit suicide," whined Dan.

Dr. Lehman started to laugh.

"But it's okay to molest little boys?" she asked.

"I didn't touch them," declared Dan.

Blades wasn't sure what to do. He couldn't believe what he was hearing. He decided to back away from the house and make a call. He went behind what he thought was a shed and called the department. He immediately asked for backup and then asked to speak to the Chief.

"Chief, I'm at a farmhouse in Rochester and I'm pretty sure the good doctor is about to kill a man," whispered Blades.

The blood drained from the Chief's face unbeknownst to Blades.

"What are you talking about, Blades?" he asked.

"I'm at a farmhouse in Rochester, I followed Dr. Lehman

here. I need you to call the local cops and back me up here," Blades said urgently.

"I'll send some of our own," replied the Chief.

"That will take too long. I need backup now," insisted Blades.

"Blades, how were you able to track the doctor?" asked the Chief.

"I put a GPS on her car. I know I should have got a warrant but I was on to something," explained Blades.

"This won't hold up in court, Blades," remarked the Chief.

"It's too late now and she's about to kill someone, Chief!" exclaimed Blades.

"Hang tight, Blades. I'll make the calls. Don't go in without backup," warned the Chief.

Blades hung up. The Chief immediately called Officers Kilroy and Scott and told them to head to Rochester. He told them to do what they had to do to protect the group. They didn't like the implication but knew if they had to kill Blades they would. The Chief didn't call the local police.

Blades went back to the house and waited to hear more conversation. The man continued to beg for his life but Dr. Lehman wasn't moved by his pitiful promises. Fifteen minutes went by and then there was silence. Then he heard Dr. Lehman's voice.

"I hope you're terrified. This is how you made those boys feel," she said.

Blades didn't hear the man reply. He moved closer to the house and looked in the side window. Dr. Lehman's back was turned and she was holding a big needle. He waited for backup. Several minutes went by. Blades couldn't understand why the local police hadn't responded. It was a small town and they shouldn't be taking this long. Dr. Lehman continued to terrify the man. He found it strange that the man was no longer begging for mercy.

Blades decided he couldn't wait for backup. He ran around to the front of the house and burst in the front door.

"Lehman!" he yelled. "Put down the needle."

Blades walked towards the bedroom and as he did a man raced to the bedroom door. Blades pointed the gun at the man and told him to back off. Jay stepped away from the bedroom.

"Go to the back of the bedroom so I can see you," ordered Blades.

Jay went to the back of the room. He looked at Kelly.

"Blades, this is none of your concern. I'm trying to save this man," said Kelly, thinking quickly.

"I heard what you said to him, Doc. You're going to kill him. If you were trying to save him, why is he zip-tied to the bed?" asked Blades.

"I know who he is and I didn't want him to escape. He's sick, Blades. He needs this needle," insisted Kelly.

Blades looked at the man who was wide-eyed but not moving.

"I'll arrest him, Doc. But I have to arrest you, too," replied Blades.

"We'll handle her," said a new voice.

Blades looked to his right and saw Officers Scott and Kilroy.

"What are you two doing here?" asked Blades.

"The Chief sent us as back-up," said Officer Scott.

"Where are the local police?" asked Blades.

"I don't know," said Officer Kilroy.

"I'm taking the doctor in," said Blades.

"I have to give him this needle or he'll die," yelled Dr. Lehman. She looked at Officers Scott and Kilroy who were pointing their guns at her. Jay stood against the wall saying nothing. He knew what Dr. Lehman was doing. She had the antidote but knew Blades thought it was a lethal injection of some kind.

"Don't move a muscle," said Blades. "Put down the needle!"

As Dr. Lehman moved to give the man the needle, Officer Scott dove into the room and landed on top of Dr. Lehman. The needle flew out of her hand and ended up at Jay's feet. She whispered to Officer Scott not to move. He didn't.

Blades looked at the man on the bed and Dr. Lehman on the floor.

"Scott, get off her!" yelled Blades.

Scott got up and pretended to be dazed. Officer Kilroy helped Dr. Lehman up. He took his time, knowing he had to stall in order for the original injection to kill the pedophile.

Blades told him to hand-cuff her and then hurried to see the man on the bed.

"What did you do to him? Why isn't he moving?" asked Blades.

The man wasn't moving. The light slowly went out of the man's terrified eyes. He was dead.

"What did you do?" yelled Blades as he looked at Dr. Lehman.

"Nothing at all. That was the problem, Blades. I was trying to inject the antidote to save him. You stopped me so he's dead," said Kelly.

"What?" yelled Blades.

"You heard me. You prevented me from saving this man," she yelled.

"I heard you telling him you were going to kill him. I know who he is. He's the football coach from New Hampshire," Blades yelled back.

"I had no idea. He just staggered in here asking for help.

He said he was having some sort of allergic reaction. He had a seizure so I zip-tied him for his own safety," explained Kelly.

Blades looked at everyone in the room. They were all involved somehow in something. He called the local police for backup and an ambulance.

CHAPTER 88

Local backup finally arrived. Officers Scott and Kilroy escorted Dr. Lehman to their squad car. Jay followed behind. Blades talked with the locals for a few minutes and walked towards Dr. Lehman.

"She's coming with me," he told the officers. "You take Jay."

"Yes, sir," said Officer Kilroy.

Dr. Lehman was placed in the back seat of Blades' car. The ambulance left with the dead pedophile. There would be an autopsy performed immediately. Blades and the locals gathered all of the evidence from the farmhouse that suggested there was more to the dead man than having an allergic reaction.

It was a relatively quiet ride back to Boston. Dr. Lehman was quiet but she and Blades looked at each other through the rearview mirror several times. She would shake her head and just mumble. From what Blades could comprehend she kept saying, "You just don't get it Blades."

Blades didn't react. He drove in silence because he wanted to sift through all that he had heard and witnessed. As they arrived at the precinct, Dr. Lehman asked for her phone call.

"You can make your call when we get inside," said Blades. "I'm assuming you're calling a lawyer."

"Yes, I am. I'm calling Stanley Francis. Do you know him?" she asked coyly.

Blades knew what she was doing. She knew he knew Attorney Francis.

"We've met, thanks to you. So, you even have a lawyer involved in your so-called good work," commented Blades.

Dr. Lehman didn't answer. She just smiled. Blades parked the car and escorted her into the precinct. He took her directly to an interrogation room. She sat down. He handed her the phone and let her call her attorney.

"What am I being charged with Detective Blades?" she asked as she held the phone to her ear.

"Attempted murder and possibly first degree murder," Blades replied.

Dr. Lehman relayed this information to her attorney with a smirk on her face.

Blades read Dr. Lehman her rights but she didn't remain silent.

"Detective Blades, you have no idea what you're doing. I was trying to help that man so I could turn him in," said Kelly.

"Really? He just happened to find the farmhouse," said Blades.

"Yes, he did," explained Kelly.

"All the way from New Hampshire," replied Blades.

"He was trying to get away, Blades. It makes sense," she retorted.

"Nothing makes sense, Dr. Lehman but I'm going to make sense of it. I heard what you said to the man in the farmhouse. You wanted him to suffer and die," said Blades.

"I said no such thing," replied the doctor.

Blades knew she would never admit what she said and he had no actual proof. It was hearsay. However, Blades had a good reputation and everyone knew he wasn't a liar. Unfortunately the doctor had a good reputation, too. A more serious issue was that he had planted the GPS without a warrant. A judge could easily throw out any evidence collected at the farmhouse.

"You have no idea what you're getting into here, Blades," said Kelly.

"I think I do and it has to stop," he replied.

"Don't give me the song and dance about the system, Blades. We both know it sucks. You almost lost your boys a couple of times," Kelly reminded him.

"But I didn't because of the system," Blades shot back.

"You think the system did that all on its own?" asked Kelly.

Attorney Francis walked into the room before Dr. Lehman could say anymore.

"Okay, Kelly. No more talking," said Attorney Francis. "Hello, Detective. Nice to see you again."

"Not really," said Blades. "Your client here is in a lot of trouble."

"I don't see how. I understand she was trying to save a man and your interference caused his death," said the lawyer.

"That's not what happened and you know it," replied Blades.

"I know what my client told me and what the evidence shows," said Francis.

"There's going to be an autopsy," Blades said.

"I know but it will show that the man was having an allergic reaction to a bee sting," replied the lawyer.

"The hell it will!" yelled Blades.

Blades looked at the doctor and then back at the attorney.

They both looked frustrated but not about the arrest which was soon to come. They looked frustrated with Blades.

"You didn't have a warrant for the GPS, Blades. The judge is going to squash your case. I suggest you walk away. You won't be held liable for that poor man's death," said Attorney Francis.

"Are you threatening me?" asked Blades.

Before he could answer Dr. Lehman chimed in.

"How are the boys, Blades?" she asked.

Blades' head swung in her direction. Why was she asking about the boys again?

"They're fine. Why are you asking?" he asked.

"I know they went through some trauma. I hope they don't re-live it in their minds," replied Kelly.

"They're fine," said Blades.

"I'm just saying it's good that you and Clare have legal custody of the boys. But that really doesn't matter, right? Dennis is dead after all," Kelly remarked.

"Yes, he's dead," said Blades in a weary voice.

The door to the room opened and the Chief walked in.

"I'll take her to booking, Blades," he said.

"Why are you taking her, Chief? Isn't that below your grade?" asked Blades.

"I want to make sure she's treated right, Blades. She's done a lot for the community."

"Yes, she sure has," said Blades sarcastically.

Dr. Lehman stood and started towards the door to the Chief.

"I was just telling Blades that he must be happy that Dennis is dead. He can't bother them anymore. The boys are lucky to have Blades as their father. They'll have a peaceful and happy upbringing," said Dr. Lehman.

"What's she doing?" asked Blades as he looked at the lawyer.

Dr. Lehman looked straight into Blades' eyes.

"Officer Scott has quite a good shot, doesn't he?" she asked him.

Blades looked at her attorney again and then at the Chief. Both said nothing and looked right at him.

"How do you know who shot Dennis?" asked Blades.

Dr. Lehman looked at the Chief.

"Just a lucky guess," she said not taking her eyes off the Chief.

The enormity of the situation hit Blades like a ton of bricks. He was speechless. How far did this go?

Blades looked at the Chief.

"You ordered the shot?" asked Blades incredulously.

"No, I didn't order the shot, Blades," declared the Chief.

Blades was confused. Dr. Lehman was trying to confuse him.

"Just get her out of here," said Blades. "I have to think."

CHAPTER 89

The Doyen hung up the phone. Dr. Lehman was in a bit of trouble but the autopsy would show the pedophile died of a bee sting allergy. The Doyen had made several calls and the coroner was instructed to attest to the allergy and the fact that Dr. Lehman did have the antidote in her hand.

The farmhouse would have to close or simply be stripped of any evidence of wrongdoing. Detective Blades had not been allowed to remove anything from the house except for what was in the bedroom but that would be thrown out since he had no warrant. Plus, the Doyen was sure they could handle the judge if it went that far.

The Doyen was worried about Dr. Lehman. She was doing too much and had slipped up. The group would run interference and suggest that Dr. Lehman take a vacation. Detective Blades was getting too close to her. The group would have to call another meeting. It didn't help that so many children were abused on a daily basis. Dr. Lehman was relentless when it came to protecting them but she was clearly burnt out. The Doyen silently reprimanded herself for not stepping in earlier and ordering Dr. Lehman to take a break. She sighed and then heard her phone ring.

The Doyen answered the phone and was informed that the good doctor had made bail. She was going home with Jay. Detective Blades had been informed that he violated procedure and there was nothing he could use against Dr. Lehman. The Chief explained to the Doyen that Blades was furious and probably wouldn't let it go. The Doyen informed the Chief that Dr. Lehman would be taking a vacation and the group's activities had to stop in their area for a bit.

The Chief agreed and shared that they all needed a break. He also reassured the Doyen that he would handle Blades.

CHAPTER 90

Reilly thought about Blades' questions about her family. Who was her father? Did she want to know? Her mother was artificially inseminated so her father was kind of artificial. Her mother never really discussed it with her and she died when Reilly was little. Reilly hadn't asked Aunt Loretta about it in a long time. She decided to try and research information on artificial insemination. She had her mother's name, Lorna Simonsen, but had no idea where to start regarding the sperm donor.

The first thing Reilly did was to try and find out how she could access her mother's medical records. She decided to ask her Aunt Loretta that question. Next she researched how to identify sperm donors. The law was pretty straight -forward in Massachusetts. The donor could be completely anonymous, the donor could be identified but have no legal access to the child, or the donor could be identified by a donor number which is normally included in the mother's medical records. This didn't mean Reilly could automatically get a name but she might be able to get information about the donor's eye color, height, weight, etc.

Reilly sat back on her chair and asked herself again if she

really wanted to identify her artificial father. In the midst of her thoughts, in came Aunt Loretta. She was impeccably dressed as usual as if she just returned from church. Her hair was perfect and she was smiling.

"Hello, Reilly. What are you up to today?" asked Aunt Loretta cheerily.

Before Reilly could decide whether or not to tell Aunt Loretta, she heard the words coming out of herself.

"Actually, I'm trying to find out who my artificial father is," replied Reilly.

Aunt Loretta stopped in her tracks and turned around.

"Why would you want to know that, dear? The donor signed off on all of his rights," asked Aunt Loretta.

"I'm just curious, I guess," replied Reilly. "I hardly remember Mom and I am intrigued by my father's identity. I don't want a relationship; at least I don't think I do but I would like to know who he is."

"Well, that will be difficult since the donation was anonymous," declared Aunt Loretta.

"Maybe," said Reilly. But if I can access Mom's medical records, there might be a donor number."

"I don't think there is, dear. I saw your Mom's medical records when she was ill," explained Aunt Loretta.

"Okay, but I would still like to see them," stated Reilly. "Do you have a copy?"

"I don't but I could get you a copy if you give me a couple of days," replied Aunt Loretta.

"Thanks, Aunt Loretta!" exclaimed Reilly. "You're the best!"

"My pleasure, dear," Aunt Loretta replied.

"Let me know when you have them," said Reilly.

"I will, dear," replied Aunt Loretta.

Reilly turned back to her laptop and Googled her mother's name, mainly out of curiosity. Not much came up besides her mother's death from breast cancer. Reilly had never before researched her mother. She scrolled down as Aunt Loretta brushed past her to go to the kitchen. Reilly continued to read the article about her mother. At the very end of the article, there was a faded picture of her mother. Reilly had to really look at the picture in order to visualize her mother. The picture looked nothing like her mother. Reilly scrolled to the top of the article to double check her mother's name. It was Lorna Simonsen. The birthday and date of her death was correct. She scrolled down again and examined the picture again. The picture was not her mother's. The wrong picture must have been used.

"Hey, Aunt Loretta, I just found an article about Mom but the picture is not hers," yelled Reilly.

Aunt Loretta came back into the living-room, looking surprised.

"Let me see, dear," said Aunt Loretta as she peered over Reilly's shoulder.

"You're right! That's not your mother's picture. The article is right but not the picture. It's probably just a mistake," said Aunt Loretta.

"It's weird that it wasn't corrected," said Reilly.

"Yes, but it was a while ago and I don't even remember this article," said Aunt Loretta.

"I guess it's not a big deal," decided Reilly.

"What are you looking for?" asked Aunt Loretta.

"Nothing really. I just wanted to read about Mom," said Reilly.

Aunt Loretta patted Reilly's shoulder reassuringly.

"I'll get that information about the donor as soon as I can," promised Aunt Loretta.

"Thanks," said Reilly, looking affectionately at her aunt. "I'm going to head to the office for a while. I'll see you for supper."

"Okay, dear. Have a good day."

Reilly left and Aunt Loretta decided to re-read the article about Reilly's mother. She went on her home computer and within a few seconds, retrieved the article. All of the information was correct but the photo was not of Reilly's mother. She decided to call the publisher and request a new photo. She managed to talk to the current editor and promised to send in a new photo of her niece.

Aunt Loretta then made a call to the doctor's office that housed Lorna Simonsen's medical records. She asked to speak directly to the doctor. She was on hold for a minute or two and then was greeted by her old friend.

"Hello, Loretta! Nice to hear from you!" exclaimed the doctor. "What's up?"

Aunt Loretta got right to the point.

"Reilly wants to see her mother's medical records because she's interested in the identity of her father," explained Aunt Loretta.

"Really? What brought this on?" asked the doctor.

"I'm not sure but you're going to have to go through Lorna's records and make sure Reilly can't identify her father," instructed Aunt Loretta. "After you do this, send a copy of what is left to me and I'll give the information to Reilly."

"Okay, no problem. I'll do that today and have it sent right over," promised the doctor.

"Reilly can never know her real father," said Aunt Loretta with conviction.

"I agree and will take care of it. There'll be no way Reilly can find out who he is. I will take care of the official birth records, too."

"Perfect," declared Aunt Loretta. "I appreciate it."

"See you soon, Loretta."

CHAPTER 91

Dr. Lehman made bail and was picked up by Jay. She was very agitated but had been assured by the Chief that the charges would go nowhere. They just had to figure out how to explain the farmhouse and control Blades.

"What do you think of the situation, Kelly?" asked Jay.

"I'm not sure. Blades is definitely onto to us but really doesn't have any proof," replied Kelly.

"I thought you'd be more worried than you are," said Jay.

"The Doyen will handle everything. We're meeting later tonight and I really will take a break," stated Kelly.

"Is the whole group meeting or just you two?" asked Jay.

"Just us, I think," Kelly said.

"From what you told me, Blades could be a real threat to our organization," said Jay with concern.

"We have things we can hold over his head. We helped him get custody of his boys and we eliminated Dennis. We could implicate him in these so-called wrongdoings, if we choose. He's not going to put his family through anything else," explained Kelly.

"That may not stop him, Kelly," cautioned Jay.

"Then he'll have to either walk away or join the organization," stated Kelly.

"It might not be that easy," said Jay.

"We'll deal with it when we have to. Let's get some dinner," said Kelly.

"Okay," said Jay as he reached for Kelly's hand. "Everything will be fine. I'll make sure of it."

Kelly smiled at Jay and immediately felt at ease.

"I love you, Jay," said Kelly softly.

Jay looked at Kelly with relief.

"I've been waiting five years for you to say that," declared Jay. "I've loved you from the moment I saw you."

Kelly leaned in for a kiss and they drove away.

CHAPTER 92

Blades' head was spinning. What the hell was going on? The coroner's report indicated that the man really had died from a bee sting and Dr. Lehman really did try to give him the antidote. Blades had interfered but the coroner assured him that the man was dead before he arrived. This made Blades feel a little better but didn't explain why the man was there in the first place. He knew he didn't imagine what Dr. Lehman said to the dying man.

Blades found out that the man was a sex offender. He was about to be arrested in Stoughton where he was last seen but fled the area and somehow ended up in Rochester. He couldn't figure out a connection. The Chief told him that the farmhouse belonged to Jay Hastings, a friend of Dr. Lehman. She was there with Jay. This made sense because Blades met Jay at the clinic where Kelly was attacked. Maybe it was all a coincidence but something wasn't right. Blades could feel it in his gut. Is it possible that Kelly was simply relaying to the pedophile how she felt about his misdeeds?

Blades pulled into his driveway and entered the house through the garage. Clare and the boys were home. He smiled when he saw Clare.

"Well hello, little lady," said Blades as he pulled her into him.

"Hello to you, my favorite detective," said Clare with a giggle.

The two kissed until they heard the boys yell at them to stop.

They both laughed as they separated.

"We're just kissing guys!" said Clare.

"Yeah, well it doesn't have to go on that long," said Eric. Tyler agreed.

"Come on boys, what's better than kissing a pretty girl?" asked Blades.

"Gross," said Tyler as he hugged Blades.

"Dinner is five minutes," yelled Clare. "Go wash up."

The boys went upstairs to wash up. Blades turned to ask Clare a question.

"Clare, I know you told me Audrey helped us get a lawyer. Did she ever mention Dr. Lehman?" asked Blades.

"No', said Clare. "Why?"

"I'm not sure why but when I saw Dr. Lehman at the hospital the other night, she mentioned the lawyer," explained Blades.

"Maybe she was the friend Audrey knew," suggested Clare.

"Maybe. Could you ask Audrey?" Blades asked her.

"Sure," said Clare. "I can call her now if you want," said Clare.

"Yeah, do that. Thanks," said Blades.

Clare left the room to get her cell phone. Blades could hear her talking to Audrey but couldn't make out what she was saying. Clare walked back into the kitchen.

"Audrey said her cousin knows Stanley Francis," explained Clare.

"That's all she said?" asked Blades.

"Yes, but she did ask me why I was asking and seemed a little weird about it," said Clare. "I also asked her if Dr. Lehman knew the lawyer and Audrey said she wouldn't know and then hurried off the phone."

"Interesting," said Blades.

"What's going on?" asked Clare.

"I don't know yet," said Blades.

Just then Blades' cell phone rang.

"Hello, Blades here," said Blades.

"Hi Blades, it's Reilly. We need to meet," she said with urgency.

"What's up?" asked Blades.

"Remember when we were talking about the missing kids the other day?" asked Reilly.

"Yeah," responded Blades.

"Well, I'm one of them," said Reilly in a low voice.

"What? What do you mean?" asked Blades.

"I'm a missing kid. I was taken from my father when I was six. My father wasn't a sperm donor. He's alive," declared Reilly.

"Where are you?" asked Blades.

"I'm home but I can meet you at the café," said Reilly.

"Okay, I'll be there in fifteen minutes," said Blades.

CHAPTER 93

Aunt Loretta wasn't sure about what to do about Reilly. Reilly was so agitated lately. She wondered why all of a sudden she wanted to know who her father was. Aunt Loretta did everything she could to shield Reilly from the truth. Her mother really did die of breast cancer and her father was a son of a bitch. He hadn't seen Reilly for years and Reilly wasn't even her real name.

Reilly's mother, Lorna, had fled Vermont with Reilly when Reilly was six. Her ex-husband had been given visitation rights by a backwards judge even though it was apparent Reilly's father was abusive. He had abused Lorna for years and Lorna knew that Reilly would soon be a victim. She didn't want to wait until it happened. She shared her fears with a friend from her work and her friend immediately helped Lorna get in touch with a social worker that would help her disappear.

Lorna was a very educated woman, a chartered accountant. But any woman can be a victim of domestic violence. Lorna knew that the most dangerous time for a battered woman is when she tried to leave her abuser. She had to have a plan. Lorna had money but had no idea how to escape. Nina, her friend at work, promised to help. One night when Lorna's husband was at work, Lorna and Reilly grabbed what they could and left in Lorna's car. They drove to a spot designated by Nina. A very nice man named John helped her transfer her things from her car to his truck and drove them to Massachusetts. They changed their names and their looks and settled into the town of Milton. Lorna was very attached to her aunt who lived there. Lorna's husband would never find them because he thought her aunt lived in Colorado, plus he was in prison.

Years later, Lorna was diagnosed with breast cancer. It had spread aggressively. Lorna battled the cancer for years but died when Reilly was six. Aunt Loretta was listed as Reilly's guardian. Aunt Loretta decided to tell Reilly that her father was just a sperm donor in order to protect Reilly. Maybe it was time to tell Reilly the truth thought her aunt. Her father was still alive and still a son of a bitch. He had never even looked for Reilly.

Aunt Loretta made a few phone calls to confirm Reilly's father's whereabouts. He was still in prison in upstate New York. He had been convicted of a double murder he didn't commit. He had "murdered" his wife and daughter but the bodies had never been found. The prosecutor was handed a lot of evidence that strongly suggested he had murdered them and burned their remains. The jury saw a lot of evidence convincing them he was an abuser, so murder wasn't a great leap for him to make. They convicted him in less than four hours. He was sentenced to life in prison with no possibility of parole. In Aunt Loretta's mind, that was justice enough for abusing Lorna. As long as he stayed in prison he couldn't find or hurt Reilly again. Aunt Loretta still had to think about how to handle this situation. After a few moments, she made a decision and also made a phone call.

CHAPTER 94

Reilly was visibly upset by the time Blades arrived at the café.

"What's going on Reilly?" asked Blades.

"I have been researching my real father and I found this," said Reilly as she handed Blades a newspaper article she copied from the library.

Blades read the headlines and skimmed the story. The headlines showed an image of a very beautiful woman holding a little girl on her lap. The caption read, "Missing Mother and Daughter Feared Dead."

"Is this you, Reilly?" asked Blades.

"Yes, and that's my mother. I have seen this photo before in Aunt Loretta's closet. It seems my real name is Sarah."

"Why would your aunt lie about you," asked Blades.

"I found a second article in Aunt Loretta's closet detailing how my father went to prison for life for killing us, except that he didn't," said Reilly.

Blades read the article. Reilly's father had a violent past. He probably deserved to be in prison but not based on lies. Blades began to put things together in his mind and didn't share these thoughts with Reilly.

"It looks like people were trying to protect you and your mother from your father," explained Blades.

"I know that but why now? Mom is dead, he can't hurt her," Reilly claimed.

"Your aunt obviously wants to protect you, too," said Blades.

"So are you saying we should leave this alone? I shouldn't confront Aunt Loretta or see my father?" asked Reilly as she tried to fight back tears.

"I'm not saying that, Reilly," said Blades softly. "But maybe your mother needed to protect you and it looks like she had good reason."

Reilly started to cry.

"I feel like I don't know who I am," said Reilly shaking her head.

Blades touched Reilly's hand.

"I don't know what to say," he said.

"How did my mother get away? She must have had help," exclaimed Reilly.

Blades thought about this for a minute.

"My God," he said. "She must have had help."

Blades turned to Reilly.

"Does your aunt happen to know a doctor named Kelly Lehman?" asked Blades.

"Yes," said Reilly. "That's my doctor."

Blades ran his hands through his hair.

"This is getting crazy," said Blades.

"What is?" asked Reilly.

"Everything. You have to go home and ask your aunt about your father. Ask her about how you and your mother left him," instructed Blades.

"Why?" asked Reilly. "Will my aunt get into trouble?" I'm not doing this if she will."

"No," said Blades. "I promise she won't. She saved your life and your mother's life. I get it but I need to know her connection to Kelly Lehman."

"Alright, but if I think it's going in a direction where my aunt can get into trouble, I'm done," declared Reilly.

"Fine," said Blades. "I'll fill you in later."

Reilly went home to an empty house. Aunt Loretta left a note saying she was at a meeting and would return late evening. Reilly slumped on the couch and thought about what she had discovered. On one hand, she wanted to meet her father just to see what he was really like. On the other hand, she didn't want to meet him at all because of what he did to her mother. Just the same, Reilly decided to call Riker's in New York and ask about visiting hours. She got through to the main desk. A woman's voice came on the phone.

"Riker's," said the receptionist.

"Yes," said Reilly. "I'm calling to ask about visiting hours."

"That depends on the prisoner, m'am," replied the receptionist. "Who's the prisoner?"

Reilly hesitated. She tried to remember her father's last name.

"Rick Sanders," said Reilly.

"Rick Sanders?" asked the receptionist. "Is this a joke?"

"No," said Reilly who was now very confused.

"Rick Sanders died earlier today out in the yard," explained the receptionist.

"What? Are you sure?" asked Reilly. "How?"

"He was stabbed by one of the prisoners. Who's this?" asked the receptionist realizing she may have said too much.

"No one," said Reilly and hung up.

CHAPTER 95

Blades was onto something. He was sure Reilly's aunt got help from Kelly Lehman or someone she knew when she took in Reilly and her mother. He decided he would talk to the Chief about how he should proceed. He headed into the direction of the station. His phone rang.

"Blades, it's Reilly. My father's dead," she said calmly.

"What are you talking about? How do you know that?" asked a bewildered Blades.

"I called the prison to check on visiting hours in case I decided to meet him and the receptionist told me he was killed in the yard today," explained Reilly.

"That's no coincidence," said Blades. "Let me look into it. What's his name?"

"Rick Sanders," said Reilly.

"Where are you now?" asked Blades.

"Home," replied Reilly.

"Is your Aunt home?" asked Blades.

"No, she's at a meeting," answered Reilly.

"Do you know where?" asked Blades.

"No," said Reilly. "The note didn't say."

"Okay, stay put and I'll be in touch," instructed Blades.

Blades called Riker's himself and was directed to the warden who confirmed Sander's death. The warden didn't have any more information and had no idea who killed Reilly's father. It was an open investigation. Blades continued to drive to the station.

Blades parked his car and headed to the Chief's office. He knocked on the Chief's door and let himself in.

"I need to talk to you, Chief," said Blades.

"Not now, Blades. We have to go to the hospital," said the Chief.

"What's up?" asked Blades.

"There is a seven year old boy in a coma there. His father was just arrested for abusing him. The boy has a lot of injuries, is dehydrated and malnourished. It's bad, Blades," explained the Chief.

"Okay, let's go. You can ride with me," stated Blades.

Blades and the Chief drove quickly to the hospital, sirens sounding. Once there, they were directed to the floor where doctors worked on the little boy. There were a lot of police officers there already and a couple of social workers. Dr. Lehman came out of the boy's room, visibly upset.

"Kelly," said Blades. "How is he?"

"He's dehydrated and starving. He's seven years old and weighs thirty-eight pounds. He has burn marks on his body from bleach exposure and bruises. Where's his father?" asked Kelly.

"He's in jail, without bail," explained the Chief.

"Someone should shoot that son of a bitch," stated Kelly, clearly angry. "How does someone do this to kids?"

"I know it's awful, Dr. Lehman," said the Chief. "He won't get out."

"He better not get out," raged Kelly.

"Will the boy be okay?" asked Blades.

"He'll never be okay, " explained Kelly. "He's been abused for seven years by his fucked-up father. His teachers filed four 51A's on the father and the father retained custody. How's that possible? Should we just chalk it up to overworked social workers or to a society that doesn't give a shit about kids? Let the system fix it, huh, Blades?"

Kelly was starting to lose it. Blades decided to try to calm her down.

"I understand your anger, Kelly, but the system will keep his Dad in jail," promised Blades.

"Oh, so now we get a great reaction. Wait until the kid is near death and then step in. Sweet move," said Kelly sarcastically.

"Kelly, why don't you and I get a coffee," said the Chief.

"Fine," said Kelly as she walked away.

The Chief turned to Blades.

"Hey, gather as much information as you can from anyone here. I'll handle the doctor," said the Chief.

Blades nodded at the Chief as he watched Kelly walk away. He saw her reach into her pocket for her cell phone and make a call. The Chief hurried to catch up with her. Blades watched as they shared a heated conversation. He watched as the Chief took Kelly's arm and she ripped it away from him. Blades knew the Chief knew Kelly more than he let on. He spoke to a few people and then went to find the Chief. Blades heard them in the staff room.

"If you don't order a hit, I will!" seethed Kelly.

"You need to calm down Kelly. We can't just kill the boy's father. He's in jail," said the Chief.

"So, you don't have a problem with that boy having to see

his asshole father again? The system sucks and you know it!" exclaimed Kelly.

"Yes, I know, but we are going to talk to the Doyen first," whispered the Chief.

"When?" asked Kelly. "It better be soon."

"I'm not sure," said the Chief, "but soon."

Blades listened intently. Who was the Doyen? What was a Doyen? The word sounded familiar to Blades but he looked it up on his phone. A Doyen was the most prestigious member of a secretive group or organization. Blades lifted his head up from reading. So, there *is* an organization playing God. Then Blades came to the horrifying realization that the Chief was involved. Everything made sense now. Dennis was probably murdered. Captain Froio did say Dennis would be handled but Blades didn't really think the police would murder him. There was so much more making sense. The lawyer made sure Blades got custody of the boys. No backup was sent to the farmhouse. The problem remained that Blades couldn't prove anything. Who would he tell? For all he knew the organization included the police commissioner.

Blades listened as the Chief tried to calm Kelly down. Then he heard someone call his name. It was Reilly.

"Blades, what's going on? The paper sent me to cover this story," said Reilly as she tried to catch her breath.

"There's a lot going on but I can't tell you anything yet," said Blades.

"How's the boy?" asked Reilly.

"Not good," said Blades.

"Prick," said Reilly.

"I take it you're not talking about me," said Blades.

"I'm talking about the kid's father," said Reilly. "I guess now I understand why Aunt Loretta did what she did."

Blades watched as Kelly and the Chief moved the meeting into her office and close the door. He turned to Reilly.

"This is serious stuff, Reilly. I have to think about who to talk to," said Blades as he nervously paced.

"What do you mean?" asked Reilly.

"I can't tell you yet or maybe ever," Blades realized. "I need to talk to the doctor and the Chief again."

Blades walked to Kelly's office and knocked on the door.

"We're busy," yelled Kelly.

"It's Blades. Let me in!"

"Not now, Blades," said the Chief.

"Oh it's now," said Blades, "or I'll start talking to the press. I'm with Reilly Simonsen from the Boston Globe as we speak."

Blades pulled a surprised Reilly next to him. The doctor's door opened slowly. Kelly beckoned them in and shut the door again.

"What are you talking about, Blades?" asked the Chief.

"I know what's going on. I know there's a group playing God. I know you kidnap kids and kill abusers. This has to stop!" demanded Blades.

Before Kelly could reply, her phone rang. She answered the call and listened without saying a word. She then closed her phone and looked at the Chief. He understood the look. Blades looked at both of them and he knew, too. He took his cell phone out of his pocket and called the jail where the boy's father was being held.

"Don't do it, Blades," cautioned the Chief.

It was too late. Blades asked the officer on duty how the father was doing. Several minutes went by and then the voice came back on the phone confirming the father's death. Apparently, he committed suicide by tying a garbage bag over his head while in custody. Blades closed his phone and stared at Kelly and the Chief. Reilly was baffled as she looked at everyone.

"Who ordered the hit, Chief?" asked Blades.

"What are you talking about, Blades?" asked the Chief.

"Who ordered the hit on the boy's father? Who's the Doyen?" asked Blades.

Kelly's face went white and she looked surprised at Blades mention of the Doyen. She looked at the Chief who was beginning to look defeated.

"What are you talking about, Blades?" asked Reilly.

Before Blades could answer, the door to the office opened.

"I'm the Doyen. I ordered the hit," said the person coming in.

Blades didn't recognize the person or the voice. Reilly's jaw dropped.

"My God, Aunt Loretta, what's going on?" asked Reilly.

CHAPTER 96

Aunt Loretta and Reilly had a long talk and Reilly understood why Aunt Loretta did what she did. She was protecting Reilly and her mother from a very dangerous man. Reilly's birth name was Sarah but she didn't remember ever being called that so she would stick with her current name. She was still overwhelmed that her aunt was one of the top people in the group who helped kidnap kids and kill pedophiles.

Reilly had no choice but to become part of the group. As she heard details of its history and present activities, she knew she would never turn on her aunt. She was, after all, a saved child. Over the next few months Reilly and her aunt spent a lot of time with Kelly and Jay. They told Reilly everything about the group. Reilly could join or not. Either way, Reilly would remain silent about the group's activities. She grew to realize that the eccentric part was Aunt Loretta's way of never being suspected of anything other than an aunt to Reilly. It was an act, one that Reilly loved.

Every now and then Reilly would find herself staring at her aunt. Aunt Loretta would respond with a somewhat sympathetic smile. Reilly usually asked more questions about the group when she had the opportunity. One night, Reilly point blank asked her aunt why it didn't bother her when she participated in taking someone's life.

"Aunt Loretta, as long as I've known you, I can't see the side of you that ends people's lives. How can you be so comfortable with that?" asked Reilly.

"Reilly, I know you understand why I help abused children escape from their abusers. I can't stand that the system fails so many children and I'm not one to wait for it to rehabilitate itself while children continue to be abused or killed. However, I have no sympathy whatsoever for pedophiles. I think they are evil. Imagine a grown man luring children into a boy scout group or gathering as many altar boys as he can. Imagine a coach assaulting young girls. Imagine how terrified these kids are and imagine those bastards telling the boys if they talk, they will tell people they are gay."

"But, Aunt Loretta," said Reilly.

"Let me finish, Reilly, please," said Aunt Loretta. "You and I both know that there is absolutely nothing wrong with being gay but these abusers place homosexuality in a negative space. These pedophiles tell their victims that their parents will die if they say anything about the abuse. Parents who sexually abuse their kids tell them this kind of love is normal and special. Kids know the difference but can't verbalize their fear because they are supposed to be able to trust their parents. Most kids know their abusers."

Reilly sighed and waited for her aunt to continue because she knew she wasn't finished.

"Pedophiles who get caught have already molested children on a regular basis. They don't always get long prison terms because some doctors think they can cure them. They can't. Pedophiles' sexual preferences are children just like yours are males. Pedophiles are sexually attracted to children. Think about that. They are also the most self-centered people on earth because they clearly have no regard for children. Many say they want to stop but they don't. There is no cure, Reilly. I don't lose a wink of sleep when I know we are killing another pedophile. Some people would think I'm disturbed. I'm not disturbed at all. Killing them is the only logical answer to me and it doesn't bother me on any level. They are vermin. However, I will never ask you to be involved in the group in any way. I'll always respect your opinion and as far as I'm concerned we never have to talk about the group again," promised Aunt Loretta.

Reilly signed again and looked at her aunt. Aunt Loretta had matter-of-factly told her she didn't have an issue with killing pedophiles. In some weird way, Reilly understood but didn't necessarily agree.

"Aunt Loretta, why did you have my father killed?" asked Reilly not in a sad way but more so in an inquisitive way.

"Your father was in prison for killing you and your mother. If he somehow found out you were still alive he would be released from prison and would undoubtedly look for you. He's an incredibly dangerous man, Reilly. He abused your mother in ways that I cannot speak about. He has no regard for women. You would not be safe around him no matter what you think. Another reason is that I would likely go to prison because I framed him for murder. I know that sounds selfish but I couldn't live without being around you every day. I would worry that he would somehow get to you. We normally only kill pedophiles but every now and then but not often, we kill other abusers," explained Aunt Loretta.

"Why didn't you just have him killed and my mother and I would be okay?"

"Your mother ran with you, Reilly. She came straight to

me and wanted to get away from your father. She was terrified of him. She couldn't go back and I knew he would look for her. The system wasn't protecting you and your mother. If I had your father killed, your mother would be the first person the police would suspect because that's how it goes."

Aunt Loretta chuckled sarcastically and continued.

"The police would respond fast to a dead abusive husband but not to a battered woman at that time. The best plan seemed to be to relocate you and your mother and frame your father for your murders. He needed and deserved to go to prison," explained Aunt Loretta.

Reilly couldn't help but still love her aunt. She went to great and risky lengths to protect Reilly and give her a good and safe life. She was very conflicted about the group but wasn't bothered enough to be upset at this time.

"Thanks for telling me, Aunt Loretta. All of this is so overwhelming but I'll be fine and I'll always love you no matter what," said Reilly.

Aunt Loretta pulled Reilly into a strong, warm hug and kissed the top of her head.

"I'll never let anyone hurt you, Reilly," she whispered.

EPILOGUE

Blades, Clare and the boys loved the Bahamas. Blades was in great need of a vacation. It had been a rough number of months. The little boy who was viciously abused by his father was doing very well. He was with a wonderful foster family arranged by Dr. Lehman through the great work of the very social worker that had worked with Elaine Craven. Blades watched as Reilly played Frisbee with the boys. It turned out that she needed a vacation, too. She was overwhelmed by her aunt's role in "saving" children as she called it. Aunt Loretta passed on a vacation because she was busy, so to speak. Clare had taken to Reilly immediately and Reilly, in turn, loved Clare.

Blades heard more about what Dennis had done to Clare and the boys and it was ugly. He would lock them in a closet for hours. He would verbally abuse Clare and make the boys listen to every word. He would tell the boys that all women were evil. He got away with it all of the time because he was a lawyer who knew how to manipulate everyone. He abused his role as a lawyer, too. He could play the role of a devoted husband and father at the drop of a hat. Clare was losing every ounce of self-esteem and was never sure if she should stay with

Dennis or leave him. Then Theresa stepped in. She got Clare out of that relationship and helped her heal. It took years but Clare was back to her normal happy self. The system failed Clare and her boys. That pretty much explained why Clare didn't blink an eye when she was told about the group.

Blades and Clare laughed as Reilly dove in the water to catch the Frisbee. The water was refreshing in the almost unbearable heat. Clare motioned to the waiter that they wanted two more pina coladas. Blades chuckled.

"Are you trying to get me drunk so you can take advantage of me?" asked Blades.

"I doubt you need alcohol," laughed Clare.

Blades leaned in for a kiss. Clare kissed Blades and then sat up quickly.

"They're here, Dana," said Clare as she pointed behind them.

"It's about time," said Blades.

Blades stood up to greet their guests.

"Where the heck were you two?' asked Blades. "You newlyweds are a pain in the ass."

Kelly and Jay laughed as they hugged Blades and Clare.

"We have drinks coming," explained Blades. "Clare is trying to get me drunk."

"So is Theresa," proclaimed Jake as he joined them on the beach.

They all laughed and got settled into their lounge chairs.

Jake and Theresa had belonged to the group for many years and had never divulged this to their family. Blades thought about Jake and what he had been accused of. Jake had killed those rapists and Blades had to accept or at least pretend to even though he knew in his heart that it was a possibility all along. Jake agreed to serve time in prison to make his claims of innocence concerning the rapists' deaths look believable. Joining the group seemed surreal for Blades but he had lost so much faith in the system, especially when it came to children. If the system didn't move fast enough, the group would. He was in deep as far as everyone was concerned and was gradually accepting his involvement.

Everyone in the group that Blades had already known, were a bit surprised at his willingness to join the organization. It was either that or have conflicting relationships with everyone in his big, new family. Part of Blades couldn't believe what he was doing but he had convinced himself that if the group continued its work, maybe the system would get a dose of reality and then the group would not have to exist anymore. He wanted to believe he was helping children and potentially revamping an increasingly failing system that was supposed to protect children at risk.

"I know we all need a vacation," said Blades. "Let's try not to talk about work."

Theresa plopped down next to Clare and they clinked glasses.

"You alright with everything, Clare?" asked Theresa. "I know this has been a lot to take in, especially Jake's role."

"Honestly Theresa, I only know one Jake and he is a loving father and husband. I'll never judge him for what he did because quite frankly, those men deserved to die. You and I both know that they wouldn't get life sentences if they were convicted," replied Clare.

Theresa nodded in affirmation.

"Dana has never brought it up, Theresa and I doubt he ever will. As I said, Dana and I won't be involved in the "extermination" role of the group but I'm with you one hundred percent when it comes to keeping abused children safe. We both feel even stronger about it given our experiences with Dennis," said Clare.

"Well then," said Theresa. "Bottoms up!"

"Well, we have two more kids on the move," said Kelly as she read her latest text. "Plus we'll have one less pedophile on the street by this time tomorrow. Okay, no more work talk, Blades! I promise!"

Blades smiled and agreed. He was about to make a toast to the newlyweds when his phone rang. It was the Chief who wasn't supposed to bother them on vacation.

"What's up, Chief?" asked Blades shrugging his shoulders to the others.

Blades listened intently and then hung up.

Everyone knew that look. Something bad happened again.

"Drink up, guys. The unidentified little girl who was found in a trash bag months ago has been identified. The Chief wanted us to hear it from him but to stay put. He has people on it until we get back," said Blades.

Everyone shook their heads and gestured in ways that indicated their interference with the system was a necessary evil. The fact that they had lured Blades in was a bonus because he had many connections and was well respected. They raised their glasses in a silent toast to their dedication to protecting children.

Blades raised his glass and looked at everyone around him. It was too easy convincing them he had willingly joined the group. His undercover work was just beginning.

CPSIA information can be obtained at www.ICGtesting.com
Printed in the USA
BVOW08s1653050616

450700BV00001B/1/P